The Players

Also by Barbara Sherrod
in Large Print:

Daughter of the Dreadfuls
Gamester's Lady

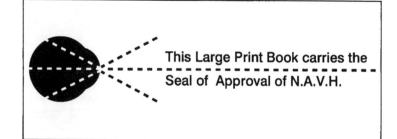

The Players

Barbara Sherrod

Thorndike Press • Waterville, Maine

Published in 2004 by arrangement with Maureen Moran Agency.

Thorndike Press® Large Print Romance.

The tree indicium is a trademark of Thorndike Press.

The text of this Large Print edition is unabridged.
Other aspects of the book may vary from the original edition.

Set in 16 pt. Plantin by Christina S. Huff.

Printed in the United States on permanent paper.

Library of Congress Cataloging-in-Publication Data

Sherrod, Barbara.
    The players / Barbara Sherrod.
      p. cm.
    ISBN 0-7862-6554-X (lg. print : hc : alk. paper)
    1. London (England) — Fiction. 2. Sisters — Fiction.
  3. Large type books. I. Title.
  PS3569.H43495P57 2004
  813'.54—dc22   2004045983

The Players

As the Founder/CEO of NAVH, the only national health agency solely devoted to those who, although not totally blind, have an eye disease which could lead to serious visual impairment, I am pleased to recognize Thorndike Press* as one of the leading publishers in the large print field.

Founded in 1954 in San Francisco to prepare large print textbooks for partially seeing children, NAVH became the pioneer and standard setting agency in the preparation of large type.

Today, those publishers who meet our standards carry the prestigious "Seal of Approval" indicating high quality large print. We are delighted that Thorndike Press is one of the publishers whose titles meet these standards. We are also pleased to recognize the significant contribution Thorndike Press is making in this important and growing field.

Lorraine H. Marchi, L.H.D.
Founder/CEO
NAVH

* Thorndike Press encompasses the following imprints: Thorndike, Wheeler, Walker and Large Print Press.

Chapter I

The four Sparks sisters never ceased to delight the families of the surrounding county. Their combined beauty brightened every morning visit and country dance. Their manners were universally charming and a credit to their noble family name. But most notably, the Misses Sparks were generally supposed by their kind neighbors to be marked out for tragedy.

Miss Irene, the eldest and most elegant, stood the tallest. A moss of honey-colored curls set off her fine-boned face. Unfortunately, she was reputed to be bookish. Certainly she looked bookish. Not yet three and twenty, she bore the serious expression of a much older woman. Her dignity and mode of dress did little to soften her appearance. Irene's neighbors attributed her severe aspect to the heavy responsibilities she had shouldered at the age of seventeen — upon the death of their mother, Irene had undertaken the task of rearing her three younger sisters.

All the villagers of Botherby knew that Lady Sparks had died of a broken heart, the result of her husband's reckless ways. Irene, undaunted by her youth, had taken on the full burden of running Hopewell, formerly a fine estate, now crumbling from neglect. She had forestalled the complete ruin of the mansion quite creditably under the circumstances. Robert, the steward, approved her sensible plans for modernization and even went so far as to admit that Miss Irene had "quite a head for business." If the chickens escaped into the pasture and the housemaid ran off with the footman and the plate, the fault could not be laid at Irene's door.

Botherby society knew very well where to settle the blame for the shameful decay of Hopewell — on Lord Sparks, who devoted as little attention to his house and lands as he did to his daughters. The baron's neighbors might be willing to pay him all the respect due his title, but they could not be blind to the single occupation that engrossed his entire life — namely, squandering away nearly all of his fortune. Had milord done his duty, Miss Irene would not have been so clearly destined for spinsterhood.

By contrast, Martha was born to be married. Irene may have acted the mother's part, but it was Martha who looked the part. The villagers nodded and beamed at the sight of the second Miss Sparks, with her round, full form, her pink cheeks, and her shy smile. Martha's tenderness for children was proverbial. The townsfolk frequently came upon her in the act of bestowing sweetmeats and wondrous tales upon the local urchins. What a pity that such a one as she should live to "waste her fragrance on the desert air," as the vicar's wife so poetically phrased it.

"But so it must be," the good woman mourned, "for a daughter of Lord Sparks cannot stoop to marry a farmer or tradesman; neither is she likely to attract any respectable man of means, without so much as a pittance to her name."

In principle, the two youngest sisters were not yet out. In practice, however, they went everywhere with the elder two. Ordinarily the leading families of Botherby would have turned a cold shoulder to such a violation of morality. But the ladies of Hopewell presented so irresistible an opportunity for condescension that it proved impossible to snub them. Moreover, the exquisiteness of Caroline and the good humor of Mary — called Muffin by one and all — saved many a gathering from insipidity. Their approval was further guaranteed by the distinguished name of Sparks, which, despite the present lord's dissipation, had graced that part of Somersetshire since the time of the Restoration.

At sixteen, Caroline embodied all the loveliness of budding womanhood. Instinctively she understood the manner of lowering the lashes in the company of gentlemen and of enlivening a morsel of gossip in the company of ladies. Caroline had the makings of a heartbreaker, though little good it would do her, sighed the good people of Botherby. However, in spite of the girl's bleak prospects, rather a few local swains could be observed dangling after her on the streets of the town, begging to be allowed to carry her basket.

When eyebrows rose at the sight of one of the Sparks sisters, the cause might always be found in Muffin. She promised, at only thirteen, to carry on the family tradition of recklessness, effrontery and wild horsemanship. The neighborhood still noised about the child's scandalous brawl at the Fair, though the incident had occurred in Muffin's eleventh year. Irene predicted that the squabble would take on the proportions of a legend, owing to the fact that Muffin had planted numerous powerful blows on the faces of several strapping lads, who sported purple eyes and puffy lips for a great many days afterward.

To the enormous satisfaction of their neighbors, the Misses Sparks met with their long-anticipated tragedy on a rainy afternoon, when their father, thrown from his mount on the London road, suffered a head wound from which he never recovered. The pomp of his burial rites, along with the speculation that they would never be paid for, inspired the baron's neighbors to philosophize high-mindedly on the irony of Fate.

Philosophy was a luxury for which Irene could spare no time. Nor was there a moment for recrimination or self-pity, for it immediately fell upon her to consult with the family lawyer. Mr. Uffingham traveled from London expressly to tell her, in high-flown phrases, what she already knew — that her father had left no provision for them. All the family lands had long ago been sold off to support the baron's gaming habits. He had drained the whole of the capital that generations of Sparkses before him had taken great pains to amass. Ponderously, Mr. Uffingham imparted to Irene the only piece of news that surprised — nay, shocked her. Hopewell was entailed away from the female line.

He seated himself in the library's most

uncomfortable carved chair and regarded Irene's serious expression. "The estate falls to the Earl of Hammond," he told her, "and very sorry I am for it, too; for while I have never met his lordship, I am given to understand that he is not quite the thing." Mr. Uffingham's eyebrows rose in disapprobation.

Taking a chair opposite the solicitor, Irene replied evenly, "I cannot pretend to be surprised. As a relation of my father's and a member of his idle set, he could hardly be a gentleman of very estimable character."

Lifting his eyebrows once more, Mr. Uffingham shook his head gravely. "I am told by his very own brother-in-law, Lord Selby, that he promises to disgrace his family and is likely soon to bring scandal upon all their heads."

The solicitor then turned to other business, saying nothing further in regard to the Earl of Hammond. Nevertheless, the little he had said was sufficient to convince Irene that the new master of Hopewell was certain to follow in the rackety footsteps of the old.

"I shall tell you the worst right off," Irene announced to her sisters as they huddled before the fire in the drafty sitting room. "We must quit Hopewell within the month."

"Quit Hopewell!" they cried out as one.

"But it is our home," Caroline protested. She turned her tear-filled eyes toward Martha, who searched for words to soothe her.

"In point of fact," Irene went on in tight-lipped determination, "it is not our home any longer. It now belongs to Stephen, Earl of Hammond."

"Who the devil is he?" Muffin demanded.

"The heir to Hopewell, I am sorry to say."

"The Earl of Hammond?" Martha wondered aloud. "I never heard him mentioned by our parents."

"Nor I," declared Muffin. "Though I suppose I hardly saw either of them above a dozen or so times in my life. Still, we ought to be the heirs, you know, not some rum earl who never set eyes on the place."

Irene smiled ruefully. "The explanation is very simple. We each had the lamentable presumption to be born female. Hopewell is entailed upon the next male heir, who, as it happens, is your 'rum' earl. His father was distant cousin to ours, I am told."

"It's a flaming cheat!" fumed her youngest sister.

"Muffin!" Martha reproved in a gentle

13

whisper. "Is it not your turn to see about the tea?"

"No amount of tea will wash away the injustice of it," Muffin retorted.

"What are we going to do?" Martha asked, sighing.

Irene looked into the three faces which had turned to her for an answer.

"One thing we shall not do," she stated evenly, "is continue to bemoan our fate in this fashion."

"I would like to meet this Earl of Hammond," Muffin said. "I would tell him exactly what I think of him."

Irene laughed humorlessly. "Be sure to tell him, while you are about it, that Hopewell is rightfully ours, that he may sign it over to us at his earliest convenience, and that he may visit in the hunting season if he notifies us well in advance of his coming. Tell him, too, that we have no income and are therefore strapped for funds to repair and maintain the estate. Perhaps he may settle an annuity on us. After all, what does it profit us to have Hopewell if we cannot afford to patch the roof?"

"Very well," Muffin countered, "I shall write him at once!"

Unable to repress her tears any longer, Irene murmured, "You will do no such thing. Even if Hopewell had been left to us, we should have had to give it up. Don't you see that?"

Seeing their sister so uncharacteristically shaken, the three sat as if frozen, until Muffin roused them again by running to Irene and hugging her violently. Laughing and crying at once, Irene said gently, "Would you go and see if the tea is ready? There's a good girl."

Moving to obey, Muffin sniffed noisily, "I am not a good girl."

The remaining three sat in silence for many minutes, listening to the hollow chimes of the clock on the mantel.

Then Caroline brightened, as a flash of inspiration seized her. "We might hire out as governesses," she offered. "We are not without accomplishments and learning to recommend us to some respectable family."

"I'm not sure I would like being a governess," Martha said.

"Of course you would!" Caroline stated. "You adore children. Everyone says so. And I am sure I should think it an adventure. Moreover, it is truly a practical scheme. Irene's drawings would gain her a fine position. Your skill on the pianoforte and mine at the harp would recommend us likewise. Perhaps we might find some dark and stormy castle in the north, with a brooding master and a terrible secret hidden in the attic."

"It is not very likely that the gentleman would employ all four of us," Irene pointed out. "Nor is he likely to take on a girl of sixteen as governess, no matter how troubled he is in his attic."

"I am nearly seventeen," Caroline said, pouting.

"Suppose we did manage to place ourselves," Martha added. "What would we do about Muffin?"

"I daresay," Irene observed wryly, "she might make an excellent stable hand, except that — like the law of entail — gentlemen who keep horses generally give preferment to males."

Again Caroline brightened. "Well then, I could be a seamstress. We could sell off the furnishings which belong to us, and with the proceeds we could set up a shop in London. What an adventure that would be!"

Falling in with her sister's enthusiasm, Martha said, "London! It would be a dream come true. Carrie would have no difficulty in stitching the latest fashions. Why, you saw how she worked my blue silk, just from seeing a drawing of the high-waisted bodice. I've always wanted to go to London."

"It's the very thing," Caroline exclaimed, encouraged by Martha's speech. "I wish you would not look so stern, Irene. It would answer famously. We could take rooms above the shop. I would sew gingham curtains to brighten our cozy poverty. Martha would see that we were all fed and bathed. Muffin would act as our bill collector. And you might find a family in the district in need of a governess. Oh, do say you will at least think about it," she begged.

"I will think about it," Irene promised. "Indeed your plan cannot be entirely discounted, though the idea of Baron Sparks's daughters setting up in trade would severely shock our acquaintances in Botherby. I confess, I am reluctant to entertain them so hugely."

Here she paused to imagine the expressions such news would inevitably provoke on the faces of their neighbors. The thoughts of her sisters apparently bent in the same direction, for all at once they burst into gales of laughter.

Martha, the first to recover her composure, said softly, "It may be that our little adventure will not do after all. London might not wish to patronize our shop, once society comes to know the origins of the proprietress."

"They would swarm to us, I suspect," Irene remarked, "out of curiosity to see a lady sunk down in the world."

"Then it is settled," Caroline declared cheerfully. "The cream of London society will flock to my door, and I shall do them up magnificently."

"You amaze me." Martha sighed. "I wish I were daring enough to risk all on such a doubtful scheme." Then, seeing Caroline at work inventing another solution, she wondered where Muffin could have disappeared to. "Do you think she forgot all about the tea?" she asked. "Shall I go fetch it?"

"In a bit," Irene said. "We have not quite done. There remains one alternative we have not discussed."

At this juncture, Muffin arrived clamorously with the tea things. Martha and Caroline had to suppress their curiosity long enough to serve up the bread and butter while Irene poured. That done, Caroline implored Irene to tell them their final alternative.

The eldest sister lowered her eyes. "To tell the truth," she said in much distress, "I hesitate to put forward such a suggestion. I am afraid you will find the idea repulsive, and I could not blame you in the least if you did."

"What on earth is it?" Muffin cried breathlessly.

"Now, now," Martha calmed her. "All in good time." Looking fondly at Irene, she said, "Nothing you could say would repel us. If we have not learned by now that you are thoughtful, prudent, and good on our behalf, then we shall never learn it."

Irene bit her lip. "I wonder if it is ever thoughtful or prudent or good to suggest such a cynical and mercenary scheme as I have in mind."

"Oh, do tell us what it is," Muffin pleaded. "We are perishing with curiosity."

"More important," Caroline added, "we scorn to flinch from anything merely because it is arduous and requires bitter sacrifice!"

"Very well," Irene relented with a heavy sigh. "My scheme is this: One of us should marry as rich a man as we can scare up in the shortest time possible."

Chapter II

The Earl of Hammond entered his breakfast parlor to discover Charles Dale, his youthful secretary, already in the act of scanning the morning's letters.

"Efficient as ever, Charles," Hammond greeted him. "May I interrupt you long enough to bid you good morning?"

"Good morning, my lord," the secretary replied somewhat absently.

The earl smiled, perceiving that Charles was engrossed in a piece of correspondence which produced a furrowed brow and an expression of uneasiness. He walked to the sideboard, where he helped himself to sausage, biscuit, and tea.

"You are much to be pitied, my young friend," he said as he set his dishes on the table and took his customary seat.

"Indeed?" Charles responded. He placed the worrisome letter at the bottom of a pile of papers and looked for the first time at his employer. "I have been used to thinking myself most fortunate."

Hammond sipped his tea, then attacked his sausage. "You would be so much more fortunate," he remarked between bites, "if you had entered the employ of some tulip of fashion, a gentleman who slept the morning away after a night's dissipation and did not require your services at unholy hours, a gentleman who did not banish his servants from the breakfast parlor in order to do business over morning tea."

"I should consider it an immense bore," Charles stated.

Amused, Hammond observed the young man. "In that case you would be very much in vogue," he said. "Boredom is all the rage at present. To betray enthusiasm or purpose is to declare oneself decidedly out of the way."

Charles laughed. "That is why I prefer your employ to that of others. I have not the knack of being in the way."

"Nor have I," the earl remarked.

Hammond referred, Charles knew, to his reputation for eccentricity, a reputation he took care to uphold on every occasion. London society whispered that he rarely allowed his dark hair to be dressed, because it fell naturally in the Brutus cut. It was also said that his tailor had much to do to accommodate his lordship's great height and broad shoulders. Although he insisted that his trousers and coats be made of the finest cloth, his mode of dress was a study in moderation. His resistance to exotic cravats, high-starched collars, and other extremes of fashion was proverbial, as was his resistance to pressure from his sister to marry, produce an heir, and live the idle life of his father and grandfather before him.

"You may not consider yourself so fortunate in your employer when you hear what transpired yesterday evening at White's," said the earl. "I was approached by my esteemed brother-in-law and his cronies."

"Ah, Selby," Charles said with a groan.

"Exactly," Hammond said. "It was strongly hinted that I had better mend my ways, or I should suffer the consequences."

Charles's brow furrowed.

"Do not frown so, Charles," his lordship continued. "I was greatly amused, particularly when I heard the thrust of their grievance. You can never guess the reason behind the threat."

"I am sure I cannot," Charles agreed resentfully. He felt ready to take Hammond's part even without hearing the grievance.

"I am informed that members of the club — as well as the whole of London — have until now kindly overlooked my fanatical attendance at sessions of the Upper House. However, it appears that now I have gone too far. Rumor has it, you see, that I mean to give a speech in the House. Naturally my friends and family are in an uproar."

"Naturally!" Charles repeated in some disgust.

"They assure me that it is my solemn duty to avoid any commitment that might offend the Prince Regent. I have been warned, you understand," Hammond went on dryly. "I will no longer be received in the illustrious drawing rooms of London. I shall certainly be cut wherever I presume to go."

Smiling at his employer's irony, Charles remarked, "I daresay, the Prince is far too good-natured to take offense at a speech on currency reform. And the hostesses of the town have more sense than to snub an earl of the realm, especially such an eligible one. London is far too curious to know who will catch you at last."

"What a comfort you are, Charles!" the earl exclaimed. "You have enabled me to see my true value in the world — not as a member of Lords or even as a man who hopes to be more than a parasite on the nation, but as a catch for some simpering miss and her rapacious mother. I thank you, my friend."

"Your lordship is pleased to be satiric, I see," Charles noted. "Will you give up the speech?"

"Only if the party chooses another member in my stead to deliver it," Hammond answered. He drained his cup and pushed it aside. "Nor do I intend to give up White's; I think I can withstand sanctimonious lectures from that quarter so long as the port there continues excellent. My sole reservation is my sister. She will tax me more than ever with my iniquities."

"I have a note from her here," Charles said. "She means to wait on you this morning."

A flicker of amusement crossed the earl's face. "That was to be expected. What does she say?"

"It seems she has a matter of the greatest urgency to discuss with you."

"That too was to be expected," Hammond said. "Depend on it, Charles. She means to fleece me. But now to business. What news?"

For the better part of an hour the two men reviewed the earl's correspondence and business while the servants unobtrusively removed the breakfast cover. Hammond's projected speech to the House of Lords was reviewed as well. Finally, when they had disposed of these concerns for the moment, Charles handed Lord Hammond a heavily scrawled and much-blotted paper.

"I know not how to prepare you for the contents if this amazing letter," he began. "For some weeks I have been looking into the matter, as you asked. Now this arrives."

Taking the letter, Hammond unfolded it and read:

To His Grace Lord Stephen,
Earl of Hammond,
Grosvenor Square, London:

It is some weeks now since you have come into our property, and my sisters and I have been at a loss as to how to proceed so that we shall not starve or be forced to go to the workhouse, where we should certainly die of typhoid or the pox.

"Who the devil is this person?" Hammond demanded. "I cannot make head nor tail of this."

Nodding sympathetically, Charles begged him to read on.

To avoid suffering such a pathetic end, which must touch the heart of even such a one as yourself, my sisters and I have agreed that one of us must marry an extremely rich gentleman who will provide for the four of us. Far be it from me, your lordship, to remind you of your moral obligation to fellow creatures you have wronged. But if you have any wish to make amends and so mitigate your consciousness of having inflicted harm on innocent mortals, then surely you will find such a husband for us. With all your connections in town, you should have no difficulty locating an unexceptional gentleman for the purpose.

Irene, our eldest sister, ought to be given first preference, for she is not only handsome, wise, and practical, but she thought of the scheme to begin with. Martha, our next eldest, is plump, fond, and agreeable, and everyone hereabouts thinks she will make an excellent wife. Caroline is thought a great beauty. For myself, I don't see it, but the young scarums in Botherby evidently do, though she is just sixteen. Finally, there is myself. My name is Mary but I am called Muffin. If you should find a rich nob who fancies a girl of thirteen for his bride, I shall not falter at the sacrifice. I ask only that he keep a good stable. I beg you will send the gentleman to Hope-well at once, as we are on the point of quitting it and can afford to waste no further time. Please instruct the gentle-man to say nothing of this letter, as my sisters are ignorant of my intention to write you.

Kindly disregard any disrespectful ex-pression herein. I pray that you may be brought to a sense of your duty in this.

Yours, etc.
Mary Sparks

Laughing heartily, Hammond lay down the letter. "Very well," he said to Charles, "you have had your little joke. You will ex-plain to me who that mad child is and why she attacks me so bitterly."

With a sigh, Charles began, "You may re-call the communication from Mr. Uffing-ham, the lawyer." When Hammond evinced an impatient sign of recollection, the secre-tary inhaled deeply and went on, "And you recall as well that you have inherited Hope-well, the estate of the late Lord Sparks."

"I told you then I had no idea who the deuce Lord Sparks is — or was — and wanted no part of his estate," said the earl.

Gravely, Charles continued, "I believe I

27

explained at the time that the estate was entailed on you."

"You know what I think of entails, Charles," his lordship stated irritably.

"Indeed I do," the young man said, "but that does not alter the case — you are heir to a crumbling, worthless estate."

"According to this remarkable letter," Hammond said, "Lord Sparks left his daughters homeless and penniless. What a bounder the fellow must have been."

"Mr. Uffingham made no mention of daughters," Charles apologized. "Had he done so, I should certainly have apprised you of their condition at once."

"I do not doubt it, Charles," Hammond reassured him. "Well, there's nothing for it but to give them back their precious Hopewell. I certainly have no use for another country house."

"If you consider all the facts, my lord," the secretary went on, "I think you will see that it is not a simple matter of refusing the inheritance. Your solicitor, Mr. Pettibone, has made a number of inquiries at my request. It develops that the young ladies cannot afford to keep the estate any more than they can afford to leave it. In short, sir, it is a devil of a pickle."

"Are you saying," the earl inquired with a

steely look, "that I must now begin to interview perspective husbands for one of these females?"

Charles shrugged apologetically. "You must confess, my lord, that Miss Muffin Sparks is a singular young person."

The earl's lip curled appreciatively. "If the fashion nowadays is to be bored," he said, "one would be decidedly unfashionable in the company of such a formidable little lady."

The door opened at that moment to admit Bunkers. The elderly butler announced, with several upward rolls of his eyeballs, that the Lady Louisa Selby awaited his lordship's attendance in the large sitting room.

"I have been instructed to inform your lordship," Bunkers sniffed, "that my lady will not sit cooling her heels above five minutes."

His eyes alight with mischief, Hammond leaned back in his chair. "Thank you, Bunkers," he said smoothly. "Be so kind as to inform her ladyship that I shall be six minutes at the very least." He drew his watch from his waistcoat and made note of the time. Then he set the watch before him on the table.

Solemnly Bunkers cleared his throat. "As

you wish, sir," he intoned, and left to brave the wrath of the earl's sister.

"Ordinarily I am the most tractable man alive," Hammond told Charles, "but Louisa makes it so tempting that I can never resist crossing her." He paused thoughtfully. "You know, I am also tempted to have a look at the three starving ladies and their mad sister. What think you, Charles?"

The secretary smiled. He had no doubt that the earl would end by providing somehow for the Sparks sisters and that the provisions would be arranged with the utmost tact. "Will you bring along a husband with you?" he inquired archly.

"A husband?" Hammond repeated, replacing his watch and rising from his chair. "Now that I think of it, I might enjoy the novel experience of being on the hunt for one. I've spent so many years evading the hunters myself that I know all the ploys and snares." He bade farewell to the young man, then made his way slowly to the large sitting room and the entertainment that awaited him there.

Lady Louisa paced the sitting room, stopping now and again to inspect a pretty Limoges snuff box. The piece ought to grace her own parlor instead of her brother's, she thought. She recognized it as the one that her mother had presented to Stephen recently upon the attainment of his thirtieth year, an event Louisa considered grotesque, given her brother's single condition. She thought it gross folly on her mother's part to permit her only son to ignore his obligation to marry and produce an heir. To reward such disregard for the claims of society constituted an affront.

Had she been a selfish woman, Louisa congratulated herself, she would be doing everything in her power to assure Stephen's continued bachelorhood. Her own offspring — two marriageable daughters — would thus stand as beneficiaries to a sizable portion of the Hammond wealth. Instead, she put aside her own interest, taking every opportunity that presented itself to upbraid him for his laxity. Her mother would not urge him, and so she must. In any case, from what she saw, he was more than likely to bequeth his fortune to an institution for wayward orphans or some such nonsense. Indeed, she felt there was no enormity of which he was not capable if it meant outraging propriety or thwarting his sister.

These ruminations, coupled with her present mission, gave rise to Lady Louisa's feeling of general ill usage on this occasion. She suspected that Hammond was not likely to receive her latest request with the amiable benevolence one might expect in a rich brother. Because their mother had in no uncertain terms declined to intervene, her mission was almost surely doomed to failure. To beg a favor in the face of such obstacles went sorely against the grain. Louisa pouted at the Limoges box, setting it down on the table with a thud.

Thus it was that when Hammond finally made his appearance in the room, she greeted him with more than her usual shrillness.

"Stephen," she scolded, "Selby tells me you have made a scene at White's. He was dreadfully mortified."

Urbanely the earl approached her and kissed her hand. "Good morning, Louisa," he said. "You look charming in that bonnet. It is new, is it not?"

"Why, yes," she answered. "I bought it from that new milliner in Hill Street. Lady Volteface will patronize no one else, you know."

"Ah," he exclaimed with great interest, "is the marchioness now our arbiter? I should think Lady Jersey will be quite put out at being supplanted."

Louisa paused to glare at him. "Do not think to change the subject," she warned. "I am not so easily deceived as that. I know perfectly well you don't care a fig for bonnets or arbiters."

"I did not know we had a subject," Hammond said laconically. "Do sit down, my dear. If there is to be a subject, you really ought to sit down."

She hesitated a moment, considering whether sitting down would give Stephen the upper hand. At length it occurred to her that she ought to strike a more conciliatory note than that with which she had begun. Therefore, she seated herself on the sofa, daintily spreading the folds of her skirts about the cushions.

"The subject, I take it, is my speech," the earl said.

"It is absurd!" Louisa charged. "What do you mean by it?"

"Do you wish to peruse the text?" Stephen inquired blandly.

"You know very well I do not," she retorted. "Selby simply does not comprehend your aligning yourself with a party at a time when the Prince himself appears to be wavering."

Thoughtfully, Hammond replied, "I see. In your view it would be better to wait and see which way the wind blows."

"Such an inelegant expression!" his sister

said, shuddering. "I know nothing about politics, nor do I mean to know anything about them. The real business of life has little to do with that sort of thing."

"What do you consider the real business of life?" he asked.

Louisa gaped at him. Testily she replied, "I never think about it. It is unladylike to dwell on such subjects."

The earl sat down in a comfortable Chesterfield opposite the sofa. "Then the subject is closed," he stated.

"What subject?" she demanded to know.

"The subject you just accused me of trying to change," he explained patiently.

Realizing that she had lost considerable ground, Louisa retrenched. "How do we always manage to embroil ourselves in these debates?" she asked demurely, turning upon him her most adorable smile. "I'm sure I don't know how we end up in a wrangle when we are as fond of each other as a brother and sister may be."

The earl stifled a smile. "I am sure I don't know either," he said.

"Well then," she went on briskly, "let us forget all that, shall we? My subject has to do with Beatrice and Chloe."

"I hope my nieces are well," he stated politely, his dark eyes narrowing.

"Wonderfully well!" she declared. "That is, they would be wonderfully well if one could introduce them into society in a proper way."

"My dear sister, you are everything that is proper," he responded. "I believe there is no one better suited to launching young ladies with propriety than yourself."

Louisa frowned. "You mistake my meaning," she said. "I have been wishing that Selby and I could absorb the expense of a proper ball for their debut, a magnificent occasion, one that the cream of the ton would speak of for months afterward."

"You don't mean a proper introduction," the earl said smoothly. "The ball to which you refer is more in the line of an extravagant, wasteful affair, and it would be a mistake for you to think that I will underwrite it."

Furious, Louisa rose from the sofa and marched halfway to the door. Facing him stormily, she cried out, "But you are their uncle! It is your obligation to do what you can on their behalf."

"They have a father," he reminded her quietly, "and while he may not have the means to hire a hall the size of Saint Paul's, he will do all that is required."

"These are not some strangers, you know," she retorted. "These are your nieces!"

"And two more brainless toads no uncle could wish for," Stephen observed languidly. "Really, Louisa, can you actually believe that a splendid display will get them husbands?"

Her ladyship bit her lip. She still hoped that by quelling her anger she might yet bring her brother around. "You are trying to provoke me, as you always do," she said. "I am sure you will think it over at your leisure and see your way clear to doing your duty."

"I cannot promise anything of the kind," Hammond said, rising and walking to the door. "My duty is spoken for; I have an obligation that takes me into the country."

Her anger rekindled, Louisa demanded to know what sort of obligation could inspire him to cast off his own flesh and blood. Opening the door, he called, "Bunkers, will you show Lady Louisa to her carriage."

Her ladyship had no choice but to leave, which she did with a great show of indignation. Following her departure, Lord Hammond instructed Bunkers to seek out his valet with directions to make immediate preparations for a journey.

A short time later, Lord Hammond left his house, pausing on the doorstep to look about him. He observed with satisfaction that the clouds had cleared, and it promised to become a fine March day. Perhaps he would have good weather for his journey on the morrow. With that cheerful thought, he dismissed his coachman and walked to his destination.

The footman who answered his knock confided to him in a significant whisper, "My lady will be glad to see you, sir."

Hammond knew that hushed tone. "Did she have a bad night?" he asked.

A sorrowful nod confirmed his suspicion. Swiftly he climbed the winding staircase, taking the steps two at a time. He rapped twice on the door to the sitting room and went inside.

The dowager sat at an open window, throwing crumbs to the finches and pigeons that flocked to the sill. Her still-beautiful face lighted when she saw who her visitor was.

"You are very naughty, Mother," he said.

"Naughty!" she objected. "Why, I am nothing short of wicked."

Hammond closed the window firmly, saying, "It's not yet warm enough for that. Your friends will have to fend for themselves a while longer."

The dowager sighed. With a mixture of pleasure and resignation, she allowed Stephen to fuss over her.

"I suppose you are going to hand me a lecture," she said.

He glanced down at her legs, which were raised on an ottoman. A wool blanket covered them.

"You have had your legs wrapped," he said.

"Only for an hour or so," she replied, "until Miss Simpson returns to hover over me. How very charming it is to be ill. The attentions one receives are quite overwhelming. Had I known what a stir I should create, I would certainly have acquired an affliction much sooner."

Hammond kissed his mother on the brow. Gently moving her feet to one side of the ottoman, he sat down on the other and took her hands in his.

"You are nearly as intractable as Louisa," he murmured.

"How odd," Lady Hammond said with a laugh. "She says I am nearly as intractable as you."

"How did it happen," he asked, "that such a mother had two very different children?"

"All children are different," she responded. "That is what makes families tolerable. Besides, your father spoilt Louisa shamefully. He thought of you as his heir, requiring only the tutor and the rod to equip you for your station in life. Louisa, however, was his daughter, requiring only indulgence and a husband who would carry on the work of spoiling her."

Hammond smiled. "Thus it became my life's work to unspoil her."

"You two have been at each other's throats again, I see."

"Never mind," he said. "I have come to say goodbye. I leave for Somersetshire tomorrow and expect to be gone three or four days. You will miss me?"

"I certainly shall," she agreed merrily, "even though your scoldings are nothing to Louisa's. But what takes you into the country?"

Stephen related the story of his recent inheritance. His description of Muffin's letter amused his mother greatly.

"You know," she said thoughtfully, "it seems to me that I once met Lord and Lady Sparks. He was a distant relation of your father's. Yes, I remember them well now."

"That explains the entail, I suppose," Stephen said. He rose and walked to the window. "It is a vicious system that palms off property on a male heir and bypasses a man's nearest relations because they are female. It is especially vicious when the male heir is myself and squirming under the obligation it entails. It is no wonder they call it an *entail*."

"As I recall," his mother said, "Lady Sparks's family threw her off. They did not approve of Lord Sparks, and from what I saw, he was a rank fish."

"Your language, Mother!" his lordship said, laughing. "Louisa will be shocked to fainting."

"Only if you tell her," the dowager remarked sagely. "In any case, Lady Sparks stands out well in my memory. She was one of the loveliest creatures I have ever seen. If her daughters favor her at all, they will have no difficulty whatsoever in securing a husband."

Walking to the center of the room, Hammond replied that he was relieved to hear it. "But I do not presume to be able to find them one," he added. "I know of no gentlemen in London who is so eager for a destitute wife that he will travel into Somerset to get her. And I know no one at all in that county save that oily squire who is so sweet on you."

"Then there is only one thing to do," Lady Hammond declared.

Her son looked at her quizzically. "There is?" he asked.

"Of course." She chuckled. "How very fortunate you are, my dear, to have a mother who can tell you what it is. I declare, I amaze myself."

"I do not need you to tell me how fortunate I am in my mother," Hammond said. "But what is it? Must I flatter you to extort the answer?"

"I am not averse to flattery," she teased, "but I shall not keep you in suspense. When you wish to hunt, you go to Scotland, where the grouse are. In the same way, you must bring these Hopewell ladies to London, where the husbands are. Here they may hunt the quarry themselves."

Hammond grinned. "Yes," he agreed, "that is a solution, but what in blazes shall I do with four females? You are not well enough to chaperon them; therefore, they cannot stay with you. I might hire rooms for them, but they would still need some respectable lady to take them about. Could I find another like your Miss Simpson, it might answer, but she is a most singular personage and one of a kind. I don't see how we should manage it."

Fondly, the dowager smiled at her son. "I cannot do everything for you," she said. "I have exhausted my cleverness. Besides, it is a mother's first duty to set her children on the road to independence, especially when she is at a loss for an answer and knows not what else is to be done. This puzzle you must needs unscramble yourself."

Lord Hammond was still trying to unscramble the puzzle when he returned to Grosvenor Square. He was recalled from his brown study by Bunkers, who announced that all was in readiness for the next day's journey and handed him a note. Recognizing his brother-in-law's seal, Hammond opened the paper and read the terse warning.

> Give up this nonsense about a speech, and I will say nothing to the Prince. I call on you to remember your duty to King and family.
>
> Yours, etc.
> Selby

Hammond thanked the butler, then added before the man departed below stairs, "Bunkers, if anyone else should call or write to remind me of my duty, you will kindly inform him that I am dead."

Chapter III

Amid a flurry of packing and crating, Hopewell seemed to Irene even more chaotic than usual. She had just left her sisters engaged in mending and pressing and folding in the upstairs bedroom. Now she stood in the middle of the library and gathered together her energies. It was her task to sort the books. There were a few with which she could not bear to part, and there were many which would have to be sent to the vicarage.

From the look of the high, crowded shelves, Irene had a good deal of dusty work to look forward to. She was glad she had thought to bring the feather duster, and glad, too, that she had thought to pin up her hair. Perhaps she ought to have worn a cap, she thought. But the knot she had pinned at the nape of her neck would have to do. It felt sturdy enough to the touch. Only a few curls had managed to work their way loose.

She moved the ladder to the farthest corner, wishing that the one narrow window in the room yielded more light. The dimness would add to the difficulty of making selections, she knew. Climbing the first step, she found it awkward to carry the duster and still maintain a firm grip on the unsteady ladder. Descending again, she caught her boot heel on the hem of her skirt and nearly fell.

"This will never do," she declared.

Laying the duster on the desk, she pulled the folds of her skirt to one side and tucked them under her sash. As she inspected the results, she nodded in satisfaction. Her petticoat was long enough to ensure decency and short enough to ensure safety.

The feather duster was not so easily disposed of, however. She tried putting the handle between her teeth, in the manner of a pirate about to board a frigate. Assuming a piratical expression, she leered ferociously, but the final result proved disappointing, for the feathers tickled her nose and made her sneeze. A more efficient method, she discovered, was to slide the handle of the duster beneath the bow of her sash where it tied at the back. As she observed the effect of this device, she laughed. The feathers plumed out like a tail.

"I look like a shorn peacock," she told herself and climbed the ladder without incident.

The books lining the shelves in the corner were not what she had hoped they would be. They included writings by many of her sisters' favorite authors and her own.

"Oh, why could they not have been sermons!" she said with a sigh. "Then, at least, I might have marked them out for the vicarage without a pang."

Reaching behind her, she drew the duster from her sash and whisked it along the shelf. A cloud of motes drifted over her, causing her to shake her head and cough. These motions loosened several more curls from her head knot and reminded her abruptly of the ladder's shaky construction. But, determined to persevere, she returned the duster to its place in her bow and surveyed the titles once more.

One heavily worn volume proved irresistible. She drew it from the shelf and with her fingers wiped the remaining dust from its cover. It was a slim, heavily marked folio. Its binding had come undone, and several of its pages slipped halfway out. She opened the book, aligning the errant pages with care. As she did so, a well-remembered line caught her eye. Soon she was engrossed in reading. So rapt did she become in the scene, in fact, that she did not hear the door open to admit the Earl of Hammond.

He looked about him, allowing his eyes to adjust gradually to the dimness of the room. The little kitchen maid who had answered his knock at the house had told him that Miss Sparks was to be found in the library. In a timid flutter, the maid had led him to the door and had then disappeared down the corridor. She had not only neglected to tell him which of the Misses Sparks he would find in the library, but she had apparently led him on a fool's errand, for he saw no one in the room. It occurred to him that he might wait there for hours, or even days, before someone in that ramshackle household came to his rescue.

The sound of a page turning caused him to glance up. There, standing atop a ladder, was a young woman poring over a book. An odd way to read, he mused, but not nearly so odd as her appearance. Her hair was wildly disarranged, half of it tightly knotted, half of it tumbling down her back in golden curls. She had made a great lump of her skirt, revealing yards of petticoat, and she appeared to have a bird's tail. In addition, she displayed a profile that impressed him with its fineness and strength.

To announce his presence without alarming his hostess, Hammond gently cleared his throat. Irene started violently. As she

46

looked toward the source of the sound, two of the pages escaped from her book and drifted down to the foot of the ladder. He moved to retrieve them immediately, glancing at the print as he did so and smiling at the familiar passage.

"I did not hear anyone come in," Irene said with a gasp. She brushed a stray lock of hair from her face, leaving a dark smudge of dust across her fiery cheek.

Hammond looked at the page in his hand, then up at her. Mellifluously he intoned, *"She speaks! Oh, speak again, bright angel! For thou art as glorious to this night, being over my head, as is a winged messenger of Heaven."*

Irene laughed with pleasure. *"What man art thou that so stumblest on my counsel?"* she declaimed.

The earl searched in the pages for the appropriate reply. *"I know not how to tell thee who I am,"* he answered. *"My name, dear saint, is hateful to myself because it is an enemy to thee."*

Enchanted, Irene blinked her eyes. As if by sorcery, a handsome, elegantly dressed stranger had materialized in her shabby library. Now he spoke poetry to her with playful grace. His voice was rich and deep, his knowledge of the play nearly as complete as her own, his eyes alight with amusement.

"Art thou not Romeo, and a Montague?" she said.

Taking swift note of his line, he replied, *"Neither, fair saint, if either thee dislike."*

Irene stared at him, wondering if she had perhaps created him out of her imagination. No, he was perfectly real, she assured herself, and therefore, it was incumbent on her to forget Shakespeare and remember her manners.

"You are welcome, sir," she said. "I shall be down directly."

"Capital!" he exclaimed. "I was afraid I would have to climb up to you, in the manner of the Romeos everywhere. How much more sensible for Juliet to come down directly."

As Irene began her descent, her boot caught in the lace trim of her petticoat. The book flew out of her hand, and in her effort to grasp it she lost her balance. She would have fallen on top of her book had not Hammond caught her in his arms.

He did not hurry the business of steadying her on her feet. Nor did he give any indication of releasing his hold on her very soon.

Feigning a lightness she was far from feeling, she asked, *"How camest thou hither, tell me, and wherefore?"*

He replied from memory, *"With love's*

light wings did I o'erperch these walls." He stopped, wrinkling his brow in thought. "To tell the truth, it was on horseback from the inn at Botherby. I confess, I cannot remember the rest of the lines." Reluctantly, he released her.

"Thou knowest the mask of night is on my face," she said, smiling, *"else would a maiden blush bepaint my cheek."*

"Yes," he said, "it does rather resemble a mask of night. But in point of fact, I believe it is a smudge which bepaints your cheek."

Irene's hand flew to her face. Hammond withdrew a handkerchief from his coat and gently began to wipe off the smudge. She gazed at him, feeling silly at what she imagined must be her daft expression, yet unable to tear away her eyes. She permitted him to dab her cheek with the soft linen, a work that he prolonged until he had accentuated the rosiness there well beyond nature.

When at last he had finished, he said seriously, *"I am afraid, being in night, all this but a dream, too flattering sweet to be substantial."*

Irene smiled softly. "The dust on your handkerchief ought to reassure you," she said. She took the linen from his hand and looked puzzled when she saw the monogram. "Well," she declared, "it's plain as a pikestaff you are not a Montague, not with the letter *H* embroidered on your hand-kerchief."

His smile faded. "You have found me out," he acknowledged ruefully. "The name is Hammond." He bowed gracefully and added, "May I know with which of the Sparks sisters I have the pleasure of play-acting?"

Her face clouding over, Irene stiffened. She stepped away from him and answered curtly, "Irene." Then, suddenly conscious of her improper appearance, she tugged at the folds of her skirt and smoothed them down around her petticoat. Uneasily she attempted to tidy her hair, which fell rebelliously over her shoulders.

"I beg you will pardon this reception," she apologized shakily. "We no longer have a footman, nor indeed any servants besides Annie. Do you find the inn to your liking? Oh, where is my book?"

Hammond fixed her with a look. *"What's in a name?"* he asked, a challenge in his voice. *"That which we can call a rose by any other name would smell as sweet."*

"That is Juliet's line," she responded unhappily. Then spotting the book where it had fallen by the desk, she stooped to pick it up. When she rose, she faced him with recovered dignity. "As you see," she said, "we are in the throes of packing. We shall be out of your way in no more than a few days."

"I have not come to evict you, Miss Sparks," Hammond said.

"It is not a question of eviction," she replied formally. "Hopewell belongs to you. There is no more to be said."

"*Alack,*" he quoted gravely, the playfulness entirely gone from his voice, "*there lies more peril in thine eye then in twenty swords.*"

Silently she took the pages from his hand. She placed them inside the book and put it firmly on the desk.

"I shall fetch my sisters," she said. "They are above stairs and will surely want to extend their greetings." She moved toward the door.

"*Wilt thou leave me so unsatisfied?*" he asked in a voice of such strength that it stopped her in the act of pulling on the doorknob.

She turned to look at him, distress visible in the thin line of her lips and the heave of her bosom. Something in her told her to reply in a softer vein, but she quelled it. Another, more habitual instinct warned her that she was in danger of making a complete fool of herself. If she did not keep her wits about her, the voice whispered, she and her sisters might well end up like the besotted

Juliet. That would no doubt please her neighbors in Botherby, but she had no desire to play the tragic heroine for their amusement, nor for the Earl of Hammond's either.

"What more satisfaction canst thou have?" she answered in Juliet's words.

For some time he looked at her with deep intensity. At length he spoke angrily. "Dash it! I have forgot the line!"

"No matter," she said, moving to leave.

"One moment!" he commanded. He crossed to her and took the duster from the back of her sash, his face coming alarmingly close to hers in the process. With a gallant bow and a flourish, he handed the duster to her as though it were a bouquet. "Your feathers, madam," he said with an ironic smile. "I apologize for ruffling them so."

Breathlessly, Irene made her escape from the room.

When she had gone, Hammond went to the desk and picked up the book she had flung there. He turned to the place where they had left off. What more satisfaction did Romeo desire, Juliet had asked. Romeo ought to have replied, *"The exchange of thy love's faithful vow for mine."*

It was a bit much, Hammond acknowledged. But then, Romeo always seemed to

52

have a lamentable tendency to go beyond the bounds of good sense whenever he could. A lovesick calf, Romeo was impulsive, unthinking, moonstruck. He had made a bad end, too, Hammond reminded himself. Of course, Romeo's age must serve as his excuse, for he had been little more than a schoolboy. In contrast, the Earl of Hammond had seen thirty summers. What, in the name of heaven, he wondered, was his excuse?

With such misgivings, the earl read the remainder of the scene. He paused over one part in particular, rereading it many times until he had committed it to memory. Then, clapping the book shut, he smiled roguishly at the ceiling. *"All these woes shall serve for sweet discourse in our time to come,"* he vowed.

The sisters gathered in the front parlor, tidying whatever came to hand in order to render the room suddenly presentable, as well as to soothe their nervous anticipation. Caroline tucked a tear in the drapery behind a pleat, while Martha, seating herself on the sofa by the tea table, inspected the napkins for stains.

Irene paced restlessly before the fire, stopping to poke it now and then. Although it was warm outdoors in the March sunlight, Hopewell's drafty rooms retained a wintry chill. As she fanned the flames, Irene assured herself that the importance of their visitor justified the luxury of a fire.

Only Muffin was still, sitting silently in the most obscure corner of the parlor, partly hidden by an outsized candelabrum.

"I suppose he is very smartly dressed," Caroline said. "Did you notice his cravat, Irene? How was it tied?"

Irene eyed her sister moodily. "I don't recall," she replied, stooping to stab the poker at a log.

"I am sure he is 'all the crack,' as Muffin would say," Martha added. "Is he not, Irene?"

"I suppose he is," she answered.

Caroline flung the drape away in despair. "He will see the tear soon enough anyway." She sighed. "There is no use in trying to disguise it." She went to warm her hands by the fire, observing Irene's preoccupation in some puzzlement. "I wish you would tell us what he is like," she said. "Your refusal conjures up the most horrid speculation. Is he an overfed ogre or a black-bearded ruffian?"

"You read too many Gothic tales," Irene said. "I do believe, Caroline, that you will be disappointed if he does not turn out the veriest monster."

"I shall be disappointed," Martha interjected, "if you do not tell us anything. Annie will show him in at any moment and we hardly know what to expect."

"Annie certainly seems to be taking her time about it," Irene said. "Was it not fifteen minutes ago I sent her to the library to bring him here? I expect she has forgotten him completely."

"Please do not complain of your impatience," Caroline reproved. "We are fidgety enough as it is, especially so because you make him out such a mystery."

Irene looked at her regretfully. She did not trust herself to describe the earl. If she once alluded to his dark, expressive eyes, her composure would fly instantly out the window. If she referred in even the most casual way to his graceful bearing, his strong shoulders, or his square jaw, her sisters would set up a howl and tease her unbearably. Caroline would be sure to mistake her uneasiness for something tender and foolish.

It was imperative, Irene felt, that she not allow herself to be distracted from her duty. The others might succumb to Hammond's manifold charms. Indeed, they could hardly fail to do so. But she must and would keep a clear head. This was a resolution more easily made than kept, she knew, for the earl had turned her own head with astonishing swiftness.

She thought back to the young woman who had enacted Juliet in the library. That Irene had permitted herself to be lively, mischievous, and unabashedly smitten. Such comportment, however, did not belong at a meeting with the new master of Hopewell. The situation required Cleopatra — a queen wholly in command of herself — and not Juliet — a simpering girl with nothing better to do than to fancy herself in love.

Caroline seated herself next to Martha and said, pouting, "She is not going to say a word, no matter how much we beg her. I take her obstinate silence as permission to imagine whatever I like. And I think he must be hideously ugly, covered with red scars and brown warts."

Irene laughed. "You are mistaken," she said. "He is very handsome." To distract her sisters from following up this piece of news with more questions, she asked, "Where has Muffin gone?" Searching the room, she at last spotted her in the corner. "Are you not feeling well?" she asked kindly. "You are white as a sheet."

"I am dreadfully ill," Muffin said, groaning, as she came near the fire. "I ought to go to bed."

Alarmed, Irene said, "Of course, you shall go at once."

But the door opened at that instant, and Hammond entered at the maid's behest, thus preventing Muffin from escaping a meeting with him. Muffin had no sooner set eyes on the earl's shiny Hessian boots than she darted back to her hiding place, daring only once to peer out as Irene introduced Martha and Caroline.

These two young ladies, who had risen from the sofa at the first sound of a step at the door, now curtsied prettily. Caroline gawked openly at the earl's classical mien, while Martha bashfully returned his smile with one equally warm.

"And Muffin," Irene added, surprised to find that the girl had left her side.

With shoulders hunched and her chin down, Muffin performed a hasty curtsy from behind the candelabrum.

"Muffin?" the Earl said, stifling a smile. "What a charming name."

"I ought to have said *Mary*," Irene said. "We are so used to calling her by our pet name."

Cordially, Martha invited him to sit

down. He took the most comfortable chair, as she had indicated, and firmly set his eyes on the two friendly faces in the room.

"Please excuse Muffin," Martha said. "She is not feeling herself just now."

"I understand completely," his lordship replied. "I too have not been entirely myself this afternoon, and your sister, who so kindly entertained me in the library, called me by another name at first."

He was gratified to see Irene blanch.

"Muffin is probably just afraid of you," Caroline confided in a loud whisper.

Hammond studied Muffin, who squirmed in the corner. Then he glanced at Irene, who squirmed behind the sofa. He wondered if he ought to jeopardize his amusement by putting them more at their ease.

"I fully understand that, too," he said. "Having acquired her childhood home, I no doubt appear to Miss Muffin in the role of a villain." Directing a charming look at Martha, his most sympathetic listener, he continued, "I assure you all, I am really a delightful fellow, known everywhere for my good nature and my devotion to Shakespeare." He noted with satisfaction that Irene grew very pink. "But my most illustrious quality," he went on silkily, "is my ability to keep a secret. I am quite famous for it, in fact. I have never in my life betrayed a confidence or revealed anything that might cause embarrassment to another."

Muffin came out of her hiding place and stared at him. Caroline remarked, "Why, what a disagreeable reputation to have! I'm sure we should all die of boredom if everyone in Botherby kept their own counsel and would not tell a secret."

Out of the corner of his eye, Hammond noticed Muffin creeping closer. "I'm afraid I disappoint you, Miss Caroline," he said.

"Oh, not at all!" she contradicted eagerly. "I declare, you are the handsomest man I have ever seen."

Gravely, his lordship thanked her.

Irene urged Martha to pour tea, hoping that such a distraction might prevent Caroline from further outbursts. All watched quietly as Martha placed a piece of bread and butter on a plate and handed it to the earl. When everyone had been served, the sound of china cups tinkling on saucers was all that could be heard.

Irene cast about in her mind for some innocent pleasantry, but it was Hammond who finally broke the stillness. He apologized for coming upon them so unexpectedly, without first writing or sending a messenger.

"The truth is," he said, "I only learned of

your existence two days ago and felt that too much time had been wasted already."

"But how did you learn of our existence?" Caroline asked excitedly.

Irene added quickly, "I hope Mr. Uffingham did not alarm you needlessly."

Watching Muffin inch back to her corner, the earl explained, "An excellent young lady informed me that my inheritance had left Lord Sparks's daughters homeless."

"Your wife?" Caroline asked,

To her vast relief, he shook his head. "I am not married," he assured her.

"Then who could it be, I wonder," Caroline persisted.

"It is not for nothing that I am renowned for keeping confidences," he replied. "I will say only this: She is a friend to all of us, and, for my part, I am much obliged to her."

He was rewarded with Muffin's brightest smile. She hastened to the sofa, snuggled up to Martha, and accepted a proffered scone with alacrity.

"My curiosity is insatiable," Caroline said. "Who can she be?"

"I too am curious," Irene intervened, "but not about your friend's identity. Obviously, she wishes to remain anonymous, and we shall not press you." She then aimed a look full of meaning at Caroline.

Her speaking more than two sentences prompted the earl to look at Irene steadily for the first time since he had presented her with the feather duster. Feeling his eyes on her, she nearly faltered in her speech, but pressed on bravely. "I am curious to know why you did not come when you first heard of the inheritance. Have you come expressly to see us?"

"Yes, it is a mystery!" Caroline agreed.

As he framed his answer, Irene recalled what Mr. Uffingham had said in regard to Hammond's reputation. Like her father, he was "not quite the thing," and, like her father, he was utterly charming. Therein, she knew, lay the danger.

"I've come to see you," he explained smoothly, "to ask a favor of you."

The sisters looked at one another, astonished at the notion that they could perform a favor for one so richly endowed in every possible way.

"We shall do anything you like!" Muffin announced. Her sisters glared at her, aghast.

"I thank you," the earl said solemnly. "But perhaps I ought to tell you what it is before you decide."

"Perhaps you ought!" Irene agreed with asperity.

"Well then, you would oblige my family and myself by coming to London for an extended visit with my sister."

Stunned, Irene watched the three on the sofa clap their hands in ecstasy. Their cries of "London! We shall go to London!" filled the room. Imperturbably the earl allowed them to rhapsodize without interruption. Irene's eyes met his over the heads of her sisters. She gazed at him in the hope of penetrating the mask of his mild expression and discerning the motive behind the invitation.

He saw only that she looked at him with even greater iciness than she had displayed in the library. Damn her! he thought. Damn her for a missish, contrary female, above being pleased by the most benevolent of gestures. It was not often that he took the trouble to make himself agreeable to a woman in such a fashion. Generally, his nobility and charm spoke for themselves. When he did exert himself to win a woman's favor, he was accustomed to gaining his point.

"I'm afraid that would be a dreadful imposition on your sister," Martha said modestly.

"Not at all," he answered. "It is precisely what she needs. She has two daughters your own age and would welcome whatever might distract them from ripping each other's hearts out. No, indeed, it would be no imposition whatever. Louisa has everything to gain, I assure you. And she likes nothing better than to dress up young ladies and marry them off."

"Marry them off!" Caroline repeated in rapture. Turning to Irene, she sighed and said, "It is perfect, is it not? It is like a dream!"

"It certainly does seem fantastic," Irene said. "And your sister, my lord, appears to be an unbelievably generous woman."

"So she appears," his lordship concurred. "But I sense a note of skepticism. Perhaps Miss Irene has an objection?"

Too full of their joy to have sensed anything like skepticism, the other three loudly disputed this suggestion. They insisted that Irene was as thrilled at the prospect of going to London as they were themselves.

"It is only that she worries so much," Martha explained. "She is always thinking what will be best for us. Isn't that right, Caroline?"

"You do want to go, Irene, don't you?" Caroline pleaded.

Irene looked down at her hands, which were folded primly before her. "It appears to be a practical plan," she allowed, "given the fact that we have no alternative."

Her sisters took that as indication enough of her enthusiasm.

Rising from his chair, the earl prepared to take his leave. He was reluctant to depart while Irene continued so distant, and he felt again what he had felt in the library — a wish for a word or a sign more satisfying than her cool assent. But she did mean to accept the invitation. That much was clear. The other must come in time.

Irene watched him move to the door. "Thank you, my lord," she murmured so that he barely heard her. He replied with a graceful bow.

Before making his exit, Hammond promised that his carriage would be at their disposal to carry them to town in a week's time. He would attend to all the arrangements, including their stay overnight at an inn en route. He himself would depart for London early the next morning to deliver to his sister the joyful news that her invitation had been graciously accepted. In the meantime, he hoped that they and their abigail would have a pleasant journey. Then, with a parting look at Irene, he was gone.

When the door had shut, Caroline groaned in vexation and said, "Our abigail?"

"What a hum!" Muffin complained. "Why do we need an abigail?"

"A better question," Irene sighed, "is where do we get one? They are almost as scarce as husbands."

"Perhaps Mrs. Bostwick will act as our abigail," Martha put in hopefully. "She may be anxious to visit her daughter in London."

"Freeze Mrs. Bostwick!" Muffin exclaimed. "We are perfectly able to manage for ourselves."

"I daresay," Caroline giggled, "we would look after poor Mrs. B. much better than she after us."

"The earl is right," Irene reminded them. "It is best to observe the proprieties in this. I have heard that ladies traveling unchaperoned may be subjected to the most high-handed treatment."

"Well," Martha said, "let us hope that Mrs. Bostwick is inclined to travel Tuesday next."

"And that she isn't having one of her famous spells," Muffin added.

This dire allusion set Irene to laughing. "We have struck a bargain with Lord Hammond," she said stoutly, "and we are not going to fail our appointment with him merely for lack of an abigail. If push comes to shove, we will sew one out of pillows and lace!"

The mention of their late visitor's name roused a hush of admiration. Soon Caroline began to recount the many signs of his taste and breeding. Martha nodded dreamily as her sister itemized his lordship's many fine qualities. And Muffin summed it up for all of them by concluding, "He's slap up to the mark!"

Irene refrained from encomiums, too conscious of the conflicting emotions within her to express the admiration she felt. It was exactly as she had predicted half an hour before; her sisters were wholly captivated, completely taken in. He had only to dangle the bait in front of their innocent faces, and they were ready to throw all caution aside and follow him blindly. Admittedly, the bait was tempting. London! Surely one of them would catch a husband in those well-stocked waters. He had quite simply saved them with his bait, and while her reservations troubled her, she could not but be grateful.

Abruptly Caroline recalled Irene to the present. "I don't think you knew what you were about," she scolded Irene. "You behaved as though he had come to seduce us."

Irene smiled thinly. "Perhaps he did," she said.

"Fiddle!" Muffin said.

"I wish you would tell us your reservations," Martha urged. "Do not feel, my dear, that you must keep them hidden."

"Even if they are ridiculous!" Muffin put in.

Irene walked to the chair that Hammond had so recently vacated. She looked at it thoughtfully, then sat in it. She felt the warmth he had left there and leaned back, saying, "I am plagued with questions. I wish they would take themselves off, but they are a stubborn lot. Who, for example, is this mysterious young lady that knows all about our situation? Why must she remain anonymous? Furthermore, why did the earl's sister not send us a written invitation by way of her brother? Does not a lady of her stamp know that one cannot be quite comfortable about an invitation delivered by proxy? And why, tell me please, should a woman with two marriageable daughters of her own invite four potential rivals into her home?"

The others frowned as they pondered this.

"Don't count me as a rival!" Muffin objected.

"Why," Irene continued, "should our existence matter at all to Lord Hammond? Why should he ignore Hopewell and attend just to us?"

"To be kind," Muffin declared.

"I pray you are right," Irene went on, "but when have we known men of his sort to exert themselves purely out of kindness? Recall, if you will, our father, his companions, and our mother's relations. When were they ever kind, unless they expected to get something in return? From what I am told, we may expect the same from Lord Hammond. Indeed, I have it on excellent authority that his character is such that we ought not to regard his overtures as sincere."

These doubts cast a funereal pall over her listeners. In grim sorrow they looked at one another. The answers that flashed through their minds seemed too dreadful or too preposterous to entertain for more than a second. But, having been raised, the questions refused to go away of their own accord.

At last Muffin jumped up, jostling the teacups. "If you are so determined to suspect his motives," she cried out in distress, "then you had jolly well better ask him exactly what he means to do with us."

"I fully intend to," Irene replied.

Chapter IV

Upon his return to town, the earl waited on his sister, who had just ended a morning visit with her dearest friend. Lady Volteface had complacently divulged a piece of news highly distressing to Louisa; to wit: that her daughter's ball had resulted in a betrothal that would shortly be announced in the *Times*. Naturally enough, this tidbit put Louisa wholly out of charity with her brother. She greeted him coldly, asking in a voice resonant with impatience, "Pray, to what do we owe the honor of your presence?"

Stephen looked leisurely around the sitting room. It presented, he saw at a glance, a vivid contrast to the one he had lately visited at Hopewell. Louisa's taste ran heavily to swirling velvet drapes, hard incommodious chairs, and ornate upholstery. Everywhere one gazed there were trinkets, boxes, figurines, vases, and portraits bearing the childhood likenesses of her two daughters. One could hardly turn around in such a chamber without risking real danger of knocking over one treasure or another. His lordship tried to imagine Muffin in such surroundings and, summoning up an image of inevitable disaster, smiled.

"Are you going to invite me to sit down?" he inquired politely.

"I am not," said Lady Selby. "I do not see that you deserve any such attention."

"You grieve me, my dear," he replied pleasantly. "I should have thought you would be overjoyed to receive the sponsor of your daughters' ball."

Louisa seemed not to have heard. "Why, only this morning," she lamented, "Lady Volteface informed me that her daughter's engagement was positively formed at her debut, and a paltry affair it was, too, I can tell you. It is beyond bearing, to see such a thin, squinty little thing married, when my own girls languish in obscurity, all because their uncle is too selfish to do his duty by them."

"Perhaps I did not make myself clear, sister. I am prepared to do all that is required."

"You've made it quite plain, I think," her ladyship went on, "that your obligations are nothing to your whims. So you take yourself off to the country with nary a thought for anyone else, regardless of their dependence on you for their future well-being."

"You may have your ball," Hammond repeated patiently, "and you may have carte blanche as well."

Lady Selby could not immediately dislodge her frown. From long and constant use, it appeared to have etched itself permanently on her powdered visage. She stared at her brother stupidly, as a series of emotions rose in her bosom. The last of these — extravagant gratitude — succeeded finally in transforming her expression.

"Oh, brother," she gasped, "you are so good, so thoughtful, so kind and generous. I knew you would come round, once you had been made to see your responsibility. I hardly know what to say, except that I am very glad I paid you that visit and reminded you of what you owe your nearest relatives. My heart is so overflowing with thankfulness that I am entirely speechless. Words fail me, and I think I would faint were it not for the fact that I know how you detest swooning females. I can only thank you with a full heart and tell you that I shall never forget this kindness. Never!"

This effusion gave Hammond not a few misgivings. He regretted heartily that removing himself from his sister's ill graces did not produce as much entertainment as receiving her set-downs. The outpourings of sisterly affection soon bored him, stemming as they did from a motive of self-interest.

"Spare me your outbursts," he said. "You've covered my waistcoat with powder, and my valet will be giving me notice on your account. No more, Louisa, if you please."

Solicitously she brushed his coat with her fingers and apologized, adding that if she did not fear to crush his cravat, she would give him a hug. "But I cannot stay," she exclaimed. "I must find Beatrice and Chloe and tell them at once. And Selby! I must make him come and thank you, too. He will offer to help defray the expense, but of course you will refuse." On that, she left him.

Anticipating more of the same when the Selby household convened, Stephen set about fortifying himself against the coming onslaught with a glass of his host's famous port. Selby might be an officious, interfering brother-in-law, but he kept an excellent cellar, and Hammond meant to avail himself of a sample. After pouring himself a glass of wine from the decanter, he sniffed approvingly and sipped the flavorful ruby.

Feeling refreshed now, he sought out the least prickly chair the room afforded and sat down in it. With each taste of port, he grew more satisfied. In less than half an hour he would have settled the Sparks sisters with his eternally grateful sibling. He would put them from his mind then, put Irene from his mind, and direct his attention to his meeting with the Chancellor of the Exchequer.

The redoubtable Mr. Dabney had groomed him these past several months to introduce the currency-reform bill in the Upper House. No one, least of all Hammond, labored under the delusion that the bill would come to a vote. One had to plant a notion in the brains of the members, allow it to be swallowed, digested, and smoked over, and then, perhaps, in ten, twenty, or thirty years, one might bring about a change. For now, the minister advised, it was sufficient to season Hammond with political speechifying, a prospect his lordship looked forward to with amusement and a determination to do well.

It was not the sort of thing his father would have approved, any more than his relatives and friends did. As master of the farmlands and tenants at Crown Leigh, the Earl of Hammond had much to do without embroiling himself in the swampy regions of government. Indeed, for several years after attaining to the title, Hammond forbore to venture beyond the safe realms of family business. Then the encouragement of the chancellor, coupled with an inexplicable restlessness of spirit, drew him out of his isolation, giving him an urge to leave some sort of mark upon the world.

Bonaparte's movements on the Continent served to confirm him in his ambition. Although the Frenchman was all that was evil, he was without a doubt adventurous and daring. The vulgarity and corruption of the upstart Corsican were bywords; yet, Stephen had to admit to a certain admiration for the man.

Draining the last of the wine, he turned his thoughts to a thornier subject — the ladies of Hopewell. Irene's face rose up before him, a vision of blue-gray eyes and flushed cheeks framed by honey-colored curls. The charming image soon dissipated, however, in the recollection of her icy stare. The younger girls, in contrast, had been more than cordial. Even Muffin, who had hidden from him at first, had ended by throwing him looks of joyful complicity. Only Irene had evinced resentment.

It did not surprise him that she felt as she did. He was, after all, an interloper, the undeserving heir to the home she had always known. At the same time, she was too intelligent to doubt that the entail, and not the earl himself, was responsible for her present straits.

He felt sorely tempted to do something, when next they met, to startle her out of her determined frigidity. But such an enterprise would prove delicate, he knew. A man of honor could hardly make love to a woman he had undertaken to protect.

A clamor outside the door roused his lordship from his meditation. He set down his glass and rose to receive the effusions of his relatives, who disputed in the hall for some time before entering. From the expressions on their faces, Hammond guessed that the gesture that had inspired ecstasy in his sister had provoked very different emotions in the others.

Selby acknowledged him with a murmur of his name and a refusal to look him in the eye. Marching to the port decanter, he held it up to the light. "I see you've helped yourself," he observed. "Well then, I need not offer you any."

With a maternal smile, Louisa pushed her children toward Hammond and bade them thank their generous uncle.

Beatrice, a near-sighted girl with dull hair and a long face, spoke first, essaying a minimal curtsy and delivering herself of a weighty observation: "Frivolity is a detriment to the mind and a noxious poison to the soul. The claims of society — in such frivolous schemes as balls and dances — are as the chaff of wheat."

"When have you ever seen a chaff or a wheat?" Chloe demanded. "You are merely quoting one of those prosy sermons you read, and you have no more idea what you are talking about than I have." She then curtsied prettily before her uncle and looked up at him with a flirtatious smile. "Beatrice insists she will not come to the ball, uncle, and for my part, I think she is being a horrible prig, for if an elder sister will not dance, then how can the younger one find any beaux? She is only afraid that I shall have all the beaux to myself while she will have none."

Louisa smiled indulgently, as though her offspring had spoken in the most intelligent, engaging manner. "Of course Beatrice will have beaux," she declared. "It is her ball, and therefore she must have beaux."

"It is mine, too!" Chloe pouted.

"Yes, indeed, my pet," Lady Selby said, "and you will both be the talk of London when it is done. Will they not, Selby?"

Hearing himself addressed, Selby jumped.

"There's no more than half the decanter left," he said, "and that's the last of it."

Subduing her impatience, Louisa coaxed her inattentive spouse. "My dear, we are speaking of the ball that Hammond has promised our girls. You have not changed your mind, Stephen, I hope?"

Hammond assured her that he had not.

"You see!" she called to her husband. "I did *not* imagine it; nor did I invent the story. You heard him with your own ears."

Selby, feeling called upon to say something in acknowledgment of Hammond's liberality on his daughters' behalf, muttered, "Very decent of you, Hammond. I should, of course, throw in some blunt from my side, but Louisa says you will not hear of it, and I do not argue with her, for on the subject of balls I say as little as I can."

"If you dislike the scheme," the earl said graciously, "I shall, of course, say no more about it."

"Dislike it?" Louisa cried. "Why, he is perfectly delighted with it, as we all are. If he seems a trifle stupid at this moment, it is only because he is too moved to speak. Is that not so, my love?"

"Do as you please, Louisa," her husband said. "You always do anyway. I ask only that you leave me out of it. I want no part of finery and arrangements."

"There, you see," Beatrice interjected in a righteous tone. "Papa agrees with me. He despises such nonsense and wishes to see his daughters engaged in more rational pursuits than flirting at a ball. Is that not so, Papa?"

With a helpless look at the earl, Lord Selby seized the port decanter and cradled it in his arm. His family gazed at him intently, in the expectation that he would settle the dispute once and for all.

"I do not like discussions," he said. "A very awkward business, discussions."

"Oh, Papa!" Beatrice exclaimed in disappointment.

"Papa likes a ball well enough," Chloe said triumphantly, "especially if the gentlemen are permitted to sit down to cards."

Shrugging his shoulders, Selby strode toward the door. He paused for a moment to shake his head at Hammond, whom he regarded balefully. "You must have taken leave of your senses, man." He sighed. "First that speech in the Lords. Now a ball. Stap me if the mad old king himself knows a hawk from a handsaw better than you do." So saying, he left the room, taking his port with him.

Louisa shooed her daughters to a corner, then turned to Hammond with a fond expression fixed to her lips. "Perhaps Selby has not thanked you as he ought," she said. "I assure you, he is perfectly aware of what you have done here today and what it means to the future of our poor girls. After I have spoken with him in private, I am sure he will make his true feelings known to you in proper form."

"He may even offer me a glass of port," Hammond said.

"Beatrice, too, will thank you when her natural modesty is overcome by the sense of what she owes to her mother and by the recollection that the allowance she is to receive upon her father's death is insufficient to support her through life."

From her corner, Beatrice glared sullenly at Hammond.

"Chloe, on the other hand," Louisa continued silkily, "is, as you have seen, fully conscious of the beneficence you have conferred upon us."

Tossing her head at her sister, Chloe favored Hammond with another perfectly executed curtsy.

"And I," Louisa concluded her little speech, "I hardly know how I am ever to repay you for your goodness."

"There is a way to repay me," Stephen said affably. "In fact, I have the very thing."

Peering into the glass above her dressing table, Lady Louisa Selby declared that she was the unluckiest woman alive. To have been born with such a brother, nay, to have been born at all — it was completely insupportable. If only their mother would curb his obstinacy. But the dowager would not speak to him; she had said so countless times. She preferred to take refuge in her ailments. And even if she had agreed to speak with him, she could not be counted on to side with her daughter. How very agreeable it would be, Louisa thought, to have a debility in one's legs so that one would not have to go about and meet with the willful idiosyncracies of the world. "If it were not the season," she told her daughters, "I would pack my trunks at once and take myself off to the country, where I should not be troubled any further."

"Fiddle, you detest the country," said Chloe. "I wish you would not take on so. It is very disagreeable."

"Not as disagreeable as falling into a trap of your uncle's making," her mother replied.

"We are still to have our ball; he has said so, and he always keeps his promises." She leaned down to her mother so that their cheeks touched, and she admired her image in the mirror. Although round faces were not the fashion, Chloe imagined that her plump face and forthright chin were most pleasing. Accustomed to comparisons with her sister, who was undeniably plain, Chloe prided herself on her appearance and even fancied at times that she resembled her grandmother. Quickly she glanced at her mother's reflection, noting that she sat in uncharacteristic silence, looking very grim indeed.

"Four!" Lady Selby exclaimed with a pitiful moan. "Four of them, no less. What could Lord Sparks have been thinking of, to be so prolific and so penniless at the same time? Have people no more consideration than to live at the expense of others?"

"Do not repine," Beatrice urged from her chair, where she struggled mightily to make sense of one of Dr. Johnson's essays. "To bear with inconvenience for Charity's sake is an ennobling sacrifice. I myself look forward to welcoming these poor creatures into our home and I do not feel at all that I condescend beneath myself by befriending them."

"I am very glad they are coming, too," Chloe stated. "I am bored to distraction with listening to Beatrice's sermons. It would be preferable to go about with young ladies who do not look down their noses at anything that isn't old and tedious."

Rolling her eyes heavenward, Beatrice assumed a martyred look. "Only one part of the plan strikes me as not strictly the thing," she said. "If we are to benefit from a charitable gesture, then where is the Virtue in it? I myself would prefer to put aside any thoughts of a ball for at least a year."

Chloe choked with indignation. "You are horrible!" she cried. "You only want to defer the ball to punish me. Your high-sounding philosophy doesn't fool me one bit."

"If I had not acquired the forbearance that derives from great study," Beatrice remarked, "I should not hesitate to inform you that you are an empty-headed goose, for all your fine features and tonnish airs."

The two young ladies then embarked upon an exchange of taunts along these lines, culminating in their mother's pleas that they be still. "You have given me the headache," she complained, "as though I didn't have enough to bedevil me."

With a lofty sniff, Beatrice resumed her reading. Idly fingering a bauble on the dressing table, Chloe gave a great yawn and cast about her for something to occupy her mind. "I cannot understand why you are in such a bother," she said to her mother. "You adore outfitting young ladies and telling them how they must not behave. I should think you would enjoy having a free hand with four more girls, especially as my uncle means to pay for it all."

Louisa eyed her daughter darkly. "Has it occurred to you," she asked, "that they might be very beautiful?"

"And so what if they are?" Chloe replied, admiring her image in the mirror once more and patting her coiffure complacently. "I am sure I shall not begrudge them any prettiness they may lay claim to, nor any beaux neither."

"I assure you, Mama," Beatrice intoned, "I, too, am wholly indifferent to physical beauty in others, for while it is said to be most pleasant to behold a reflection of beauty that lies within, still I have observed that in proportion as a maiden is beautiful, she is likely to be ignorant and insipid."

Convinced now that she was indeed the unluckiest woman in the world, Lady Selby moaned and demanded her vinaigrette. Her daughters obediently helped her to the divan, where they propped her up on satin pillows and exhorted her not to play them a Cheltenham tragedy. For a time she sniffed her potion and blinked her eyes, until she was suddenly restored to excellent spirits by the reflection that her obligation to her brother and his orphans from Somerset would end immediately after the ball.

Chapter V

"It's all arranged," Hammond told his secretary as they dined alone in Grosvenor Square. "They will go to Louisa, and I have salved my conscience." As if to emphasize the finality of the plan, his lordship speared a roasted potato with his fork and contemplated it thoughtfully.

"I confess," said Charles, "I am surprised. I did not think Lady Selby could be brought to invite four ladies into her home, not with her ambitions for Miss Beatrice and Miss Chloe."

Lord Hammond smiled. "I have very persuasive methods at my disposal," he said. "Some are pleased to call them *bribery*. I prefer the appellation *bargain* myself, implying as it does a fair exchange."

"You have not given her the Hammond diamonds?" Charles asked in distress. "Surely, sir, you have not bribed her with the jewels."

"The diamonds are safe, my boy," said his lordship, "and they shall remain in my possession until such time as I have a wife to hang them on. No, my bribe was even more expensive, if that is possible. I have agreed to sponsor a ball for my nieces."

Charles blanched. "That is a powerful bribe indeed. But will it be worth it, do you think? Lord and Lady Selby are widely known to be prudent in their expenses, but not when the bills are to be sent elsewhere."

"Your euphemisms are delightful," Hammond said with a laugh, slicing his beefsteak and pudding. "By *prudent* I take it you mean *niggardly,* and you are saying, in your uniquely diplomatic way, that they will do their best to leave me with pockets to let. Perhaps it is you, not I, who ought to undertake a political career."

A blush crossing his handsome young face, Charles begged to know what Hammond had found at Hopewell. Was the estate in a condition of decrepitude, as Mr. Uffingham had represented? Had the four ladies actually agreed to come to London to seek a husband? Did the sisters match the descriptions Muffin had given in her letter?

Hopewell, his lordship reported, lay in the worst possible state of decay. Indeed, he had begun to refer to it in his private thoughts by the name "Hopeless," for its fallow lands and neglected mansion seemed beyond restoration. If Mr. Uffingham had exaggerated at all, it was on the side of optimism.

The four ladies had actually agreed to travel to London, Hammond said, now addressing Charles's second question. He had ordered the coach into Somersetshire to bring them to town. They and their abigail would be deposited on Louisa's doorstep in little more than a day's time. At first there were some objections to the plan put forward by the eldest sister, he said, but she had come round at the last.

"That would be Irene, would it not?"

"I'm afraid it would," Hammond replied in a tone that caused Charles's eyebrows to arch, for while he was accustomed to his employer's irony, he could not recall ever hearing it so underscored with ruefulness. "Muffin's descriptions," the earl continued, "are not quite fresh in my memory. Perhaps you recall them better than I."

"She began by saying that Irene was handsome and ought to be given preference," Charles reminded him.

Hammond gave his secretary a look of irritation. Rising from his chair, he threw his napkin onto his dinner plate. "Let us have coffee in the library," he said. "Perhaps there I can think what is the best means of giving Miss Sparks preference."

In the library, Charles handed his lordship his coffee cup. Whenever he revived the topic of the ladies at Hopewell, Hammond managed to divert the conversation. Unwilling to pursue a subject so disagreeable to the man he revered most in all the world, Charles talked on innocuously, while Hammond studied his empty cup.

"What say you to marrying?" the earl asked irrelevantly.

Although Charles was usually ready with a tactful response to every question put before him, this one left him tongue-tied. "You are not thinking of marrying *me* off to one of the Hopewell ladies," he replied at last. "I am hardly rich enough for their purposes. I do not come into my portion for another two years yet, and until then I am completely dependent on the stipend you have granted me."

"But you are young and handsome and not without prospects," his lordship mused. "You might do for Martha. Muffin, of course, is too young yet, and Caroline would find you dull and unromantic."

"What about Irene?" Charles inquired innocently.

"She would not like you," said his lordship. "Such is her dislike of me that she would dislike anyone connected with me. And though dislike does not necessarily constitute a deterrent to marriage, still, I have better hopes for you, my lad."

"Do you intend to give Miss Sparks a glove on the cheek?" Charles asked bluntly.

Hammond smiled at him and refilled his coffee cup. Then, raising it high to toast the young man, he said, "I propose to give her that — and a good deal more. I drink to your very good health."

As he replaced the cup on the table, Bunkers entered to announce the arrival of the chancellor. Mr. Dabney strode into the room, flanked by two loyal party minions who imitated Mr. Dabney's gestures and echoed his utterances in unison.

"Back at last, Hammond," Mr. Dabney said heartily. "Thought you were avoiding me."

"Not at all," Hammond greeted him. "I was taken into the country on important business; I meant to call on you tomorrow."

"No time like the present, don't you know," Mr. Dabney replied, echoed by his two cohorts.

"If you are here on the matter of the speech," Stephen said, "I assure you, I am ready. Charles, let us show his lordship what we have written."

Before Charles could walk to the desk, where a carefully inscribed copy of the address lay in a locked drawer, Mr. Dabney halted him with a raised hand. His associates raised their hands as well.

"Not necessary," the chancellor said. "It's to be postponed."

Disappointed, Charles exclaimed, "But why?"

"Why, you ask?" Dabney laughed sardonically. His followers laughed, too. "Why is anything committed or omitted in Parliament of late? Because of Boney, that's why."

"I don't understand," said Charles.

Hammond intervened here to explain to his secretary that the campaign in Leipzig no doubt occupied the members too fully for them to absorb any suggestions regarding currency reform.

"That is it in a nutshell," boomed the chancellor. He paused to allow his friends to repeat his exclamation, and then he proceeded. "It's all a farrago. Regardless of whether Wellington can contain Bonaparte on the Continent, life in England must go on, don't you know. But to convince the members of that would take more oratory than I am master of."

The two party members looked at each other, despairing to duplicate such a lengthy speech.

Hammond approached Mr. Dabney and

shook his hand warmly. He liked the wise old eccentric and admired his ability to defer his chief causes until the time was ripe. Although Hammond was nearly as disappointed as Charles over the postponement, he thought he would do well to emulate his mentor's patience. "When the time comes," the earl said, "I will be ready."

"You have learned a useful lesson this night," the minister announced.

"Night," his followers chanted.

"You have learned that members and ministers do not control events, contrary to what the newspapers would have you believe. And now I must be off, don't you know." Stopping his faithful echoes with a raised hand, Mr. Dabney bid his lordship a very good evening and departed, his loyal shadows marching in time to his step.

When they were alone, Charles sighed in dissatisfaction. "Damn!" he pronounced, hitting his fist on the desk.

"Damn!" Hammond echoed, exactly imitating Charles's tone and gesture.

The two gentlemen exchanged an irreverent look and then laughed heartily together.

Outside the dowager's chamber, Hammond accosted Miss Simpson.

"I am sure she has awakened from her nap," whispered that venerable lady. "She will be so pleased to see you; your visits are a tonic."

"Like your kindness and care," said Hammond. He kissed her hand, causing her to giggle. Then he went into the room.

He found the dowager looking rosy and refreshed. Miss Simpson had arranged her legs comfortably on a hassock, and, to Hammond's delight, they were neither wrapped nor covered.

After presenting his cheek to be kissed, he related the story of his visit in Somerset and his negotiations with Louisa. Her ladyship listened with amusement and ruminated over the bargain her children had struck. She wondered aloud whether it was provision or punishment to install the Sparks sisters in Berkeley Square.

"A little of each, I suppose," said Hammond. "You need not worry, though. I shall keep a close eye on them all."

"How so?" she asked. "You will be preparing to speechify, I have heard."

"Ah, Louisa does gossip," he said. "No, the speech is to be postponed. I shall be able to devote myself to assisting my poor relations on their hunt for a Smithfield bargain."

"I should never have thought of settling them in Berkeley Square," said the dowager. "It is dreadful to say this of a daughter, but I don't think I would have trusted Louisa."

"Well, I don't either," said the earl. "She will buy every ribbon and gewgaw on Bond Street, just to avenge herself on me, and then, when the ball guests have drunk up the champagne and gone home, she will cast the Sparks sisters into the street without so much as a fare-thee-well."

The dowager gazed at him incredulously. "And yet you bring them to her anyway?"

"I am prepared, Mother," he assured her. "I shall hold off paying her bills until I am ready to move the ladies to a more hospitable lodging."

Laughing, his mother devoutly hoped that not all brothers and sisters conducted themselves so disgracefully.

"We are nothing to Beatrice and Chloe," said Hammond. "I've not seen anything to equal their hatred of each other."

"Is it always thus?" the dowager asked.

"No, I have seen a very different picture of sisterly affection. I saw it at Hopewell and admired it. To find four such different and opinionated females in one family is uncommon, but to find them able to exist in harmony and affection is rare indeed."

"I am very glad to hear it," his mother responded. "To what do you attribute such sisterly attachment?"

Hammond pondered this now as he had done many times before. "It comes, in part, I suppose from their being orphans," he said.

"Gracious!" her ladyship declared. "Do you mean to tell me that when I shuffle off, you and Louisa will make your peace?"

" 'Shuffle off'!" the earl said, laughing. "Where the devil did you pick up that expression?"

"I have been reading Shakespeare, my love. He uses it, so I am sure it is highly poetic. Are you still so fond of Shakespeare?"

"More than ever," Hammond replied. "From family harmony to Shakespeare. That *is* a leap."

"Yes, yes," she said impatiently. "We were speaking of sisters and brothers. And you were telling me that I might bring you and Louisa together by making you orphans."

"I said no such thing," the earl corrected. "You are disposed to quiz me."

"I am disposed to hear more. Why do these sisters dote on one another when all over the kingdom sisters are ever at war?"

"I suspect it is the influence of the eldest — Irene. She is a strong, determined young woman with a powerful influence over the younger ones."

"She sounds positively fearsome," the dowager observed. "I very much want to meet her."

Hammond promised her that she would, as he proposed to escort them to London himself very shortly. He meant, he said, to surprise them by joining their party at the Bluebird Inn, where he had arranged for them to stop overnight.

"Is it wise to surprise them?" his mother asked. "When I was a young girl, I preferred the opportunity to adjust my hair and pinch my cheeks until they blushed."

"I have made up my mind," he said. "Besides, I want to deliver them to Louisa in person, so that I may witness her rapture with my very own eyes."

Although she knew her sisters awaited her impatiently in the carriage, Irene descended the staircase slowly. She looked about her as if she meant to commit the very walls to memory. Unable to hurry her leavetaking, she paused at the entrance to the parlor.

She threw open the doors and gazed around at what had been the scene of so many intimate family occasions. But nostalgia soon gave way to quite another sensation as she rested her glance on a comfortable high-backed chair. There the Earl of Hammond had sat, she recalled, and there he had smiled at her over the chatter. Amusement had shone in that smile — and something else besides, something that caused Irene to smile now as she had not been able to smile then.

Closing the doors, she walked toward the front entrance. A sudden recollection, however, made her turn on her heel and run through the hall to the library. Stepping across the threshold, she sighed to see the room shorn of its books, furniture, and mementos.

In a moment, the room appeared to her imagination as it had when she first set eyes on the Earl of Hammond. She felt herself perched precariously on the ladder again, taking in his deep voice and merry eyes. With a slight shiver, she remembered the strength of his touch as he prevented her fall.

For some time, Irene permitted herself the luxury of anticipating her next meeting with the earl. She devoutly hoped he would take that opportunity to dispatch all her doubts. It was not only for the sake of her sisters' safety that she cherished this hope. She knew it would also add materially to her happiness if she could think well of her family's benefactor.

Putting a cool hand to her hot cheek, she scanned the room again. Recollecting her sisters' attendance outside, she pulled down the heavy veil of her hat and adjusted it under her chin. Then — without another backward glance — she rushed from the house.

Chapter VI

His lordship's carriage rumbled into the courtyard, where it was welcomed by a number of barking dogs and scattering hens. The landlord, who had lain in wait for the coach's arrival, elbowed his goodwife, saying, "They have come. Prepare the joint of mutton and the fowl. Not a moment to lose!"

He rushed outside to welcome the earl's guests, noting with pride the crest emblazoned on the carriage. He wished that it were not so dark, so that his neighbors might behold that emblem of nobility, designed by the first earl, who had reveled with King Harry in the London stews and had fought with him at Agincourt. With its menagerie of roaring lions and growling canines, the signet never failed to inspire assiduity in every species of landlord.

The stable hands attended to the horses under the supervision of Muffin, who had ridden aloft with the coachman. Mr. Small, the landlord, opened the door so that he might hand out the ladies. Caroline was the first to alight. Exultantly, she took in the spectacle of an inn on the London road, the inmates of which all scurried to attend to her needs. "I am famished," she announced.

The next to emerge was Martha, who peered about in the dark to ascertain the whereabouts of Muffin and to thank her host for his kind welcome.

The last to step down was a large lady of domineering aspect. Her wide black hat and heavy veil hid her face from view. She wore a coarse woolen shawl gathered thickly under her chin and a pair of unframed spectacles on the tip of her imperious nose.

"Miss Proutie," the woman introduced herself to Mr. Small in a deep, commanding voice. "I will see to the girls, my good man. You will go inside and prepare the beds for inspection."

The landlord gaped. He could not see Miss Proutie very well, and she averted her face when he held up his lantern, but he had the distinct impression that she was the fiercest female he had ever laid eyes on.

"Well, are you waiting for your beard to grow?" Miss Proutie snapped.

Mr. Small hurried inside to warn his wife that the ladies had arrived with a dragon in lieu of an abigail. "She means to look over the bedsheets," he said portentously.

His wife watched him as he dashed up the staircase and called anxiously to the chambermaid to remove the coverlets. Peeking out the door of the kitchen, she saw the formidable abigail lead her three charges into the main parlor. She tiptoed in behind them, wiping her hands on her apron and looking worriedly at the fire.

"I shall tend to that," said Miss Proutie. Thereupon, she picked up the poker and thrust it at the logs until the flames roared.

"I'm parched," said Caroline. "Perhaps our kind hostess would bring us some ratafia."

"She will bring tea," amended Miss Proutie.

"Pooh!" Muffin groaned.

"Tea!" the abigail said, silencing all protest with a forbidding stare.

Mrs. Small hustled from the room, patting her heaving bosom and crying aloud for tea.

"I think you like being a hideous old harridan," Caroline said to Miss Proutie.

"What a lark!" Muffin laughed.

With a tentative knock on the door, Mr. Small entered and bowed several times. "The beds are prepared, ma'am," he said, addressing the abigail. Straight as a ramrod, he stood at the entrance for her to pass.

"Let us go then," Miss Proutie ordered her charges.

"Fiddle," said Muffin. "I mean to see if the chestnuts have been properly combed." Then, smiling at the landlord, she asked if she might obtain a carrot from the kitchen for them. "They are the leaders, after all," she explained. "A special reward is due, in my opinion."

Mr. Small begged her to avail herself of all the carrots his humble kitchen could provide.

When Muffin left, Caroline informed the others that she would stay and await the tea. "I am hungry to fainting," she declared.

Miss Proutie and Martha allowed Mr. Small to escort them to the sleeping chambers, while Caroline warmed her hands in front of the fire. The room was pleasing, for though it was not overlarge, it was commodious. Its dark wainscoting produced a cozy atmosphere, enchanced by pewter tankards along the mantel top.

After a time, a gentleman entered wearing a fur-lined cape and a roguish riding hat. Seating himself at a distant table, he stared at Caroline. Modestly she turned to the fire.

The stranger gave the impression of a dark man, whose neatly trimmed beard achieved a somewhat satanic effect. His clothes were of the finest weave, and to Caroline's unpracticed eye he looked a very tulip of fashion. From his table, the gentleman gave her a leer, and she looked away.

She was startled suddenly to hear his voice in her ear. Standing close behind her, he whispered, "I hope you are not unattended, my dear. If you are, I am yours to command." He performed a bow and a sweeping flourish, while she took a step back toward the fireplace.

In his turn, he stepped forward.

"I am traveling with my abigail," she said breathlessly. "Miss Proutie will be here in a moment."

Coming still closer, he murmured, "I am very glad of it. It is dangerous for lovely young ladies to travel alone. Who knows what rude advances they may be subjected to?"

Caroline thought for a moment and then replied in an unsteady voice, "I beg you, sir, to return to your table. The landlord will be here to see to your wishes this very instant."

"Ah," he said, his lip curling sardonically, "I was told he was above stairs and would be some time yet. Indeed, his wife informed me that he was inspecting the beds with an old hag and might be occupied for a full half-hour."

★ ★ ★

From the recesses of the largest bedroom, Miss Proutie heard something amiss. She had just poked her forefinger into a pillow slip when a faint sound reached her ears. Pausing, she listened for it again. Mr. Small, who had heard nothing, inferred that the old dragon had spotted something alien on the pillow and, in her disgust, had turned momentarily to stone. But instead of upbraiding him, as he expected, the abigail said only, "Come, my man," and traversed the hallway to descend the stairs in a flash. To the landlord's mind, she moved with a speed remarkable in one so apparently aged.

Miss Proutie flung open the door to find the satanic gentleman struggling with Caroline in his arms.

"Unhand that maiden!" she cried in a stentorian voice.

"Good God!" the gentleman exclaimed when he beheld the awesome abigail.

Miss Proutie strode to the fireplace and took hold of the poker. "My name is Proutie, sir," she said ominously. "Do you fence?"

Laughing uproariously, the gentleman bowed. "Egad," he declared, "I have never seen such a female in my life!" He pushed Caroline away.

"I trust you have seen enough females in

your life to distinguish between a lady and a doxy," Miss Proutie said. "You have behaved badly, very badly, sir, and I must now ask you to quit these premises at once."

He glanced at Caroline, who peeped out from behind the landlord. Assessing the looks of horror on their faces, he next considered Miss Proutie, who brandished the raised poker in her hand and had a murderous gleam in her eye. It was prudent to retreat for the moment, he bethought himself. After bowing, he went to his table, swept his cape over his shoulders, and was gone.

On his way out, he brushed up against Martha, who was just then entering the parlor.

"Did the gentleman want something?" she inquired.

Mr. Small buried his head in his hands. "Lord Hammond will have no further business at the Bluebird after this," he cried woefully.

"He need never know about it," Miss Proutie said. "Now buck up, man, and go see about that supper you promised."

With a grateful bow, he exited to oversee the preparation of the finest joint in the county. Miss Proutie swiftly apprised Martha of the circumstances that had led to her desertion of the bedsheets.

"Let me fetch you some tea," Martha urged her younger sister.

"I have lost my appetite now," Caroline said.

The abigail induced her to sit. Then, positioning herself next to the shivering girl, she put her arm about her shoulder.

Muffin burst in the door with Hammond's coachman hard on her heels. "There has been a set to!" she exclaimed. "All the servants are buzzing about it. Have I missed it?"

Martha told her that matters were in hand now and that it was time to enjoy the repast that Mr. and Mrs. Small intended to set before them.

The coachman apologized to the ladies, digging the toe of one foot into the floor.

"I bespoke ye a private room," he assured them, "just as his lordship said."

"Then we ought not to be here," Martha declared. "We will remove at once to our private room."

"Nay," the man apologized, "that ye cannot. This was to be the room, for the others are small and not what his lordship intended ye should 'ave. That gentleman, if he be a gentleman, overstepped, ma'am."

"Let us say no more about it, then," the abigail declared. "He was very much at fault, while you are blameless. And no real harm has come of it. So go back to your dinner and your horses, for we have an early start on the morrow."

Thanking Miss Proutie and wondering that such a dragon could speak so sensibly, he did as she had bidden him.

As soon as the four were alone again, a sob escaped Caroline's throat. She buried her head in Miss Proutie's shawl and let spill the tale. "I have never encountered such a vile, detestable creature," she said, tears of anger and fright streaking her face. "His mustache, his teeth, that hideous laugh — I believe he is the devil himself!"

Miss Proutie murmured a comforting sound.

Sitting bolt upright again, Caroline went on, "I warned him, you know, that we traveled under Lord Hammond's protection. And do you know what answer he gave? He laughed, and said that he did not know Lord Hammond's taste ran to young girls, that he had always known the earl to select his mistresses out of Drury Lane!"

Hearing this, Miss Proutie trembled a little and stood up. Solemnly she looked at each of the others. "That gentleman and Lord Hammond are evidently acquainted," she said. "I cannot tell you how sorry I am to hear it, though I cannot say I am surprised.

The manners of London gentlemen appear to be as much at fault as their morals."

"Surely not every London gentleman behaves in such a fashion," Martha said.

"I think Lord Hammond's manners are perfect," Muffin added.

Before the discussion could proceed further, Mr. and Mrs. Small entered bearing trays laden with simple but hearty fare. The dinner somewhat restored the young ladies' energies and cheeriness. Their hosts exerted themselves to the utmost to please the three pretty maidens and their generous abigail. The good offices of these functionaries were received so graciously that Mrs. Small felt inspired to declare to her husband that of all the females they had accommodated at his lordship's behest, these were undoubtedly the most charming.

The two youngest excused themselves early and repaired to their bedchamber. Martha remained with Miss Proutie while the cover was removed. Then she, too, made her good nights and sought repose above stairs. Mrs. Small hovered about the abigail, seeking ways of ingratiating herself further in that lady's favor, until she was called from the room by a loud knock at the door.

Hearing that knock, Miss Proutie moved

at once to the fireplace and seized the poker. If the rude gentleman had returned, he would find her ready. But the gentleman who entered the room proved to be none other than the Earl of Hammond, who, seeing a large black specter in a grotesque hat poised with a fire iron, stopped in his tracks.

Immediately Miss Proutie adjusted her shawl about her chin and set down the poker. Hammond wondered if he would ever pay a visit to the ladies of Hopewell without meeting with a highly unconventional reception. He gazed at Miss Proutie's odd attire and made her the most polite greeting he could muster under the circumstances. "Mrs. Smart told me I should find you here. You are Miss Proutie?"

A civil nod confirmed this.

"And have all the ladies retired for the night?"

"They have," came the reply.

Hammond removed his cloak, revealing an elegant deep blue coat. His waistcoat was ice-blue and his cravat a soft shade of rose. Miss Proutie could not help but steal a glance at the earl, who, by accident, caught her eye and started. Something in that eye seemed familiar, but the source of this flash of recognition eluded him.

"Have we perhaps met before, ma'am?" he inquired.

"I do not think we travel in the same circles," she replied.

"I suppose not," he mused. "Still, I have the oddest feeling that I know you."

Miss Proutie turned her back to him and warmed her fingers over the fire. Several honey-colored curls had escaped from under her hat and tumbled down her back. Recollecting these rebellious locks very well now, Hammond smiled and approached a little nearer.

Turning abruptly, she said, "I must bid you good night, sir, and beg you will excuse me."

"Pray, do not go!" he said, stopping her en route to the door. "I wish you would stay, for I need your help." He smiled engagingly.

Unable to resist that smile, Miss Proutie found a chair in the darkest corner of the room and sat down on the edge of it.

"Do you have a near relation in the theatrical profession?" he asked. "You put me very much in mind of an actress I saw not long ago."

"I have no family," Miss Proutie murmured.

"Dear me, another orphan," observed his lordship. "Then I suppose we have never met, and I must take this opportunity to further our acquaintance."

"The hour grows late," the lady said, shifting about uncomfortably in her chair. "How may I serve you, my lord?"

Hammond sat down on a bench across from her and leaned forward slightly. "I will be much obliged to you, Miss Proutie, if you will help me ascertain the character of the four Misses Sparks."

"To what purpose?"

"Why, to discover how I may best ensure their success in London."

Miss Proutie gave a calm nod that belied the emotions warring in her breast.

"For example," his lordship said, as though deeply perplexed, "do you anticipate any difficulty with Miss Mary Sparks?"

"Difficulty?" she repeated.

"I know no particular harm of the girl," he explained. "Yet, from what I have observed, she may grow restless in the confines of the city. I should not like to see her unhappy."

"Her sisters will keep her in check," the abigail said, with a good deal more hope than certainty.

"Well then, I am satisfied on that head," he said pleasantly. "As for Miss Mary's sisters, I hope they may fare as well, and that none of them will be induced to elope with the first scoundrel who offers marriage and a castle on the moors."

Miss Proutie bridled, retorting, "I assure you, sir, even though the Misses Sparks were born in the country, they are not fools. Nor will they give you any cause to be ashamed of having taken them under your protection."

"I intended no insult," he said smoothly, noting with a gleam that Miss Proutie seemed on the point of bolting from the room. "I only wish to spare them the embarrassment of a faux pas — or something worse. Miss Irene, for example, gives an impression of most forbidding reserve. It will be misunderstood in society, and many will think her above being pleased. Certainly it will frighten off her suitors."

After a pause, during which she gripped the arms of her chair until the knuckles showed white, the abigail managed to reply with tolerable equanimity, "Miss Irene has no desire to marry, my lord. She will be quite content to see her sisters comfortably established."

"She casts herself in the role of the protector, I see. A pity, I think, for when she is not scowling, she is one of the handsomest women I have ever seen."

Miss Proutie caught her breath and could not answer.

"I wish Miss Irene were here now," Hammond continued. "I would caution her that the role of protector is singularly dull as well as damnably inconvenient."

"I wish she were here now, too," said the abigail.

Moving nearer, his lordship said, "Miss Irene dislikes me, I fear. It is the inheritance, I suppose. Will you tell her for me, Miss Proutie, that I neither expected nor wished it?"

"You are mistaken," the abigail said in a low voice. "Miss Irene does not dislike you."

Pleased with this answer, he went on, "Yet she eyes me with dislike, as though she suspects me of harboring some nefarious motive."

"What is your motive, my lord?" she could not help asking.

"A most honorable one, my dear lady. The moment I heard Miss Sparks's rendering of Juliet, I knew we were destined to enact *Lovers' Vows*."

"You are not serious. Miss Irene will think you are quizzing her."

"Indeed? And how can you be so certain?"

This question caused Miss Proutie to

flush. She cast about her for an answer that would put an end to the interrogation and permit her to leave.

"I cannot speak for Miss Sparks," she said. "But I believe she seeks reassurance."

"I mean to give her exactly that, at the earliest opportunity," he said in a low voice. "Meanwhile, I solicit your counsel, for I hardly know what to tell her if she will not believe that I am perfectly sincere in the matter of *Lovers' Vows*."

"Tell her the truth," she advised.

"She does not know me very well," he pointed out. "Therefore, it will be impossible for her to know whether I am what I represent myself to be or merely a dissembler."

The lady paused, apparently shaken by this logic. "I do not think you are a dissembler," she said at last, "and so I shall tell Miss Sparks." Feeling that this answer sufficiently signaled a period to the interview, she swept to the door.

"Miss Proutie!" he called, walking to her and raising her hand to his lips. "You are most kind to sit up with me and advise me on these matters. May I write to you in Botherby if I have further need of your help?"

Sensible of his firm touch, the abigail

stood flustered. Then she replied in a shaky voice, "You may choose to write to me, sir, but I may not choose to answer."

When she had gone, he remarked to no one in particular that parting was sweet sorrow indeed; whereupon he sought out the landlord with a request for some viands and a bed for the night.

Chapter VII

Muffin ran ahead of her sisters and burst into the main hall, hoping that the breakfast was in readiness and that Mrs. Small would serve up beef and jam along with more homely fare. She was in the midst of imagining this repast when she spied a gentleman already seated at the table. Recognizing him at once, she halted suddenly, forcing Martha and Caroline to bump into her.

"This is capital!" she cried merrily. "Look who has come! Lord Hammond is here!"

Her two sisters could see very well that he was there. Ill at ease, they each dropped him a dainty curtsy and thanked him for having arranged for their comfort on the journey. Hammond noted that they appeared nervous. By exchanging a number of courtesies with them and confining his remarks to generalities, he managed to calm them a little. Satisfied that the carriage ride had been tolerably comfortable for the ladies, that none of them had been made ill by the coachman's swift pace, and that the Bluebird had accommodated their every wish, Hammond inquired after Miss Irene Sparks, who was nowhere to be seen.

This politeness produced consternation among the three ladies. They searched the floor and one another's faces in turn, until Muffin summoned up the presence of mind to reply, "She is out of sorts this morning. I expect she'll keep to her room awhile yet."

Irene's appearance in the doorway just then contradicted this allegation, but if Hammond saw anything amiss, he gave no indication of it.

Wearing a rich brown frock that set off her fair complexion to advantage, Irene entered the room gracefully and assumed a look of marvelous surprise. "My lord! I am amazed to see you here."

"So I gather," he said.

"You need not have troubled yourself on our account," she added cordially. "The journey has been uneventful."

"Except for the row," Muffin put in. Instantly she received Caroline's elbow in her rib.

"The row?" said his lordship.

Irene murmured that it was nothing for him to concern himself about.

The earl guessed by their looks that the row had been a good deal more than they were willing to say. Irene was blushing bright pink, while Martha and Caroline were using surreptitious frowns, nods, and kicks to quiet their youngest sister. Muffin squeezed her lips together as if to prevent any further untoward revelations. Amused by their efforts to prevaricate, Hammond smiled. He could not help but admire their ability to organize a conspiracy without so much as a word.

Appearing to accept Irene's explanation, he invited them all to join him for the morning meal. Mr. and Mrs. Small entered, bearing an assortment of dishes on a serving tray, among them a slab of smoked beef and a pot of gooseberry jam. Muffin crowed happily at finding her wishes granted and waited only for a signal from Irene to address her victuals.

"Oh, but where is Miss Proutie?" Hammond asked. Martha's fork clattered onto her plate.

"You have not met Miss Proutie?" Caroline exclaimed in alarm.

"Indeed I have," he replied, "and a fine-looking, intelligent personage she is, too."

Muffin choked on a piece of buttered toast. After patting her on the back and persuading her to drink a glass of water, Irene reported calmly that Miss Proutie had left the inn at dawn. It had been brought home to the abigail, she said, that Hammond's presence rendered her own superfluous. She had found a cart for hire and had taken it back to Botherby.

The earl observed that Miss Proutie was a very resourceful lady to have found a cart in the middle of the night, that he was deeply sorry to learn she had gone, that he liked her excessively, and that he hoped the ladies would favor him with her direction so that he might call upon her during his next visit to Hopewell.

Irene contrived to divert his lordship's attention from the unwelcome subject by overturning a pitcher of milk, spilling its contents into her lap. Coming to her at once, Hammond helped her to her feet and began blotting her soiled dress with his handkerchief. The others, alarmed at first by their sister's mishap, saw now that she was in capable hands. They began to chatter among themselves between bites of breakfast.

When he had satisfied himself that the spot was contained, Hammond laughed softly and said, "You see how useful a fellow I am. If you find a cheek smudged or a dress spilled on, I am always at the ready with a handkerchief."

Sensing him draw closer to her, Irene replied, "I am well aware, sir, of the extent to which you have been our benefactor."

"Benefactor!" he repeated. "Yes, of course. I had forgotten. Thank you for restoring me to a sense of my responsibilities. I see that you are every bit as useful a personage as myself, and that when my sister is unavailable, I may rely on you to remind me of my duty."

While she did not comprehend this sarcasm, Irene did perceive that his lordship was piqued by her response. Therefore, instead of venturing a second reply, which would surely enmesh her in further quarrels, Irene sought another diversion. The coachman, she said, had appointed an early hour for departure. Since it was nearly the time now, they had best finish their meal, collect their belongings, and forgather in the courtyard as quickly as possible.

Soon the party was trundling along the London road, with the four sisters situated snugly in the carriage and the earl astride his mount. The gentle rocking of the coach, so soon after their meal, lulled the passengers to sleep. Irene started to doze off, only to be awakened by dreams of the previous night's events.

Of the two gentlemen she had encountered during the evening, the scoundrel with the satanic beard had been the easier to deal with. Miss Proutie had resources at her command far beyond any Miss Irene Sparks might possess, and it was the most natural thing in the world for her to wield a fire iron in defense of offended beauty. To her delight, she had succeeded in sending the fellow packing.

Her duel with Lord Hammond, however, had not turned out so satisfactorily. That her disguise had completely deceived him was small consolation for the lack of reassurance she had received from him. When asked point-blank, he had declined to disclose his object in befriending the ladies of Hopewell. Instead he had teased evasively, in the exact manner of that most practiced of charmers — her late, lamented father.

Irene was even more unhappy with her behavior than she was with the earl's. The deception she had practiced on him was, in her eyes, as reprehensible as it was successful. If he should ever discover the truth, he must turn from her in disgust. While she knew that he was not the sort of gentleman whose opinion of her ought to matter a groat, she could not imagine the loss of his esteem without a powerful sense of regret.

After some hours thus spent, Irene wearied of her dispiriting thoughts. She turned her attention to the landscape which told her that they had attained the outskirts of the city at long last.

A butler ushered the travelers into the sitting room at Selby House, where Muffin promptly knocked over one of Louisa's treasures. It tumbled onto the floor, breaking into a thousand pieces. Aghast, the sisters rushed to retrieve the fragments; thus, when Lady Selby entered with her two daughters in attendance, she found the ladies of Hopewell crawling on her carpet. Above the noise of regretful apologies, Hammond briefly summed up the accident for Louisa's edification and promised to replace the vase.

"I'm glad it's broke! I detest Sèvres," Chloe said, stooping to the floor to join the new arrivals. Remembering their manners, the Sparks sisters rose at once. They performed their curtsies with lowered eyes and murmured expressions of gratitude for her ladyship's hospitality.

Before Louisa could reply, Beatrice stepped forward to welcome them with a panegyric on the virtues of charity. During this lengthy speech, the younger Hopewell ladies gaped at Beatrice, while Irene pressed her lips together to stifle a smile. When his niece had finally run out of breath, Hammond made introductions all around.

If Louisa had at first been uncertain as to the proper mode of addressing these newcomers, she now moved forward in her most daunting grande dame manner and greeted them with the appropriately empty amenities. Hammond did not stay long after that, preferring to retreat to the quiet orderliness of Grosvenor Square.

"Will you see me out, Miss Sparks?" he asked Irene. "I would have a word with you in private."

She followed him out of the room and into the hall, where he instructed the footman to have his carriage brought up. When the servant had closed the door behind him, Hammond turned to her. "I hereby give you notice, Miss Sparks," he said. "Your protection is now in the hands of my sister and her husband."

Unsure of his purpose in making this pointed announcement, Irene thanked him for delivering her family safely into the Selbys' custody.

"You see, I am no longer your benefactor, Miss Sparks," he went on. "I consider myself at liberty to cast myself in a less disinterested part." So saying, he drew near, looking as if he meant to kiss her. But at that instant the footman poked his head in the door to declare the coach awaited his lordship's pleasure.

While Hammond was occupied with glaring at the servant, Irene sought an appropriate reply. "I hope I shall never be so ungrateful as to forget my family's first benefactor," she said carefully. "Indeed, I will always think of your kindness as our protector and friend."

He considered her seriously for a moment. Then an ironic smile softened his face. "Save your gratitude, Miss Sparks," he said, "for a more grateful object. And let me assure you that in such a case as this, a lapse of memory would not only be forgiven, it would be welcomed."

In the days that followed, the four sisters adjusted comfortably to their elegant new surroundings. They were spared the embarrassment of having to answer questions about Hopewell and the events that had led to their installation in Berkeley Square, for the Selbys had no interest in anything that took place beyond the borders of London. Beatrice and Chloe declared the Sparks sisters pretty, well-behaved girls whom they were not ashamed to know, and they chattered about their town acquaintances as though the newcomers would be intimate with them all very soon. The Selby sisters also seemed to think themselves pretty, well-behaved girls whom the newcomers were glad to know. Within a short space of time, Irene was conscious that, contrary to her fears, Beatrice and Chloe thought far too well of themselves to be jealous of four lasses fresh from the country.

Lady Selby said little and looked much. It had turned out just as she had predicted — the ladies were beautiful and completely outshone her own offspring. Anticipating disaster from this dire turn of events, she spoke distantly to the sisters, in a voice that inspired awe, even from Muffin. Louisa maintained this reserve until two episodes melted it quite away. The first of these occurred during the initial visit to the dress- and hatmakers in Bond Street. Knowing that she need spare no expense, Lady Selby permitted herself to patronize the most fashionable and overpriced shops on the avenue. The fitters measured the four ladies with much praise for their figures, and these expressions of commendation were always addressed to her ladyship, as though she deserved sole credit for the existence of such well-formed females. Thus mollified, Louisa began to warm to the work of dressing the ladies of Hopewell, and it soon became apparent that the joys of outfitting lovely, modest, and grateful maidens were not to be equaled in this vale of tears.

The second episode occurred at the house of Lady Volteface, who had sent a note inviting the Selbys and their guests to an evening at cards. It seemed at first that the ladies did not properly appreciate such kind notice, and they appeared on the point of begging off, for Muffin was not at an age when she could accompany them, and they did not like to leave her alone. Lord Selby came to the rescue, however, by volunteering to keep Miss Mary company. She had shown herself an excellent student of piquet and silver loo. He would much rather, he said, play cards with Mary and drink his own Madeira than listen to Lady Volteface puff herself up over her daughter's engagement.

This difficulty settled, Louisa and the girls presented themselves at Lady Volteface's house, where the sisters Sparks were to undergo their first test in society. In the foyer, Lady Selby pinched Beatrice's cheeks and adjusted Chloe's lace over her bosom. Then, appraising the attire of the other three, she pronounced them "well enough" and herded them all inside.

Just as they had been commended in

Bond Street, so Irene, Martha, and Caroline were admired in society. A crowd of about twenty people filled the room, and most of them found an opportunity to compliment Louisa on her charges' beauty.

"You will be invited everywhere now," Lady Volteface whispered to her friend. "Each one is lovelier than the next, but the three of them together — that is a picture indeed! Thank goodness my Livonia is to be married, or I should despair of her ever attracting notice in such company!"

A circle of acquaintances soon gathered about Louisa to exclaim at the beauty of the Sparks sisters. Caroline's exquisite face was extolled, as were Martha's rosiness and Irene's tall figure. Somehow, this array of charms was attributed to Louisa's kindness, taste, and sagacity. By the time Louisa was settled once again in her coach, she realized that she had never received so much attention in her life. Consequently she leveled a benign smile at the ladies from whose beauty and manners such praise stemmed.

Flushed with excitement at being so graciously received, the ladies smiled back. Thus, the riders in the coach were supremely content with one another, the more so since they were ignorant of the report that had spread immediately upon their entrance — that the Earl of Hammond had settled an annuity upon each of the girls in the amount of two thousand pounds.

Lord Selby had passed the evening in highly unusual but highly satisfactory form. Muffin had assiduously kept his glass filled while demanding to know all the intricacies of his favorite games. In a short time, she had coaxed him into divulging his most cherished secrets of strategy, and she used them against him without a qualm. He could not recall when he had lost so badly or enjoyed it so much.

In subsequent evenings, Selby found himself forgoing the company at White's to be at home in the midst of the Sparks sisters. Muffin continued to serve as his apprentice at cards. From time to time, when they could persuade the others to join them, Selby and Muffin paired off as partners, sending their opponents down to ignominious defeat.

But this activity was only one source of his newfound attraction for his home. Irene sought permission to use his library, and, unlike Beatrice, who confined her study to sermons and dry essays, she selected plays, which she discussed with him in lively accents. Often she was moved to read a comical scene aloud for his entertainment. So charmed was he by her theatrics that he promised to take her to a play.

The intimacy among the girls blossomed. Beatrice paid her guests small attentions, such as bestowing upon them sweet tarts and pithy epigrams. Beatrice always assured her friends that she would never shirk any duty on behalf of her less fortunate fellow creatures.

Muffin replied in an undertone to Irene, "If her duty consists of dispensing sweet tarts, I have no objection to receiving her charity."

Chloe embraced her visitors as warmly as her sister did, though in a very different manner. She borrowed their ribbons and lent them her gloves. After an evening in company, she invited them to sip cocoa in her room and review the events of the night.

She perceived early on that in any crush, Caroline attracted an astonishing number of admirers. The young bucks flitted around her like moths drawn to a flame, so Chloe judged that her best interest lay in attaching herself as closely as possible to Caroline and never leaving her side. In that way, she maintained a place in the limelight. The fact that she had to share the limelight with its source did not trouble her for an instant. Limelight was a precious enough commodity without splitting hairs over how one got it.

Hammond paid several calls to Berkeley Square only to find that the ladies had gone out to be fitted for dresses or to make a morning visit. When he did manage to catch them at home, there was little opportunity to sound out Irene in private as to the progress of their visit. From the look of things at the Selby residence, all was proceeding better than he had expected. And from what he observed, he had no doubt that one of the Sparks sisters would choose herself a rich husband from among the young swains who hovered nearby at every evening party. That fortunate sister, he predicted, would be Caroline, for Martha was shy in company. As for Irene, he had other hopes for her.

The sisters themselves had little to pine about in their new surroundings. Beatrice and Chloe, each in her own way, were eager to be friendly, thankful as they were for relief from each other's society. Lord Selby beamed at them from the moment he sat down among them to the moment he nodded off to sleep. Lady Louisa's taste and advice were eminently practical, and the sisters hearkened to her as her own daughters had never done.

However, to Irene's mind, there were yet a few causes for concern. Muffin was banished from the sitting room after demolishing another china treasure, and Lady Selby was horrified to learn that the girl repaired to the stables every morning after breakfast. There was hardly a moment to spare to give Muffin her lessons, and when Irene expressed her consternation over this to Lord Selby, he expressed the hope that he would not be put to the expense of hiring a governess.

The London ton surprised Irene. She had not anticipated the kind acceptance it bestowed on four penniless country girls. Perhaps she had misjudged town society, she thought. Perhaps she had been too suspicious of noble lords and ladies — especially one of their number, whom she had regarded with distrust upon first learning his name.

Thinking back to what Mr. Uffingham had said about his lordship's character, she was not a little surprised to find that none of the solicitor's forebodings had been borne out in the past weeks. She had accompanied Lady Selby on numerous morning visits, walking parties, and evening gatherings, and at no time had she heard the Earl of Hammond spoken of as a gentleman of questionable morals, dissipated habits or insincere manners. On the contrary, he was highly regarded, and even though the encomiums she had heard emanated principally from mothers of marriageable daughters, the gentlemen of the town appeared to think well of him, too.

The discrepancy puzzled Irene. She resolved to sound his lordship further with an eye to making out his character at last. She hoped to be able to put her doubts to the test a few days hence, when a large party was to gather at the house of Lady Volteface. Hammond had talked of escorting the ladies there, and, when he did so, she meant to speak with him privately.

Chapter VIII

Lady Volteface's party threatened to put an end to the good understanding subsisting among the ladies of the Selby household. Chloe, who was not yet officially out, was barred from attending such a large formal gathering. She balked vociferously at the prospect of staying at home in the inferior company of those two indefatigable card players — her father and Miss Mary Sparks. It was grossly unjust, she pointed out, that she should be excluded, while Caroline, who was a full month younger, would be allowed to make one of the party.

Irene refused to entertain any suggestion of keeping Caroline at home on that basis. Even after listening politely to Louisa's many arguments on the subject, she still held firm to her view that it was preposterous to pretend, after all this time, that Caroline was a schoolroom miss. To force her sister to resume a status she had relinquished long ago seemed irrational to the eldest Miss Sparks, particularly in light of the fact that it was Caroline upon whom all her hopes lay for their future provision through an advantageous marriage. Much as she sympathized with Lady Selby's position, much as she grieved over Chloe's sense of ill usage, much as she would have liked to oblige them both, she could not treat Caroline so cruelly.

It was Hammond who found a way out of the difficulty. Discovering the ladies at their leisure one afternoon, he came upon them together as they sat over their embroidery in seething silence. He quickly deduced that something was the matter. When no one would tell him what it was, he sought out Muffin, who cheerfully divulged the whole.

Returning to the ladies, he said to Louisa, in a voice that all could hear, "I must extend my apologies, sister. I will not be able to escort you to Lady Volteface's crush."

Since Louisa had already worried herself into a frazzle over the party, this piece of news came as no great disappointment. She merely answered, with only a modicum of bitterness, that perhaps they would all end by declining the invitation, for if Caroline went and Chloe did not, she would never again know a moment's peace in her own house.

"I should not be surprised if you did decline," the earl replied. "Half of London has already done so."

This surprising announcement piqued Lady Selby's curiosity, and she demanded to know more.

"Did you not hear that it is to be a musicale?" he asked.

Louisa confessed that she had heard such a report but had dismissed it as an on-dit impossible to credit. After her last musicale, Lady Volteface could not have the face to arrange another, for the flatness of the champagne had been equaled only by the flatness of the soprano's high notes, and the boredom of the evening had been relieved only by the spectacle of the harpist falling off her stool. "A musicale!" Lady Selby exclaimed. "Was there ever such folly?"

"Now that I think on it," Chloe said magnanimously, "I suppose I shall not mind staying at home after all."

"But there is no need for that," Hammond assured her. "The company will not be overlarge, and there will be no dancing. I think you may go with impunity."

Chloe looked abashed at this. "I detest musicales," she said with a sigh.

"Music is the noblest of the arts," Beatrice declared. "It lifts the spirit of both performer and hearer, and, if I may indulge myself in a small vanity, I confess to feeling some pride whenever I produce a sound on the pianoforte which is not unpleasing."

Ignoring this speech, Lady Selby stated, "Then it is settled. We shall all go."

Relieved to have been extricated from their hostess's ill graces, the ladies of Hopewell collectively thanked his lordship.

"And do you detest musicales as Chloe does?" Irene inquired of Hammond. It distressed her to know that he would not attend the musicale, thus thwarting her plan for a private talk with him.

"I have business in the country," he said vaguely. He did not elaborate, even though his plan was to travel to Hopewell, where he meant to inaugurate a complete restoration of the estate. To mention the nature of his business would be to revive memories of home that might prove painful; moreover, it would remind the ladies that he was the interloper and stranger to whom their beloved home now belonged.

"I wonder that you return to the country so soon," Louisa said with irritation. "I declare, you have shown a prodigious fondness for the rural regions of late."

Hammond's lip curled in amusement. "Do you think, Louisa, that I am the sort to neglect my duty in regard to my lands? I hope I know better than to do that, especially when I have a sister who has a scold always at the ready if I forget my responsibilities. Perhaps you think I have nothing better to do than to settle disputes between contentious ladies."

"I think no such thing," Louisa snapped. "I am just thankful that you have given up that ridiculous speech."

Irene looked up from her sewing. The allusion to his lordship's speech intrigued her.

"It is not given up," the earl told his sister, "merely postponed."

Louisa declined to spar any longer with her brother. She thought it unseemly to unfold family quarrels before strangers. More important, her mind was easy now that both her daughters were to accompany her to Lady Volteface's musicale, and to argue with the bearer of these glad tidings struck her as somewhat ungrateful. She therefore excused herself to deliver the happy news to her husband.

As soon as she had gone, Chloe drew the others around her to speculate on the torments that awaited them at the home of Lady Volteface. Irene, noting that Hammond strolled to a bay window at the far end of the room, rose and joined him there. Side by side, they looked out on a foggy spring day.

"I had hoped to find a moment to talk with you," Irene said to him. "I thought perhaps Lady Volteface's party might prove an auspicious time, but I see now that I shall have to postpone the interview."

"I am growing quite used to postponements," Hammond said.

"Yes, Lady Selby mentioned your speech just now. Are you thinking of taking orders?"

He laughed and assured her it was not the sermonizing variety of speech he intended to make. He told her the purpose of his address, and as he spoke his face revealed an animation she had not before witnessed. For reasons that she did not stop to ponder Irene felt more pleased with every word he uttered.

"I did not imagine you had ambitions of that kind," she said, not without admiration.

"How should you?" he said. "You are far too occupied with imagining that I am your protector and friend."

"Please do not say that as though I had insulted you, Lord Hammond. I meant to pay you a great compliment."

"It is not compliments I want from you," he said.

She fixed her gaze on his reflection in the window. After a moment, he spoke, coming so near that she felt his breath on her hair. "Do you recall our reading of *Romeo and Juliet?*" he inquired. "Thinking of it a day or two ago, it occurred to me that we ought to essay *Antony and Cleopatra.*"

Irene inhaled quickly.

When she did not respond, he continued, "What say you to comedy instead? I infinitely prefer it myself. No one dies for love at the end."

Earnestly, Irene said, "Do not ridicule me in this fashion anymore, I beg you, my lord. I do not have the way of the London flirts as yet. In another month I may know what reply is proper in such an instance as this, and in two months I shall be prepared to feel less and spar more. But just now I cannot."

"Ah, so now I am no longer a benefactor; I am a flirt, am I? My versatility would quite overwhelm me, had I not lately lost the taste for flirting."

She searched his dark eyes, to see if he meant it.

He smiled at this. "If we were not in company," he told her, "I would demand that kiss I was cheated of some time ago."

"Perhaps you would not need to demand it," she replied. "Perhaps I would give it freely."

On this, he took her hand in his, raising it

almost to his lips. From this vantage point, he inspected the outline of her fingers. "I will not stay long in the country," he said. "Indeed, I am fairly tempted to avail myself of yet another postponement."

"Postponement!" cried Louisa, who, upon reentering the room, had caught the word, causing Hammond to let go of Irene's hand. "Selby says, and I quite agree, that it is a veritable blessing. We should die of mortification if you did your absurd speechifying before the ball."

The interruption effectively ended further communication between Irene and Hammond, for her ladyship so dominated the flow of talk with her plans for the ball that only looks could now pass between them. The earl took his leave soon afterward, bidding a soft goodbye to Irene and receiving her warm wishes for his safe return with a creditable appearance of tranquility.

Irene spent the remainder of the morning smiling and sighing over a piece of embroidery. But she was abruptly jolted out of her quiet contentment by the housekeeper, who proceeded to unfold to her a tale of disaster.

One of the stable hands had been cajoled into looking the other way while Muffin mounted Lord Selby's new gelding. The girl had ridden some considerable distance before the frisky animal dropped her in a puddle. The housekeeper discovered the catastrophe just as Muffin was returning the horse to the stable. When the good woman clapped eyes on Miss Mary's dirty and disheveled condition, she had run to inform Miss Sparks at once.

"Where is my sister now?" Irene asked in distress. "I must go to her." Whereupon she followed the good woman down the hall, wondering all the while how she would manage to contain her sister's high spirits in the midst of so many temptations.

The soprano gave no indication of liberating her audience anytime soon. Uncomfortable and hot in the stuffy room, the listeners had but two choices — either to doze off or to shift about in their seats, coughing as frequently as they dared.

Feeling her throat parched, Irene could not restrain her coughs. She glanced toward a nearby door, which led out of the drawing room and into a large salon where champagne and lemonade were laid out. The image of the cool drinks would not leave her, try as she would to concentrate on the performer. In vain did Madame Amoretti sing of the ecstasy of love and the torture of betrayal; Irene thought only of drink.

She eyed Lady Selby, who sat far from her on the aisle engaging in a struggle to keep awake. At last, succumbing to sleep, she napped with her mouth open, while a gentle noise escaped her nostrils.

Beatrice elbowed her mother. "You are snoring!" she admonished.

"Don't be ridiculous! I never snore," her ladyship replied, and immediately resumed making her slumbering sounds.

Irene could bear it no longer. She would die if she did not find a cup of water or some other liquid. At the rumble of the next snore, she slipped away into the salon and made straightaway for the refreshments table.

The room appeared empty. At the far end of it stood a small balcony ringed on the outer edge by French doors and on the inner by a semicircular staircase. As Irene poured a goblet full of lemonade and started to drink it down, she heard voices coming from the balcony. She would have made a hurried exit then had she not been riveted to the spot by the sound of one of the voices, a menacing growl that she recognized instantly.

Because she stood below the balcony, a

little to the side of the stairs, Irene knew she would not be seen if she stayed where she was. She did not wish to eavesdrop; yet she wished above anything to avoid attracting the notice of the man with the ugly voice.

In this quandary she heard that dreaded voice tell his interlocutor, "I make no threats, Colton. You know my reputation well enough and do not need additional inducements to bring you round. I say only that I have carried vouchers of yours for some time now. I am a most obliging fellow, but after all, this is the outside of enough. How is a man to support his frailties if his friends do not pay up what they owe?"

"You are a devil, Molyneux," said the other gentleman, an observation that impressed Irene with its truth and Mr. Molyneux with its risibility. He laughed humorlessly, the same sinister laugh Miss Proutie had provoked at the Bluebird as she prepared to anoint him with the fire iron.

Irene's head raced at the sound of that sardonic laugh. Whoever this Mr. Colton might be, she felt prodigiously sorry for him, for to be in the clutches of a man like Molyneux must lead to ruination.

"If I am not to have your blunt," Molyneux said, "then I expect to have your services."

"Do you think I am a lackey?" Colton retorted.

In a low, malevolent tone, Molyneux replied, "I think you are whatever it suits me to make you." So saying, he sauntered down the steps and strolled to the exit.

Irene stepped back into the shadow of the balcony, hoping to retain her anonymity. Having thought of another vicious taunt to level at Colton, Molyneux turned on his heel and saw her.

He glared at her. Then his face contorted into a smile, which to Irene's sensibilities appeared even more satanic than his menacing expression. He began to approach her, asking as he did so, "How long have you been standing there?"

At once Irene moved boldly forward and held out the goblet. "Oh, please, sir," she implored, "you will not tell Lady Volteface! I shall die, utterly die if you do. It was only that I was so thirsty and the room was so stuffy. Why I could barely breathe." As if to emphasize the suffocation she had lately undergone, she panted slightly and waved her fan at her bosom.

She saw a young man come up behind Molyneux, a light-haired gentleman of sober aspect whom she took to be Colton.

"Oh, I have forgotten my manners!" she

exclaimed in alarm. Dropping them a short curtsy, she rolled her eyes and said she hoped they would forgive her omission. Molyneux did not take his eyes off her the whole time.

"Get your drink and get out," he said,

"Oh, thank you, milord," she crooned. She took a long draft from the refilled goblet and declared, as though restored from death's door, "La, I know you will not breathe a word to her ladyship, for if you did, you would be forced to let her know that you had come in to steal a glass of champagne yourself." With a conspiratorial wink, she walked from the salon. She reached the door in time to hear Molyneux say that he had found her devilishly familiar and was certain he knew her.

When she reached the drawing room, the musicale had ended. The listeners stood about in clusters, chatting on any subject but the ordeal just passed, and waiting to be summoned to the salon for a bit of refreshment. Irene looked desperately for Caroline. She hoped to find her before the rest of the party scattered, then to persuade Lady Selby to take them home before Mr. Molyneux recognized her sister. Although the crowd was thin, Irene could not see her sister anywhere.

Lady Selby greeted her at that moment, exclaiming, "Why, my dear, you are pale as a ghost! And breathing so fast! I declare, you are having palpitations. Come, we will go inside and procure you a glass of lemonade and a breath of air. I love Maria Volteface more than life itself, but she will never open a window or properly air out a room. Come now, Miss Sparks, let me give you my arm before we have you swooning."

In vain Irene searched the sea of faces streaming before her as her ladyship led her back to the salon. There she was urged to drink glass after glass of sweet punch and take deep breaths. "I should very much like to leave," she implored Louisa, who agreed that as soon as the younger girls could be found, the coach would be called.

She had circled the salon for what seemed an interminable length of time, when, all at once, Caroline ran headlong into her arms. Irene knew by the look on her sister's face that she, too, had seen Molyneux. Without further preliminaries, she located her ladyship and begged to be taken home immediately.

There was no intimate chitchat on Chloe's bed that night. Irene took a moment alone with Caroline to discuss their future course. They must conduct themselves very cautiously in future, she advised, but they would not on any account permit the fear of meeting Molyneux to deter them from their purpose in coming to London. That said, Irene went to her bedchamber, where she spent a restless night dreaming of stuffy rooms, lemonade, and devils.

Chapter IX

Muffin's situation weighed heavily on Irene's spirits. She sought Lady Selby's counsel, but, lacking time and attention for anything save the approaching ball, her ladyship referred the matter to her spouse. As a father, Lord Selby had long ago despaired of influencing his daughters one way or the other; they regarded him as a cipher and did as they pleased. Consequently, he had left their upbringing in the hands of fate and their mother, and had concentrated on more important affairs, such as the state of the nation and the intricacies of piquet. Thus, when Irene appealed to him on Muffin's behalf, he found himself unable to sort out the young girl's pickle. But because he was fond of her, and because he felt somewhat ashamed at having failed to provide anything more substantial for her than a certain expertise in cheating at cards, he laid the matter before Hammond, who had now returned to London. With a nonchalant nod, the earl accepted responsibility for the matter, leaving

Selby with the proud conviction that he had done his very best by Miss Mary Sparks and that all would be well.

The earl sent a polite note to Berkeley Square inviting the Sparks sisters to accompany him on a morning stroll in Hyde Park. At first he had thought to take them for a drive, but recalling Muffin's penchant for horseflesh, and anticipating that any serious communication would be lost in admiration for his chestnuts, Hammond dismissed the notion in favor of a walk.

Irene answered the note at once, accepting the invitation in the name of her sisters, but an hour before the appointment she saw Martha, carrying a black satchel, leave Selby house and board the barouche.

Irene remarked on this mysterious behavior to Caroline, who supposed merely that Martha had gone out once again to the subscription library.

"Have you noticed that she is forever scribbling?" Irene asked. "And when one approaches near to her, she hides the papers away and will not bring them out again."

Caroline recalled such a thing happening once or twice, and when Irene speculated that perhaps their sister was conducting a secret correspondence, she clapped her hands in delight. One by one Caroline reviewed their acquaintances in Botherby, dismissing each candidate, in the end, as either too rowdy, too old, or too squat. At last she hit on the idea that the gentleman was probably ineligible and therefore not one whose name would readily come to mind. "Think of it," she sighed, "a forbidden attachment!"

"I pray that it is not!" Irene replied. "I have already begun to regret my idea that one of us ought to marry a rich gentleman. If Martha separated herself from a man she genuinely loved because of my scheme, I should never forgive myself. At any rate," she continued, "after a while, there will be just the three of us to walk out today with Lord Hammond."

Caroline flushed. "Did I not tell you?" she asked with suppressed anticipation. "I am to expect a visitor — a gentleman whom I met at the musicale."

Irene waited to hear the name of the visitor, but no further information was forthcoming. Unwilling to pry into what was not freely offered, she said no more. She felt much, however, for it now appeared that two of her sisters possessed secrets that they were reluctant to divulge to their nearest relation. Profoundly disappointed, Irene went to prepare Muffin for their projected outing.

At the appointed hour, Irene greeted Lord Hammond with an apology for the absence of two of her sisters. His lordship smiled by way of reply, observing that Muffin would no doubt provide enough entertainment to fill the void. With a lady on each arm, he traversed the carriage drive at the park entrance and found a path lined with shady trees.

A cloudless spring day had drawn a good many riders and strollers to the park. Irene and Hammond enjoyed the sunshine, while Muffin ran ahead to gawk at an immense dog, whose owner proudly displayed the animal to a small crowd of children. Taking advantage of this rare opportunity for privacy, Hammond informed Irene of the conversation that had taken place between himself and Lord Selby. It appeared, said his lordship, that Miss Mary could not keep herself out of mischief.

"There has been no time for us to teach her the lessons she began at Hopewell," Irene said. "By now I suppose she has forgotten them entirely."

"That is too bad," he replied. "She seems an intelligent girl."

"Unfortunately, she has no object for her intelligence," Irene said. "She has nothing to do all day but loiter in the stables, which she cannot seem to avoid, despite Lady Selby's admonitions."

"She would benefit, I think, from rigorous schooling. Perhaps Miss Proutie would agree to tutor her."

Irene flushed and made no reply.

"Or, if you prefer, she might be sent to school."

"Sent away?" Irene murmured.

"I do not mean that we should send her away in disgrace," he explained. "But there is a fine school for young ladies in Brighton, the mistress of which is a respectable woman and a personal acquaintance of my mother's. I am convinced that Muffin would thrive there."

"I am afraid we should never be able to afford the expense of a school," Irene answered with some emotion.

"That would be taken care of," he told her, "by your benefactor." There was an edge to his voice as he said it.

Irene withdrew her arm from his and stood still to face him. Resolutely, she shook her head, causing the plume in her bonnet to bob up and down. "We cannot impose on your generosity further," she said. "You have already done more than we can ever repay."

Hammond regarded her with a laconic smile. "Am I to understand," he inquired, "that your pride would stand in the way of your seeking a proper education for your sister? I do not know you very well, Miss Sparks, but I felt certain until this moment that you were not selfish."

She lowered her eyes. "Is it so very strange," she asked, "that I demur? I know nothing of schools. How am I to judge if this one will suit?"

"It would be best if you spoke with Lady Hammond," he replied. "My mother has been asking to meet you these many weeks, and we shall not put it off any longer. If after speaking with her you still do not wish to see Muffin at school, then I will say no more on that head."

"Is it necessary for me to impart my family's situation to yet another stranger?" Irene asked in distress. "I cannot see what your mother has to do with it. Why on earth should she ask to meet me?"

"Because she knew your mother," he answered simply.

This allusion to her beloved parent silenced Irene. As the eldest, she remembered Lady Sparks's gentle goodness more keenly than did any of her sisters, and she missed that source of strength and comfort more achingly as well. How often she wished that she were more like her mother. How deeply she regretted that circumstances had not permitted her to imitate that model of mildness and sense. To meet with someone who had known her, perhaps to be able to speak of Lady Sparks without fear of seeming sentimental or morbid, was a prospect too exquisite to be refused.

"I shall be glad to meet Lady Hammond," Irene replied warmly.

"Good, I will arrange for you to visit Russell Square tomorrow," he announced. "If she is well, she will have upward of half an hour to spend with you."

He took her arm in his, and they continued their stroll. So engrossed in her thoughts was Irene that she did not mark the disappearance of her sister. Hammond, who did mark it, supposed she had found another prodigy to admire farther down the path and that they would soon overtake her.

"You must permit me to thank you again, my lord," Irene said, breaking the silence. "I am fully conscious of your many kindnesses toward my sisters and myself, and although I may have appeared uncomfortable — nay, even ungracious at first — I assure you I am most grateful for your beneficence."

This expression of gratitude prompted him to reply, "I do not do it to be thanked."

Before she quite knew what she was about,

Irene blurted out, "But how else am I to repay you? I have naught but thanks to give."

He smiled at this and answered coldly, "If it will put your mind at ease, I will promise one day to exact repayment in full. In the meanwhile, I will hear no more of it, if you please."

Irene shuddered, as though a chilly gust had penetrated the fabric of her walking suit. Putting her hand to her brow, she wondered whether she had heard him aright. During the past weeks she had allowed her initial suspicions to be put to rout. Indeed, she had dismissed them as absurd, as each day made her feelings plainer to her. Now, unaccountably, he spoke coldly, reviving the memory of Mr. Uffingham's words.

He would "exact repayment in full," he had said carelessly. Had she not known that he was cut from the same bolt of cloth as her father, she might have thought he was merely quizzing her, for his attentions had hardly been those of a man intending to exact repayment. At the same time, the irony in his deep voice as he uttered the words bespoke feelings of a not very tender nature.

She caught him studying her intently, and was on the point of questioning him, when a clamor caused her to look around.

A diminutive gentleman in a morning suit held Muffin by the collar and propelled her forward. When he reached the spot where Hammond stood, he let her go roughly and shouted, "Does this chit belong to you, Hammond? You had better look to it if she does!"

Irene put her arms protectively around Muffin's shoulders. Hammond smiled pleasantly at his irate acquaintance and asked, "Has there been some misunderstanding, Hogwood?"

"Misunderstanding!" Hogwood fumed in disgust.

"Careful, my good friend," Hammond said mildly. "We shall soon have you going off on us in an apoplexy."

Hogwood waved his arms and stammered, too upset to form a coherent syllable. Muffin clung to Irene and glared at the gentleman in slit-eyed anger.

"This chit, this barbarian who has the face to call herself a female, has whipped me!" Hogwood managed to get out at last. "And with my very own whip!"

Hammond nodded as though this were a perfectly normal occurrence. He then turned to Muffin and inquired gently whether what the gentleman had said was true.

"He was beating his horse," she cried,

stepping forward and thrusting her wrathful countenance in the direction of her accuser. Hogwood stepped back, as though he feared she was about to commit another assault upon his person.

"He is a vicious brute," Muffin asserted, "and does not deserve to call himself a horseman, let alone a gentleman."

As Hogwood grew purple, Irene drew Muffin back and held her firmly.

"Is that true?" Hammond asked.

"I suppose a man may whip his own horse," Hogwood retorted.

"I suppose a man may do a good many things," Hammond replied cordially, "but if I ever hear again that you have mistreated an animal, I shall inform the members at White's that you are not the sort we like to welcome in our midst."

"Do you take her part?" Hogwood shrieked.

"I take no one's part," his lordship answered calmly. "I only say what you have heard me say. And I will add to that inducement one other — to wit, that if I hear a report of your cruelty in future, this young lady will not need to whip you, for I shall do it myself."

Hogwood stared at Hammond with a gaping jaw. Then he turned on his heel and with several loud oaths, stalked away, disappearing around a bend in the path.

Muffin threw Hammond an adoring look and then ran to him to hug his arm. "You are the highest flyer that ever was," she cried.

"And you are an incorrigible brat!" he replied soberly. "You will kindly inform me from now on of any incidents of this kind. I will not have you going about whipping my acquaintances, regardless of their iniquity. You are not too old to be spanked, you know."

"Yes, my lord," Muffin said meekly.

"Now, you will apologize to your sister for the pain you have caused her," his lordship continued, "and you will take your oath to stay out of scrapes until we have decided what to do with you."

The apology and oath duly delivered, the three walked on, very much subdued by the late crisis. Irene hardly knew what to think of the man whose arm she held. One moment he was championing her sister and acting a lover's part; the next moment he spoke of exacting repayment — and in the coldest manner. Try as she might, she could not make him out.

"Well, what shall we talk of now?" Hammond asked amiably. When neither of his companions ventured a suggestion, he continued, "May I inquire how your sisters go on in London?"

"Very well, my lord," Irene answered quietly.

"Then you are pleased with London society?"

"We have been received most kindly," Irene assured him.

"I am very gratified to hear it," said his lordship, "though I should have been shocked if you hadn't been. When three young ladies are rumored to have a dowry of two thousand pounds apiece, settled on them by the Earl of Hammond, their welcome in society is guaranteed, unless of course, they come upon the town perfectly toothless, bald, and squinty."

"Two thousand pounds!" Muffin echoed gleefully. "What a lark!"

Alarmed at this report, Irene asked how such a false rumor could have gotten started.

"Rumors abound in London," Hammond said. "I had assumed that you were the source of this particularly interesting tidbit." Turning to her with a grave look, he demanded, "Is it true?"

Stung, Irene walked quickly ahead to a rose bush. As she strove to quell her emotion, she fingered a bud, pricking herself in the process. She stared at her blood, then put her cut finger to her lips.

Muffin was speaking as she and Hammond approached.

"Irene the source of such a hum?" she exclaimed in disgust. "You are not such a high flyer as I thought, if you imagine she is capable of that. I have a good mind to borrow Mr. Hogwood's whip again."

Silently the earl handed Irene his handkerchief, and as he watched her press it to her cut, she fully expected him to animadvert on similar occasions they had shared over his handkerchief in the past. To her surprise, he said only, "Perhaps I was mistaken in Miss Sparks's character. If so, I would be gratified to hear it from her own lips."

But Irene could not speak or even look at him. For the remainder of the morning she strolled the park in numb silence. In vain did he point out to her a statue of an ancient Greek warrior and remark on the fine summery weather. She saw only one thing — that there was suspicion on his side as well as hers, and that it had prevailed over other, more tender sensations. Thus, when he deposited her and her sister at Berkeley Square, she could not even vouchsafe him a goodbye.

Chapter X

They rode in silence to Russell Square, and when Hammond opened the door to admit Miss Sparks to his mother's sitting room, her ladyship perceived at once that the two young people were considerably at odds. Irene's demeanor was coolly proper, and her lovely face showed signs of recent sleeplessness. Hammond appeared calm as usual, yet he wore an air of seriousness that was certainly far from typical.

After receiving his kiss, the dowager said, "Stephen, you have matters to discuss with Miss Simpson. You will find her below stairs."

Understanding this to mean that she wanted him out of the way, he replied, "If you say so, Mother," and with a brief glance at Irene he went away.

"Come here, my dear," the dowager invited, extending her hand to Irene. "All my visitors sit here on the ottoman. If you will just move my legs a bit, we will make room for you."

Without a word, Irene did as she was bid.

"As you see," said her ladyship, "I am prodigiously fond of having visitors at my feet."

To this gentle self-mockery Irene responded with a tight smile, wondering what would come next. If Lady Hammond resembled her daughter, she would in all likelihood say something silly and selfish. She would complain of her ailments, no doubt, as Lady Selby complained of her palpitations and headaches. If, on the other hand, she favored her son, her words would stab her in a most vulnerable place. In that case, she would find herself not on speaking terms with two of the three Hammonds.

After a pause, during which the dowager closely studied Irene's face, she said gently, "You are very like her."

This allusion to her mother so moved Irene that her eyes brimmed. She bowed her head.

Lady Hammond stroked her hair, saying nothing, waiting patiently until her guest regained control of her emotions. When Irene looked up again, she saw two wet streaks on the dowager's cheeks. Then both women found their handkerchiefs and dried their eyes. Her ladyship smiled, saying lightly, "I am glad we have managed to pass over the preliminaries. There is nothing like crying together to establish intimacy between females."

"Did you know my mother well?" Irene asked.

"No, unfortunately, I did not know her well," her ladyship replied. "We had met on only two or three occasions before my husband quarreled with the baron, severing the connection entirely. I remember that her beautiful face was lined with worry, exactly like yours, and I have always regretted the breach which prevented our knowing each other better."

"I don't know why I should be so weepy," Irene said. "You paid me a great compliment just now."

"You are distressed over your sister's situation."

Irene nodded.

"And you are angry with Stephen for suggesting that she be sent away to school."

As her feelings confused her utterly, Irene did not reply.

"My son may perhaps deserve anger, but not in this instance, my dear. I alone ought to be the object of blame, for I urged him to put the suggestion before you, and he merely obliged his invalid mother in so doing."

"He has discussed our case with you then?"

"He informed me of it before he went to Somerset."

Irene thought grimly that he had doubtless neglected to tell her of his plans to exact repayment in full from the ladies of Hopewell. "I don't think I could ever be angry with you," she said aloud.

"Excellent!" Lady Hammond declared. "Then I may speak without mincing words. At my age, it is very tiresome to have to mince words."

Gently but persuasively, her ladyship described Miss Oglethorpe's school for young ladies. It was, she said, a pleasant place, unlike the institutions one heard about so often, which put her much in mind of dungeons. There were well-kept grounds outside and cheerful rooms within. Miss Oglethorpe was not only respectable — a term too carelessly applied in this lax age — but she was also intelligent. She believed that young girls ought to know something besides how to knit a purse and entertain a gentleman on the pianoforte. Her students learned mathematics, languages, history, and composition. They had many opportunities to avail themselves of the salubrious sea air, and they profited from close association with other young ladies of good families. Added to these advantages was the fact that Miss Oglethorpe's school had a stable, which, although not large, was a palpable inducement in Miss Mary's case.

A little overwhelmed, Irene replied that hearing the description reassured her greatly.

"I have recommended the school to a number of my acquaintances," the dowager continued, "and the young people, as well as their parents, have thanked me many times over. Of course, I could not persuade Louisa to send Beatrice and Chloe there. She would have them educated at home, you know. But I suppose if she had sent them, that would not serve as much of a recommendation."

"I do not know what to say," Irene responded.

"Perhaps you are concerned about the expense," said her ladyship. "Allow me to put your mind at ease on that score. I will not permit Stephen to have any part of it. I will undertake it entirely myself."

"But your family has already been more than generous to mine," Irene exclaimed. "You say you hardly knew my mother. Therefore, her daughters cannot mean anything to you."

"Let us say that having missed the opportunity to extend my friendship to your mother, I now see a way of befriending her daughters," the dowager answered. "I must add to that lofty sentiment something a bit more selfish: I am a capricious old woman, and while I sit here, unable to move about as I would wish, I can take pleasure in imagining your sister racing over the countryside or splashing in the water."

"I do not know how to refuse such kindness," Irene said.

At that moment, Hammond opened the door and stepped inside. "Miss Simpson and I have exhausted every possible topic of conversation," he announced. "Well, what have you ladies decided?"

"I am pleased to say that Miss Sparks does not resent my interference, though well she might," said Lady Hammond. "In fact, she is most grateful."

"Miss Sparks is always properly grateful," he replied.

This hit provoked Irene into responding energetically, "I don't know how we are to tell Muffin. She will feel that we are punishing her for her misdeeds. And if we did finally prevail upon her to go, I am afraid she might run away."

Stephen regarded her thoughtfully. "You are right," he said. "These are very real difficulties. They occurred to me, too."

"It would require powerful inducement to

get her there and keep her there," Irene pointed out. "One small stable will not do it, I fear."

"But what if it had a pony in it?" Hammond asked. "One of her very own, to be kept in Miss Oglethorpe's stable and available to her whenever she can prove that she has spent at least half a day without falling into mischief."

Irene had to admit that the pony might be the very thing.

"Then it is done," he stated, putting an end to further discussion and causing his mother to worry that her son would never mend his differences with Miss Sparks if he persisted in being so high-handed.

During the carriage ride back to Berkeley Square, Hammond saw that his differences with Irene had been somewhat patched, if not fully mended. She spoke glowingly of her visit with his mother, and, seeing her quite comfortable, he refrained from references to dowries and repayments in full.

With a determined grip on her satchel, Martha contemplated the building before her. A low, narrow edifice of red brick, it did not appear particularly noteworthy, except for the legend on the door, which read: MOWBRAY & FISKE, PUBLISHERS.

166

She climbed the stairs and pushed open the door.

Mr. Mowbray greeted her with raised eyebrows. "Have you brought me more already?" he asked in astonishment. "Why, you were here only yesterday. Stap me if I have ever met such a prolific author in my life."

Martha felt her throat go dry. "Perhaps it is too soon," she apologized. "I shall return another day."

"Nonsense!" Mr. Mowbray called, taking the satchel from her. "See here, if you have something new to show me, you must not be such a mouse about it. You must be a little firmer, Miss Proutie."

"Yes, of course," murmured Martha, who could not hear herself called by that appellation without turning pink.

"Come and see what I have for you," he invited. She followed him past a line of scribes bent industriously over their desks. Stepping into a dusty room, he unrolled several long sheafs of paper by throwing them out on a table. "There! What do you think?" he demanded with considerable pride.

Peering over the sheets, Martha saw her poems leap out at her boldly. She gasped as she noted the title page: *A Gift of Maidenhood*, by A. Proutie. Turning to Mr. Mowbray in distress, she cried, "Why have you chosen such a title?"

"I merely used the title you gave one of your sonnets," he explained innocently.

"But why could we not call it simply *Poems*?"

"Mr. Fiske insisted upon the other," he said with reverence. "Mr. Fiske, as you know, is never wrong about these things."

"May I please speak with him?" Martha implored.

As Mr. Fiske had been dead these twelve years, Mr. Mowbray did not think it would do to invoke his authority further. Instead, he inquired as to why she objected so strenuously to the title.

"Do you not think," she answered haltingly, "that there are those who will consider it — unseemly? It has one meaning in connection with the poem, but quite another standing there by itself."

"I do not see how anyone can misconstrue its meaning," Mr. Mowbray lied. "Perhaps there are those whose moral deficiencies might bend their thoughts in an improper direction. But such people do not read books, unfortunately. If they did, no doubt they would be elevated out of their viciousness."

"Can you not change it?" Martha persisted.

"I don't see how I can now," he lamented. "But do not fret. Since Lord Byron published his poems, there is no such thing anymore as something improper to be published."

"You are quite sure?" she asked.

To distract her from her disquietude on the matter of the title, Mr. Mowbray said hastily, "I have happy news." He then handed her a check in the amount of sixty pounds.

Martha closed her eyes and sighed gratefully.

"You must invest that wisely," he advised her.

"I mean to keep it," she said shyly. "I shall not let it out of my hands until I am ready to put it to use."

"A pity," Mr. Mowbray remarked. "The sum of sixty pounds is not great if one must live on it. But invested well, it can do much. Why, I heard of someone just the other day who made a killing on the Exchange."

"I do not know about such things," Martha replied, allowing him to lead her back to the entrance, where the coachman waited to hand her into Lord Selby's barouche. Conscious only of the check that lay folded tightly in her hand, she rode back to Berkeley Square deep in thought.

★ ★ ★

With the ball only a fortnight away, the Selby household found itself in an uproar. Lord Selby left early and returned late every day; even the promise of an evening at cards with the Sparks sisters could not lure him to Berkeley Square. Uppermost in his mind was the determination to avoid the parade of factotums, servants, and bill collectors who streamed through his home. No stratagem was beneath him when it came to avoiding Louisa, who swept through the rooms trailing a stream of orders. He hid in corners and skulked behind screens to forestall discussions with her. More than fuss, expense, and the invasion of his privacy, he dreaded discussions.

The ballroom at Berkeley Square had at first hardly suited the grandness of Louisa's schemes. But her brother summarily refused to furnish her with the site she most desired — namely, his ballroom at Grosvenor Square, which was larger by half than her own. Nor would he permit her to give any hint to their mother of holding the ball at Russell Square. Hence, she was forced to appraise her own premises with new eyes.

Although far from ideal, the ballroom could, she thought, be made tolerable by the addition of a few clever touches. These she set about acquiring at once. She had mirrors mounted along two walls to achieve an effect of spaciousness. A new chandelier was hung, along with wall sconces, draperies, and coats of arms representing the Selby and Hammond dynasties. The thought that these fixtures would permanently grace her ballroom, and that they had not cost a groat of her own money, compensated a good deal for the limitations of space and splendor she had to endure.

Her head full of arrangements, Louisa could speak on no other subject. Thus, whenever she entered a room, its inmates fled immediately, scattering in any direction that might afford protection from her ladyship's effusions.

"I see no occasion for such fuss," Beatrice remarked to Irene. "A ball is nothing more than an excuse for vain display."

"Then stay in your room with a book," Chloe advised. "I'm sure no one will miss you."

"One has a duty to society," Beatrice stated, "and to one's parent."

"Then one ought not to be so sour-faced," Chloe retorted.

"I believe Beatrice was referring to the uproar caused by preparations for a ball," Irene said. "Indeed, I don't know when I have seen so many rushing, worried-looking people."

"Yes," Chloe agreed, "I detest all these goings and comings. Mama has not said a word about altering my gown. It is cut much too high, and though Mama sets great store by the seamstress, I have no opinion of her, for the beads are coming loose from the hem stitching."

"I will mend them for you," Caroline offered.

"You?" her friend exclaimed. "Are you clever with a needle?"

Caroline smiled. "There was a time," she said, "that I hoped to set up as a seamstress in London."

"How dreadful," Chloe exclaimed. "I hope you have changed your mind."

"Yes, I have," Caroline admitted. "I have a very different future in view now."

Irritating as Lady Selby's preoccupation was to members of her own family, it suited the ladies of Hopewell most comfortably. Martha went out in the barouche on several occasions without exciting her ladyship's notice. Muffin consorted with the grooms and the ostlers undisturbed, regaling them with tales of the wonderful pony she was to have at Miss Oglethorpe's school. Irene saw that her youngest sister's belongings were mended, pressed, folded, and packed in a trunk before Lady Selby fully comprehended that the girl would be leaving for Brighton in a short time. And Caroline welcomed a gentleman caller each morning without inspiring the least curiosity in her ladyship.

Irene's curiosity was greatly aroused, however, and she could not forbear mentioning it to Caroline any longer.

"Say you will not disapprove," Caroline begged, "and I will tell you all. Oh, how I have longed to tell you all!"

"Very well, I will not disapprove," Irene promised. "At any rate, I will not do so while you can hear me."

Caroline's eyes danced, and her cheeks glowed as she spoke. "He is so like you in that way — so full of worry and doubt. And yet, I am able to make him content. He says I am the single ray of sunshine in his cloudy days."

Although Irene did not think much of the originality of this expression, she said only, "And what do you say of him?"

"Why, that it makes me smile to think how sorrowful and tender-hearted he is under that stern brow. You will consider him, rather shy, I venture to guess. He has not the way of talking on meaningless subjects for hours on end."

"What does he talk about?" Irene asked.

"It's difficult to say precisely. Sometimes he says absolutely nothing at all. His face grows dark and moody at such times, and the vein in his forehead pulses furiously. I know that my being nearby is somehow a comfort, because I do not gabble at him as some girls might. When he wishes to be silent for a full hour, I know how to understand it."

Privately Irene thought the gentleman might be more than just shy. From Caroline's description, she concluded that he was either very uncivil or very much in love. She requested Caroline to introduce her to the young man, so that she might discover which of the two he was, and Caroline agreed.

To Irene's surprise, the caller her sister ushered into the morning room proved to be Mr. Colton. His surprise at hearing Irene introduced was no less than hers had been. The greetings made in due form, the three sat down. The young ladies looked at Mr. Colton; Mr. Colton looked at his knees. To Irene's view, he seemed nervous and ill at ease. Judging by the expression on Caroline's face, however, she found him wholly adorable.

"You see we are in a great fuss here," Irene said cordially.

Caroline added gaily, "There is to be a ball three days hence, but of course you already know that. Doubtless you will be there."

"I have not received an invitation," said Mr. Colton.

"What a horrible oversight," Caroline cried. "I shall speak to Lady Selby at once." She rose to leave, alarming Irene by her impetuosity.

"It may not be an oversight," Mr. Colton stated. "I am not acquainted with his lordship, and I saw Lady Selby only once, at the musicale."

"Nevertheless," Caroline insisted, "I shall speak to her ladyship. Once I tell her you are a great friend of ours, she will be only too happy to send you an invitation."

"Perhaps you had better consider a little," Irene urged her. "It may be that Mr. Colton does not care to receive an invitation. You have not even asked him whether he does or no."

The gentleman assured her that he was wholly indifferent, that as he did not dance his only pleasure in such an evening could lie in conversation with the two Misses Sparks. Having delivered himself of this gallantry, he produced a wan smile.

"Then it is settled," Caroline announced,

and in another second she had gone in search of Lady Selby.

Stunned by her sister's imprudence, Irene weighed carefully how to proceed next. She concluded that a direct approach might be best, and therefore she asked Mr. Colton if he had heard a rumor to the effect that the Earl of Hammond had settled a substantial dowry on herself and each of her sisters, a dowry of two thousand pounds, to be exact.

"What do you mean *rumor?*" Mr. Colton said. For the first time, he met her eyes.

"Yes, it is only just a rumor," she said. "I do not know how the report got started, nor do I care. But as your friendship with my sister appears to have advanced rapidly, I thought it right to tell you."

If she expected the gentleman to decamp at once, she was disappointed, for he only bit his lip and regarded his fingernails.

"That is certainly a most unfortunate rumor," he remarked.

"Yes, for it may make us prey to fortune hunters," she replied.

"But surely his lordship does not mean to leave you destitute?" he suggested.

"He means to see us well married, which is his way of seeing to it that we are not left destitute," she explained.

Colton did not reply, though the wrinkling of his brow and the throbbing of his vein told Irene that her information had provoked a good deal of inner conversation.

Breaking the long pause, Irene asked the gentleman if he would forgive her asking an awkward question. Although he paled a little, he gave his consent, allowing her to inquire somewhat into his circumstances.

"We have no parents or guardian to look into these matters for us," she apologized. "It becomes my office to do so *in loco parentis,* so to speak."

He nodded.

"May I ask, then, if you, Mr. Colton, are completely unencumbered?"

"What have you heard?" he asked suspiciously. "You heard something at the musicale?"

Irene maintained a calm appearance. "I have heard no gossip," she said truthfully. "But if you mean to end your friendship with my sister because you feel it may be imprudent in light of her circumstances, I should like to know, for I would wish to spare her as much distress as possible."

Mr. Colton stood up and paced before the fireplace. He leaned his arm against the mantel and gazed down at his boots.

"I do not know what effect your revelation will have," he said in perturbation. "I shall have to consult my associate to assess my position. As for encumbrances, I have in the past acquired a number of debts, as you may already be aware, but I am engaged just now in acquitting them, so that I hope to be able to offer my friendship in a purely disinterested way."

There was little in this wary speech to comfort Irene, and she would have questioned him further had not Caroline entered just then, waving a white embossed card in the air and declaring triumphantly, "It is all arranged!"

As soon as Mr. Colton made his adieux and carried himself off with the invitation in hand, Irene asked Caroline how on earth she had prevailed upon Lady Selby to grant her request.

"Well," her sister replied, laughing, "she was in the midst of reviewing the music with the maestro, and they were disputing over a piece of Mr. Handel's. She gave it to me just to have me out of the way, I think."

Because Irene had promised not to disapprove, she said nothing. She merely invited Caroline to sit beside her, for she had something of a serious nature to impart to her, and when the two of them had arranged themselves comfortably on the sofa, she took Caroline's hand in hers and told her as gently as possible what had passed between Mr. Colton and Molyneux in Lady Volteface's salon.

"So, that villain holds a threat over poor Mr. Colton!" Caroline exclaimed indignantly. "I always knew he was vile and despicable, but until this mount I never knew to what depths a human creature could sink."

"You must not tell Mr. Colton what I overheard," Irene warned.

"Of course not," Caroline answered. "I would not wound him so."

"Have you considered," Irene ventured cautiously, "that Mr. Colton's part in this may not be entirely innocent? To allow himself to fall into the clutches of such a man as Molyneux may bespeak a kind of weakness, a want of character. These things bear watching, my love."

Caroline's indignation on Mr. Colton's behalf now vented itself on her sister. "You take great pleasure in suspicioning any gentleman who offers his friendship," she cried. "First it was Lord Hammond, who has done us more good turns than your ingratitude deserves. Now it is poor Mr. Colton, who has unwillingly fallen into a desperate trap, and by so doing he loses all your compassion."

Although Irene wanted to say that she

merely desired to caution her sister, she remained silent, for it was borne in on her that anything she said would serve Caroline as an excuse for rebellion. The last thing Irene desired was to give her reasons to nurture a passion in secret. Therefore, she bowed her head in seeming acquiescence and reflected that as Mr. Colton did not dance, Caroline would, in all probability, soon weary of his company.

Respite from anxiety appeared to Irene in the unlikely form of Lord Selby, who, true to his word, did at last procure seats for a performance of *She Stoops to Conquer*. Apart from Martha, the others in the household declined to attend. Pronouncing theatricals detrimental to morals and manners, Beatrice scorned her father's invitation. Caroline had promised to make some alterations on Chloe's new ball gown; those two young ladies were therefore obliged to add their nays to Beatrice's, though they did so with considerably more regret. Lord Selby did not bother to mention the outing to his wife, except in passing, for she had by now worked herself into such a dither over the ball that she could comprehend barely a third of what was said to her at any given time. However, at the last moment, Lord

Hammond agreed to make one of the party at Drury Lane.

As he held aside the drape, Irene entered the elegant box. She saw in the gallery below and the balconies on high an audience of chattering people, most of whom stood or peered through their glasses to locate their acquaintances and salute them with bows and waves. Taking one of the front seats next to Martha, Irene admired the heavy black curtain that veiled the stage. Lord Hammond, seating himself to the right and a little behind her, assured himself of an excellent view of Miss Sparks's profile.

When the lamps dimmed, he watched her face silhouetted against the glow of the footlights. The audience hushed, and he saw her raise her hand to her white breast, as though to calm herself. A second later, the curtain parted, and he noticed her give Martha's hand a squeeze.

Throughout the opening scenes, Lord Hammond derived as much entertainment from studying Irene as he did from Mr. Goldsmith's comedy. Her eyes never left the stage. She seemed to enter into the events passing there as though she were part of it all. Merrily she laughed at the foolish characters and applauded the sensible ones. At the heroine's entrance, she leaned forward her lips slightly parted in admiration. When the curtain closed and the lamps were lit again for the intermission, she sat unmoving, still entranced. She did not notice Martha leave the box with Lord Selby to procure some refreshment, nor was she conscious that Stephen drew his chair close to hers.

"You are pleased with the play?" he asked.

Starting a little, she turned on him a pair of eyes bright with excitement, declaring that it was the finest play she had ever seen. "It is also the only play I have ever seen," she laughed, "in a proper theater, that is. My sisters and I used to produce theatricals at Hopewell for the amusement of our friends. Our mother used to say that we were, in reality, the grandchildren of Mr. Garrick; such was the excellence of our playacting skills in her estimation. I confess, we preened ourselves a little on our performances, but our poor efforts were nothing to this."

He smiled at her gay reminiscence. "And Miss Hardcastle," he said, "do you think she makes a creditable heroine?"

"Indeed I do," she stated with lively animation. "She is a wonderfully intelligent and courageous young lady; don't you think so?"

Lord Hammond frowned. "I cannot share

your good opinion of her," he said. "It is silly, I think, for a respectable young lady to pretend she is a servant and so deceive the man she loves. She ought to have trusted him with the truth."

Irene looked at him in alarm. His words had stung her guilty sensibilities. In a subdued voice, she defended Miss Hardcastle. "Kate does not deceive him for any ignoble purpose. She knows that he is shy among women of his own class, and this is her way of putting him at his ease."

"Her intentions are certainly all that is pure," he said, "but the fact is, she makes herself out to be something she is not. I regard it in much the same way as I regard the spreading of false rumors. You may call it what you will. I call it deception."

His lordship's epithet sounded a reproach in her ears. Had he known of the deception she had practiced on him at the Bluebird, she thought, he could not have found a more painful way of rebuking her. The brightness left her eyes, and her shoulders sagged a little. She turned to find Martha and saw that she had gone, leaving her alone with Lord Hammond.

With an attempt at lightness, she murmured, "Well, after all, it is only a comedy. Who could imagine such a thing actually happening?" She glanced at the closed curtain, looking deeply grieved.

Perceiving that expression of loss, Hammond suddenly felt that he had overplayed his hand. He had intended to provoke her — to give her a "glove on the cheek," as Charles phrased it. He had hoped to bring her somehow to declare her innocence in regard to the rumored dowry. But what had been meant to provoke had ended by wounding.

"Irene . . ." he said softly.

Then he saw her cheeks redden and her lips press together. Following the direction of her eyes, he noticed a young man bowing to her from another box. In a second, the fellow had disappeared. Presumably he was on his way to pay his respects to Miss Sparks. Lord Hammond had never laid eyes on the fellow before, but based on the glance that had passed between him and Irene, and the blush that it had produced on her cheeks, he disliked him heartily.

Just as the earl had foreseen, the young man entered the box and, greeting Irene formally, kissed her hand. She introduced him to Lord Hammond as Mr. Colton, then sat stiffly and silently in her chair. Martha and Lord Selby returned, and they too were favored with an introduction to the visitor.

Martha regarded with strong interest the young man she had heard Caroline mention so often and in such glowing terms.

Hammond also regarded the young man closely and perceived that he had no conversation for anyone but Irene. Colton bent over her chair and said in a nervous whisper, "I have consulted my associate, as I said I would, and my situation appears better than I had expected. I can tell you now that I am wholly unencumbered. Nothing need stand in the way."

Irene received this news as though a bolt of lightening had struck her. She swallowed hard and made a valiant effort to reply with a tranquil nod of her head. Hammond, who had overheard every syllable, reminded Mr. Colton sharply that the second act was about to begin, whereupon he left to return to his box.

When the lights dimmed and the play resumed, Irene found that her former joy in it had wholly dissipated. Hammond, who stared at her profile as though magnetized, spent the remainder of the evening ruminating upon deception.

Chapter XI

Dressed in an exquisite coat of the softest fawn, the Earl of Hammond strolled into the ballroom at Berkeley Square. Upon seeing it, he was forced to admit that Louisa had spent his money well. He had lately received a sheaf of bills she had run up in his name. Sorting through them, he had little imagined that his sister's grandiose schemes should ever come to fruition with such magnificence. Although the trappings struck him as a trifle gaudy and emulative of the opulent style favored by the Prince Regent, he was pleased that it was not any worse.

None of the family, he saw, had come down as yet. Nevertheless, the musicians played a lilting tune, their backs reflected in the shining mirrors. The new chandelier sparkled and flickered with gentle light, and the floor, polished to a sheen, caught the incandescence. In the adjacent salon, Hammond saw an army of servants standing at the ready by the tables. Laden with all manner of delicacies, the tables surrounded a kind of fountain, a gurgling feat of engineering inspired by the Regent's famous indoor waterfall. Statuelike, the servants watched his lordship explore the room, waiting to spring into action should he express a request.

Seeing Louisa enter, he went to her and complimented her on the effect she had labored so long and so expensively to achieve. Lady Selby, who was unaccustomed to receiving compliments from her brother, appeared somewhat suspicious.

"It will all have been worth it," she snapped, "if you will bestir yourself tonight to find a wife."

"I thought the purpose of this gathering was to marry off your daughters," Hammond remarked. "I had no idea you were expending yourself on my behalf."

"It is your duty to marry," Lady Selby stated, looking about her in dread of discovering some omission at the last minute.

"I cannot promise you that I will find myself a bride this night," he replied, "but I can promise you that I will dance."

"Pooh," Louisa said, "I don't believe you. I have seen you ignore perfectly charming young ladies at a ball while you stood apart yawning."

"If I have been so rude as that in the past,"

Hammond announced, "I mean to make up for it tonight."

"I am happy to hear it," she said, though she did not quite believe his protestations. "I shall do what I can to find you partners."

Stephen laughed. "I shall find my own, thank you. Naturally my nieces shall be the first of them."

Stunned by this civility, Louisa did not know what to say. It occurred to Hammond that she would be far more comfortable if she had something to fuss over, and he hit upon the idea of asking her what she could do about a small beribboned box he carried in his hand.

"Gracious! What is that?" she asked.

"Mother sent it for Beatrice and Chloe."

Ripping off the tie and opening the cover, Louisa discovered two emerald pendants inside.

"She made sure they were exactly alike," he pointed out. "No doubt she wished to avoid causing a dispute."

"As if my girls would dispute on such a night as this!" Louisa snapped.

She hurried from the room to deliver the gifts just as Charles joined his lordship. Soon after, Lord Selby arrived, wearing an expression of pleasant surprise. "It is not as bad as I thought," he confided to Hammond. Wincing only slightly at the sight of the fountain, he decided to celebrate his good fortune with a glass of something fortifying.

Within a quarter of an hour, the ballroom was filled with guests. Louisa greeted each one solicitously, poking her husband when his attention wandered, and pushing her daughters forward by way of introduction. Beatrice, looking less forbidding than Hammond had ever seen her, bobbed her curtsies dutifully and essayed a smile at every third or fourth guest. Chloe, waving her fan demurely, tilted her head so that her blond curls bounced and saved her most fetching smiles for the young bucks. To their mother's infinite relief, both girls remembered their dance steps. Hammond led each in turn onto the floor then subsequently delivered them into the arms of a succession of partners. Louisa felt tears of maternal joy well up in her eyes as she witnessed the spectacle of her daughters comporting themselves without disgracing the illustrious name of Selby.

"Where are the ladies of Hopewell?" Charles asked Hammond. "I am beginning to think they do not in fact exist. Admit it, my lord, you have invented them merely to hoax me."

Laughing, Hammond looked at the entrance for the hundredth time. "Do you really think I could fabricate such a troublesome family?" he asked.

At that instant, the three ladies appeared at the door. Martha's buxom figure was handsomely trimmed out in blue. Her fair hair set off a pair of blushing cheeks and a shy placid smile. Beside her stood Caroline in a gown of white. She glanced about her with shining eyes and an expression of irrepressible excitement. Insensible to the admiring looks her beauty attracted, she looked about the assembly, seeking one particular face among the crowd.

The last to enter the ballroom was Irene, whose honey-colored hair had already begun to rebel against the confines of the maid's coiffure and now sprayed her graceful bare neck with wispy curls. Arrayed in a flowing gown of burgundy, which clung to her slender form, she moved gracefully toward her sisters, putting her arms around their waists and leading them inside.

Hammond approached Irene with Charles trailing close behind. The earl bowed to each of the ladies in turn, then introduced his secretary. As the ladies made their curtsies, Hammond watched Irene. It was impossible, he found, to look at her luxuriant hair, her intelligent blue-gray eyes, and her tall, womanly figure and think of rumors.

Hammond escorted Irene and Martha inside, leaving Caroline in Charles's capable charge.

"Are you looking for someone in particular?" Charles asked her.

"In point of fact, I am," Caroline said, craning her graceful neck to see above the crush.

A patient man, Charles did not take umbrage at this inattention. Rather, he offered her his arm so that they might walk around the room at their leisure, until they should find the object of such urgent looks. There was no question in Charles's mind that this object belonged to the male species. Still, having no desire to relinquish his place next to such beauty, he resolved to remain at her side unless absolutely driven off.

For a time they wandered slowly without attempting to make conversation. They had just begun their second tour of the ballroom when Charles asked Caroline whom it was that she sought. "I can be of much more use to you if I know the person in question," he said.

Impressed by the logic of this suggestion, Caroline favored him with the name and a description of her beau.

"Mr. Colton," Charles said thoughtfully. "You will be disappointed in me, I fear. I have never heard the name."

Her face fell, causing him to curse his stupidity in not being acquainted with the gentleman.

He hit on the idea of inspecting the salon, in case Mr. Colton had arrived with a great thirst and had made his way directly to the tables. This plan was effected at once but yielded no better results than had the tour of the ballroom. Caroline began to grow alarmed. However, for his part, Charles did not care a groat if the fellow never turned up at all.

"Do you know," he said, "there is an old saying that a watched pot will not boil. If we joined a set, perhaps the gentleman would make his presence known immediately."

Uncertainty played on Caroline's face. "He may not like to find me dancing," she said.

"On the contrary," Charles asserted. "While he is delayed he will want to know that you have not been miserable on his account. Unless, of course, he is the most selfish beast in creation."

To prove that Mr. Colton was nothing of the sort, Caroline allowed herself to be led onto the floor. After a while she even permitted herself to enjoy the dance, noting that her partner had a light, easy step and a firm hold on her waist that encouraged her to perform a number of intricate turns with a heady swirl. By the end of the set, Caroline was laughing with delight. For all his solid, steady demeanor, she thought to herself, Mr. Dale was an energetic dancer, the kind whose intense response to the music and the movement quite matched her own. They left the floor together, laughing and panting from the exercise.

Caroline's gaiety vanished abruptly when she found her way blocked by Mr. Molyneux. He bowed and leered, sending a chill through her. Responding with the barest hint of a curtsy, she would have gone around him without a word had he not stepped into her path again.

"*Enchanté,* Miss Sparks," he said and made as if he would kiss her hand.

Charles came forward at that moment, preventing what he saw was a most unwelcome gallantry. "You will excuse us, sir," he said resolutely. "I have promised the lady a glass of lemonade."

Mr. Molyneux moved aside grudgingly and then elbowed his way into the crowd.

Caroline told Charles, in a voice filled with loathing and dread that she must find Irene at once.

★ ★ ★

With a Miss Sparks on each arm, Hammond had joined Louisa and Selby in the most crowded part of the room. By now her ladyship had seen enough to cause her bosom to swell with gladness. Numerous matrons, including Lady Volteface, had whispered a number of veiled insults in her ear, sufficient proof that they were livid with envy. The other guests openly admired the lavishness of the arrangements, one of them even going so far as to say that the Prince himself would not have disdained to grace such a ball with his magnificence.

Added to these triumphs was the unexpected success of her daughters. Beatrice danced every dance. Had Lady Selby known that Hammond was making sure to procure partners for her, the victory might not have been quite so delicious. As it was, however, she beamed in complacent ignorance at the sight of her eldest dancing with a bland-faced young gentleman who listened politely to her steady stream of verbiage. Chloe, resting her back against a post, flirted prettily with Mr. Quince, a tulip of fashion whose attention to the youngest Miss Selby was nearly on a par with his attention to the folds of his cravat.

Louisa gushed a florid greeting at her

brother, as though they had not seen each other in quite a while. Upon Irene and Martha she bestowed a gracious welcome and an embrace, thinking to herself how foolish she had been to be jealous of their beauty. They were sweet girls, she told herself, and she wished heartily that they would each find a sweet husband and settle respectably in Scotland.

Irene's heartbeat quickened with excitement. The charm of the music, the vivacity of the dancers, the rapturous embrace of Lady Selby, the admiring glances thrown at Caroline and Martha, the flickering of the lamps — all combined to heighten her animation, and as she looked up involuntarily to find Hammond's face, she trembled to see him regarding her with powerful softness. She saw him move in her direction around a cluster of people and knew that he meant to ask her to dance, but his purpose was foiled by a matron in a turban who begged leave to introduce him to her niece. This pretty young damsel amused Irene by her efforts to captivate his lordship, but from the look on his face it was clear that he was not similarly amused. He was on the point of excusing himself several times, only to be recalled by the matron's persistent cordiality. He continued to look at Irene throughout the conversation, an expression of barely suppressed impatience diffusing his handsome face. At last she saw him straighten his shoulders and ask the pretty damsel to dance, an invitation she accepted with simpering modesty. Leading the girl onto the floor, he cast one more backward look at Irene, who was vastly entertained at seeing him a little uncomfortable. She would have continued to observe him had not her attention been summarily demanded by Caroline, who tugged desperately on her arm.

"Do you know who is here?" Caroline whispered. "I would not have believed it was possible, but I saw him with my own eyes. It is Mr. Molyneux."

Irene was shocked. He did not appear to be the sort of man to form part of the Selby circle.

"Oh, the injustice of it!" Caroline cried, stamping her foot. "I think I shall go distracted. To see that villain here and no sign at all of Mr. Colton."

Although the news of Molyneux's presence had distressed Irene, the news of Colton's absence restored her again. She did not say so to Caroline, however, observing only that the hour was still very early and that he might have been delayed for any one of a thousand reasons. "I hope you do not mean to spend the entire evening fretting over him," she cautioned gently. "That would be scandalously ungrateful to Lady Selby and Lord Hammond."

"I shall continue to look for him," Caroline said, making an effort to calm her emotions.

"Mr. Charles Dale is a very fine dancer," Irene remarked.

"Yes, he is that," her sister said with a sigh. "I wish however, that I were dancing with another."

"If you recall," Irene said, "Mr. Colton told us he does not dance."

"Why, he did say so!" Caroline exclaimed. "Do you suppose that he has stayed away on that account?"

"Possibly," Irene replied. "He also said that our company would be sufficient to give him pleasure, but a man of his reserved character might feel awkward at a ball."

"He is not reserved," Caroline contradicted. "At least not with me. He is only shy."

"If that is what prevents him from coming tonight," said Irene, "then perhaps your thrusting an invitation upon him was ill advised."

Caroline confessed that she could see now what she had not seen before — that she might have been hasty. "I wanted to please myself alone," she berated herself. "I never thought how I might be mortifying him."

Irene found this self-castigation excessive, and she told Caroline that she would not listen to any more of it. "You meant the best," she reminded her. "Besides, if he did not intend to put the invitation to its proper use, he might have written you a note of explanation."

"How little you understand the quality of Mr. Colton's sensibility." Caroline sighed. "How could he send such a note, feeling as he did?"

"But we are not even sure how he felt," Irene pointed out.

"Naturally, you are not sure," her sister stated. "I, on the other hand, am quite certain."

Charles returned to claim Caroline's hand for the next set. Two young gentlemen in succession solicited the honor of dancing with Irene. After refusing politely, she sought a private word with Lady Selby.

"Did you invite Mr. Molyneux tonight?" she asked her ladyship.

"Who is Mr. Molyneux?" came the reply.

She addressed the same question to Lord Selby, who huffed, "Molyneux! Is he here?"

"Indeed he is."

"Well, I suppose he could not get in without an invitation," he said with a shrug of annoyance. "Still, I wish Louisa would consult me before inviting anyone. I could have warned her the man's a loose fish. I don't like him, and I never have."

"He attended Lady Volteface's musicale. I suppose, therefore, that he is generally well thought of."

"If he was there, then it was Volteface's doing. He's a rackety fellow who does not care whom he invites."

"Has Mr. Molyneux offended you in some way, my lord?"

"He's the rankest cardsharp I ever clapped eyes on," he answered. "His specialty is preying on young men of uncertain morals, loose fish like himself."

Irene started, wondering if Mr. Colton might be such a young man.

Lord Selby recalled her to the present by laughing. "I remember the night Hammond caught him with a card in his boot. Such a vile, transparent trick it was, too. Egad, he was furious when Hammond forced him to give back all his winnings. His luck had been in, so he had quite a fortune to give up. Hammond didn't mince words — told him in front of everybody that if he didn't give back the blunt on the spot, he would be sorry for it. Well, Molyneux gave it back in the end, but his luck was never the same after that."

While Irene deliberated over these revelations, it occurred to her that Mr. Molyneux's presence was as unexpected and unaccountable as was Mr. Colton's absence, and that this might not have been merely coincidence. She was, however, prevented from pursuing this train of thought by a question directed at her by the Earl of Hammond.

"Do you think you can spare a moment from conversation to dance?" he inquired cordially. "We are at a ball, after all, or have you forgotten?"

Irene looked him full in the face and smiled archly. "Thank you for taking pity on me," she said. "I was afraid I should never be asked to dance."

"I can think of many ways of describing the way you look this evening," he replied. "Pitiful is not one of them."

He led her to the position of honor at the head of the line, and as they danced sedately, Irene's eyes wandered to the faces of the onlookers. She scanned the crowd, hoping to ascertain the whereabouts of Mr. Molyneux, but she could not see him anywhere.

"When you dance with me, Miss Sparks," said his lordship, "I require your complete attention."

Amused by his tone of pique, she answered, "And you are accustomed to having things pretty much your own way."

"Do you mean I am spoilt?" he asked. "My mother will take issue on that head, I trust."

"I hope her ladyship is well," Irene replied warmly. "May I visit her again, do you think?"

He caught the fragrance of her hair as she circled under his arm. "She would like that very much," he said, thinking to himself that the request would please his mother almost as much as it had pleased him.

They went down the line, separated, and came back to the starting point. When they rejoined hands, he asked how Muffin had received the news of her being sent to school.

"She is in raptures," Irene assured him. "She talks of nothing but her pony. In a few days she will be gone, and there are not ponies enough to compensate us for that loss."

"You are sending her against your will, then?"

"No," she confessed. "It is only that I shall miss her so. But I am convinced it is for the best."

This admission gratified him, and he asked if he might be allowed to escort Muffin to Brighton on the appointed day.

"Nothing would please her more," she replied.

A brief shift of partners prevented further discussion, until the lines reformed their original pairs.

"Who in thunder are you looking for?" Hammond demanded.

"Was my attention wandering again?" she asked with a smile. "I am sincerely sorry."

"Perhaps you were expecting to see Mr. Colton?"

"I do not expect to see him here tonight," she said.

"Was he not invited?"

"Oh, yes," she replied, "but I have reason to suspect he was forced to decline."

The dance ended and the two of them parted, with a devout wish in his breast that Mr. Colton might go to the devil, and an equally strong feeling on her part that the only way to discover precisely the character of Mr. Colton was to confront Mr. Molyneux.

She therefore went in search of him, unaware that Hammond followed her at some distance. Mr. Molyneux showed himself at last lounging against a pillar by the entrance. He regarded the spectacle before him with a bored expression.

"I would have a word with you, Mr. Molyneux," Irene said peremptorily.

His eyes stealing along her high-waisted bodice, he made a sweeping flourish and said, "I never refuse a lady."

Chin high, Irene walked ahead of him out of the ballroom, not deigning to look back to see whether he followed. Making for the library, she went quickly inside and stepped to the fireplace, where she availed herself of the poker and hid it behind her gown. When Molyneux entered, she was standing tall and alert, facing him with a challenging look.

"You are not as appetizing at first glance as your sister," he told her, "but I daresay you improve upon acquaintance." He moved toward her, wetting his mouth.

"Stop where you are!" Irene commanded, surprising him into obeying. "I have not brought you here to make love to me. I want to know the extent of Mr. Colton's indebtedness to you."

Molyneux shifted about sullenly, giving no reply.

"Did he give you his invitation to the ball?" she demanded.

His head snapped up at this, and he gave

her a shocked look but he would not verbally confirm her surmise.

"Did Mr. Colton tell you that our rumored dowry is nothing but false gossip?" she hissed. "Did he tell you we are completely penniless and of no use to fortune hunters?"

Molyneux grinned at this. "So you may say," he laughed, "but I cannot believe that so generous a one as his lordship would leave you stranded. Besides, even if it were true, I warrant he would pay a king's ransom and then some to keep one of his protégés out of the scandal sheets."

"What do you mean?"

He stroked his beard with his fingers and declared that this line of conversation wearied him. "We are wasting time, my dear," he said with a leer, and moved closer.

"You have a great penchant for unprotected females," she said boldly.

As he moved closer to her he replied, "Ah, you think you know me well do you? Or have you been interested enough to make inquiries concerning my reputation? I am most flattered."

Instantly she swung the poker in front of her and raised it high. Responding to his leer with a determined gleam in her eye, she stated, "I must insist that you quit these premises at once."

"You!" he shouted in astonishment. "The abigail. It was you!"

"And I will not let you off so easily this time," she warned, "unless you vanish this instant!"

Molyneux broke into laughter, bending over and slapping his knee. He disported himself for some time in this manner until an affable voice behind him invited him to leave the room or be delivered into the street by the seat of his breeches.

"Why, Hammond, how very charming to see you again," Molyneux said with a sneer.

"I thought after our last encounter I was rid of you," the earl replied, coming into the room. "It seems that you are like pesty vermin, reappearing out of the dung heaps to plague us."

Mr. Molyneux's grin contorted in an ugly twist. Bowing insolently, he said, "It is dreadfully fatiguing when a lady cannot make up her mind. First I am lured into a private tête-à-tête with Miss Sparks. Then I am ordered from the premises as though I had insulted her. I wish," he said to Irene, "you would not tease a man so. It may do more harm than you know."

"If you are making a threat," Hammond said, "you do so at your peril."

"I make no threats," Molyneux answered.

"I merely point out how I have been compromised by a capricious female."

On that note, he sauntered out of the library, and Hammond watched the butler show him out. He then turned to Irene, saying in an imperious voice, "You may put that down now, Miss Sparks."

Irene replaced the fire iron and faced him, trying to guess if the expression on his face denoted concern or disapproval.

"We shall go inside," he commanded softly.

She put her arm through his and consented to be led back to the ballroom, where they took their places on the floor. The dance was so slow and the music so measured as to sound dirgelike to Irene's ears. She moved mechanically, not attending to her steps but only to her thoughts. Judging by his silence, the earl was similarly engaged.

Finally she spoke, saying earnestly, "Lord Hammond, I beg you to believe that I did not lure Mr. Molyneux to the library with any promises of the kind he suggested."

"I did not think you had," he said darkly.

"I would never have said so much as a word to Mr. Molyneux were it not for the fact that he has important information that touches someone very dear to me."

"I believe you," he replied, but his expression was so somber that Irene wondered if he truly did. Lowering her eyes, she admitted that her meeting with Molyneux alone in the library had been ill judged. "I ought to have known better," she chided herself, "for I know what he is. And if someone besides yourself had discovered us together, who knows what misunderstanding might have resulted?"

"The sight of you flailing a poker at Mr. Molyneux might have given a very wrong impression of who was the attacker in the case," he remarked. "May I add, you appear to be quite proficient with a fire iron. My compliments."

"You are laughing at me," she said.

"Do you see me laughing?" he asked. "No, Miss Sparks, the knowledge that you have braved an audience with the likes of Molyneux on the account of Mr. Colton provokes in me a very strong emotion, but it bears no resemblance whatever to amusement."

She stopped in the midst of the dance and could not continue. "I beg your pardon if my impropriety disgusts you," she said shakily. "I believe I can best make amends by my absence."

So saying, she curtsied and pushed her way through the crowd until she was entirely lost to view.

Chapter XII

Irene pulled the bedsheet over her nose and eyed the maid who had come in to draw the curtain.

"It is past noon, miss," the woman announced cheerfully. "The other ladies have not waked yet either."

When Irene did not reply, the maid went out and, a few minutes later, returned with a pot of chocolate on a tray, asking whether Miss would care to drink it in her bed. Looking ominous, Irene raised a forefinger over the coverlet and pointed to the table, where the maid set the breakfast with alacrity. Scurrying from the room then, the woman muttered under her breath that one could always tell by a lady's mood in the morning whether she had been disappointed in her partners the night before.

Her eyes focused on a point in space, Irene remained immobile for some time, reviewing in her mind the events of the past evening. Then suddenly she sat bolt upright in her bed and declared aloud, "I will not pretend another minute. I know what I know!"

Having resolved this much, she walked to the breakfast tray and addressed her toast and chocolate with appetite. As she ate, she turned over precisely what it was that she knew — to wit, that Mr. Colton was a blackguard. Despite her reputation for being overly suspicious, despite Caroline's admiration for the man, despite Molyneux's refusal to admit he had gained entrance to the ball by using Colton's invitation — despite everything — she knew with certainty that Colton was a schemer. Moreover, she meant to prove it. This thought inspired her to bite off a piece of toast and chew it vigorously.

She would need to proceed delicately, she cautioned herself. The least hint of censure could set Caroline off. Heaven knew what she might feel impelled to do in defiance of her eldest sister's disapproval. Hammond had expressed to Miss Proutie the hope that none of the sisters Sparks was capable of agreeing to an elopement. At the time, Miss Proutie had scorned the very suggestion. Now, however, it loomed as an awful possibility.

The recollection of Hammond gave her pause as she raised the cup of chocolate to her lips. How strangely things had developed between them, she reflected. They had begun in a kind of isolated enchantment, as though the library at Hopewell had loosened itself from the bonds of gravity and floated among the clouds and stars. Then he had told her his name, and the enchantment had ended. At that moment, she had regarded the earl with fear and suspicion. He had subsequently dispelled all her most hideous doubts, until the day when he had promised to "exact repayment in full."

It was with a profound sense of irony that Irene considered the reversal of their positions since then. Convinced that she had put about the rumor of the dowry, he had begun to despise her. The ball had hardened his dislike, giving him reason to think her not only a liar but a hypocrite as well, one who had spurned him in favor of the likes of Molyneux. She had lost his good opinion at precisely the instant that she had begun to value it most; and just when she would have seized the opportunity to tell him of Miss Proutie's folly, she no longer felt the freedom to do so.

These ironic reflections smacked heavily of regret, which Irene had always considered a luxury. Accustomed as she was to vigilance and penury, she could not afford to indulge herself. Rising from the table with energy, she went to the basin, threw some cool water on her face, and began to dress. It would not do to dwell on his lordship's opinion of her, she told herself, when she had determined to overset the designs of a much more dangerous sort of man.

In the breakfast parlor, Charles and Hammond picked at their braised sweet-breads with little keenness. First one threw down his fork; then the other. Charles lifted his cup for a drink of coffee and put it down again without tasting it. Hammond tapped his knife against a jam pot, glaring at it with fierce displeasure.

"You left the ball early," Charles said. "I looked for you only to be told you had gone two hours before."

Hammond adjusted his chair so that he had room to sink down into it and stretch out his legs. Studying the tip of his boots, he replied, "Sorry, lad. I ought to have said something before I left."

"I do not complain," Charles sighed. "I only wish you had taken me with you."

"To all appearances, you were happily engaged with Miss Caroline Sparks. I had no notion you required rescuing. You looked positively smitten."

"A man can play the fool for just so long,"

Charles said grimly. "Then he looks in the glass and sees a pudding-head grinning back at him."

"I can't recall when I have met a less foolish fellow than yourself," his lordship remarked.

Charles laughed. "Then it is well you left when you did, or you would have seen me dangling after a young lady who was thinking only of another gentleman. Indeed, I believe she was barely conscious of my existence."

"Dear me," said Hammond, tapping his fingertips together. "Miss Caroline has a beau, I take it. That makes two of them, then."

"Not only does she have a beau," Charles said, "but she also has an excess of ardor in praising him. That does not sit right, as far as I am concerned. When a lady must needs rise to the defense of her lover at every turn, she is trying to convince herself that she is certain of him."

"You are a deep one, my friend," Hammond responded with some admiration. "How do you contrive to smoke out these complexities? I confess, it is all too much for me. If a lady indicates her partiality for another, I bow as gracefully as I may, and exit into the wings, where, I expect, I will meet with another ingenue who will cast me in the lead."

Charles pushed his chair from the table and stood up. "That is all very well for you, my lord," said he. "You have the knack of playing your role opposite any number of ingenues. I, on the other hand, am far less of a hero. Once I have played my part, I cannot adjust to a change in the cast of players."

Hammond arched an eyebrow. "Where are you off to?"

"I am going to see her."

"It would do no good to try to stop you," the earl observed, "so I will save myself the trouble. But if the gentleman who greets you in the glass tonight bears the slightest resemblance to a pudding-head, I beg you will keep it to yourself."

"You are disappointed in me," Charles said.

With a sigh, Hammond straightened himself in his chair and moved it closer to the table. "Disappointed?" he repeated. "No, I can't say that I am. Only astonished — astonished at your perseverance, and a little envious, too."

"I am rather amazed myself," Charles confessed. On that note he left the parlor and a brief moment later Hammond heard him quit the house.

Lifting his fork in one hand and his knife in the other, the earl prepared once more to attack his breakfast. The sweetbreads lay before him, covered in a delicate cream sauce that his chef had labored many hours to prepare exactly to his taste. He carved off a slice and speared it. He then regarded it in some puzzlement, wondering why the devil he should be such a paltry fellow when his young, inexperienced secretary had gone off in pursuit of his lady fair, undaunted by her expressed preference for another. After staring inexorably at the morsel on his fork, he bit into it. To his delight, the taste was exquisite, and with his spirits considerably renewed be consumed every crumb on the plate.

At Berkeley Square, the butler announced Mr. Dale, who stormed in as though he meant to lay siege to the parlor.

Charles discerned, from the quickness of Caroline's breathing and the dark expression in her companion's eyes, that he had intruded upon a tender scene. This supposition did not discourage him, however. On the contrary, he endured the introduction to Mr. Colton with noble fortitude and planted himself firmly by the sofa.

Mr. Colton, having been interrupted, soon took his leave.

When he was gone, Caroline sighed.

"I see Mr. Colton has turned up at last," Charles observed.

"Yes," she murmured, inviting him with a gesture to sit down.

As he did so, he asked if Mr. Colton had explained his absence satisfactorily.

"Mr. Colton does not dance," she explained.

"I suppose a man may attend a ball merely in order to be among those he cares about," he said.

"Some men may do so," she replied, "but Mr. Colton is not like other men. His sensibilities are very strong and do not permit him to sham a lightness of heart he does not feel."

"You are in love with him," Charles said.

After a slight pause, she nodded.

"Then I am too late." He bowed his head.

Caroline beheld him in consternation. It had never occurred to her that the sedate Mr. Dale had conceived a passion for her. The knowledge that he had done so, while deeply flattering, sorrowed her, for she empathized with the pain she was inflicting, however unintentionally.

"You have known me only a few hours," she said gently. "You cannot love me."

"Can I not?" he replied. "And how long

have you known Mr. Colton — months, years?"

"Soon you will meet someone who will blot me entirely from your mind," she said.

"You have a high opinion of my steadiness!"

"No, no," she exclaimed in distress. "I meant only to comfort you."

"That is not how I look to be comforted," he replied.

She rose from her chair to sit beside him on the sofa. Looking sadly into his eyes, she pleaded, "Do not be angry with me, I beg you. If you care for me, as you say you do, then you will act the part of a friend."

Her nearness inflamed Charles with the idea of taking her in his arms and kissing away forever any memory of Mr. Colton. But his kisses might serve only to make her avoid him in the future, and if that happened he would lose all hope of winning her.

With a forced complacence, he moved a little away from her and said that although he was no more able to act a sham than Mr. Colton, he cared for her enough to pledge his friendship.

Caroline thanked him earnestly and asked him, to his very great surprise, what he could tell her about Vauxhall. In answer to her many questions, he told her how one got there; what kinds of ladies and gentle-men — both respectable and otherwise — frequented the Gardens at night; what sort of costume was customarily worn at the masquerade; and what intrigues attracted its visitors under the guise of longing to view the fireworks.

"You must choose your chaperon well," he advised. "Young ladies may be subjected to unwelcome advances if they are not sur-rounded by a large party or protected by an escort. I should offer you my services as es-cort, but I expect Mr. Colton already fills that office."

Caroline lowered her eyes in assent. "Yes, he has asked me to meet him at Vauxhall Thursday next, and of course I shall go. He is to be Punchinello. Will I recognize him, do you suppose?"

"I assure you," he said, "it will be difficult to avoid recognizing such a hook-nosed, hump-backed buffoon. You will find the Gardens populated mostly by dominoes in flowing cloaks and half-masks. Punchinello will stand out in such a crowd."

Relieved, Caroline conjured up an image of the masquerade, which animated her lovely face.

"How will he know you?" Charles in-quired, an idea forming in his mind.

"I am to be Columbine," she said. "I am to wear a patchwork cloak."

"Try, if you can, to find a spangled mask," he suggested, "so he will more easily recognize you."

She thanked him for the hint, saying, "You have shown yourself a true friend indeed."

Charles looked a little guilty at this. He hoped that the little deception he planned would still seem the work of a friend once it was discovered.

As he walked back to Grosvenor Square, his hands clasped behind his back, his head bent down, he took himself severely to task. It was the height of idiocy, he thought, to love a girl who was so mad for another that she flung herself headlong into scandal on his account. Still, when he recalled the beauty of her face, the sweetness of her smile, and the good-hearted sympathy that sprang from her without concealment, he sighed. One day, he vowed, she would consign this Punchinello creature to oblivion and willingly bestow her manifold charms on a thoroughgoing pudding-head.

Late that afternoon, Lady Selby surveyed the ballroom. In the light of day — light that seemed to glare cruelly on her aching eyes — the room hardly seemed the recent scene of so much noisy gaiety. The floor was littered with programs, its sheen trampled and scuffed to a gray dullness. The salon was arrayed now with crumbs and soiled linens. It echoed the hollow sounds of servants disassembling the fountain that had gurgled and splashed so prettily a few hours before.

With a great sigh, Louisa turned to the servants who had followed her into the ballroom and now patiently awaited her ladyship's instructions. As she walked back and forth between the two rooms, her minions following silently in her wake, she felt oddly let down. The ball had gone off as successfully as she could have wished. Nothing was wanting — not praise, envy, triumph, or pride — to give her pleasure in the past evening's work, nothing except the anticipation, which, now gone, left a yawning gap in its place.

Contemplation of the chandelier and sconces restored Louisa a little to good cheer. She recalled gloatingly how much these late additions had been admired by her guests. That recollection brought with it others of a bracing nature. She thought with particular satisfaction on Chloe, who had found favor in the eyes of a rich young tulip of fashion. Although Selby had dismissed Mr. Quince as a fop, she estimated his fortune at such a figure that she was disposed to find his propensity for lace and jewels a model of exquisite taste. The diamond he had worn on his pinky and the sapphire that had twinkled from the folds of his cravat had struck Selby as dreadfully dandified. She, on the other hand, having availed herself of the opportunity to scrutinize these stones very closely, had recognized at once that their combined value might furnish chandeliers and sconces for at least a dozen ballrooms.

Her listlessness somewhat alleviated now, Louisa began to issue orders to the servants, setting them bustling off in every direction, while she stood, arms folded, like a general deploying an advancing force. Warming to her work, she pushed up her sleeves, meaning to plunge herself into the task at hand, but suddenly she found her elbow tugged at and her name invoked in the most importunate manner. Without any preliminaries, Caroline begged to be taken to Vauxhall Thursday next.

"I believe I am at liberty that afternoon," said her ladyship. "Holt, is that a stain in the drapery?" she called to the butler. "Good God, how do you suppose someone managed to spill champagne all the way up there?"

"If you please, Lady Selby," Caroline said, "I wish to go in the evening, just at nine o'clock."

Louisa tore her eyes from the drapery to regard Caroline closely. "Who can have put such a notion into your head?" she asked with a gasp. "Vauxhall is no place for young girls at nine o'clock in the evening. For shame, Miss Caroline! I realize you have been in London only a short while and so cannot be expected to know everything that is fitting or unfitting for young ladies. Still, I had hoped you would have learned enough by now to spare me such a suggestion."

Dismayed, Caroline did not know what to do. She remained in the ballroom, casting about for words with which to persuade Lady Selby to reverse her position.

"Are you still here?" her ladyship cried. "Do not think to cajole me into changing my mind. Chloe has tried and failed a hundred times or more, and I will not hear of it. There, let that be an end to it."

Upon that, Lady Selby marched over to the stained drape to inspect it with her own eyes. Caroline had no choice but to hie herself from the ballroom and ponder what was to be done now.

She scratched gently on Chloe's chamber door. Invited to come in, she entered to see Miss Selby still abed.

"Oh, it's only you," Chloe greeted her cheerfully. "I feared it might be my mother come to make me get dressed. I detest getting dressed the day after a ball."

"But you've never been to a ball before," Caroline pointed out.

"Very true," replied her friend. "Nevertheless, I detest it." She motioned to Caroline to draw near and sit down.

"What did you think of Mr. Quince?" Chloe asked. As Caroline had not at all noticed him, being otherwise preoccupied at the time, she stammered a few vague phrases and then ventured to say she was sure he was a very fine gentleman. This encomium struck Chloe as so lukewarm that she felt obliged to take his praise into her own hands. She reviewed each of his excellent qualities in minute detail, particularly those elegancies of dress that had most bedazzled her. When she finished, she asked, in a voice replete with suggestion, whether Caroline had enjoyed dancing with Mr. Dale.

"I thought only of Mr. Colton," Caroline stated.

"Then why did you not dance with him?"

Chloe asked. "Is it not silly to dance with one gentleman and pine for another?"

"He was not there."

"Oh," Chloe said. "Well then, you did right to dance with Charles, for to ruin one's evening by regretting the absence of a partner is a shameful waste."

At that, a sob shook Caroline's bosom, and her lips trembled.

Chloe sat up in her bed. "Why, what is the matter?" she cried. "Surely Charles did not insult you?"

Unable to speak, Caroline shook her head.

"Did he insult Mr. Colton?"

Another shake of the head answered this.

"Well, for heaven's sake, whom did he insult?"

Despite all her efforts, Caroline could not find her voice.

"Oh, hum!" Chloe said irritably. "How am I to help you if you blubber like that?"

Caroline could not help laughing through her tears. Gradually, in a murky, roundabout way, she unfolded to her friend all the events of the past twenty-four hours, beginning with Mr. Colton's reluctance to use the invitation to the ball and ending with his desire for a rendezvous with her at Vauxhall Gardens.

As soon as she heard the name Vauxhall, Chloe jumped out of her bed and danced around the boudoir. "It is famous!" she cried. "We shall do it. Mr. Quince will escort me. I have no doubt I can make him do it. And your costume — what is it, you say — a patchwork? I know the very thing. We have such a cloak in the attic. It will be beyond anything! Oh, how I have longed to go to Vauxhall."

"We cannot go," Caroline said with a sigh. "Your mother will not hear of it."

"Naturally not," Chloe replied with disdain. "We must arrange to go without her."

"We cannot do that," Caroline said in some shock. "She will be very angry. Surely your father will not take us if he knows your mama disapproves."

"Papa!" Chloe repeated in disgust. "I shouldn't dream of asking him. As for Mama, she will not be at all angry with us if she knows nothing about it, will she?" On this question, she pranced toward Caroline wagging a knowing forefinger.

"Do you mean to steal out of the house without her knowing it?"

"That's exactly what I mean to do." Chloe grinned. "I also mean to steal back in again without her knowing."

"It's impossible," cried Caroline, who did

not feel wholly comfortable with the thought of deceiving her ladyship.

"You will not say that when you hear my plan," Chloe confided. "For months I have been thinking of the very means of accomplishing such a scheme, and now that I am out and all grown up, I mean to do it. How delicious that we may do it together!"

"But we must have a chaperon," Caroline said and sighed again. "Unless you think we may do without one?"

Chloe screwed up her face in a pout. "I suppose we must have a chaperon," she allowed. "Mr. Quince is rather persnickety on such points. He will not like it if I come unchaperoned; no, he will not like it at all."

"You see," said Caroline, "it is impossible."

"Pooh! I thought you had more spirit than that," Chloe declared, causing a blush to rise in her friend's cheeks. "We must consider who might serve us as chaperon. Beatrice will not do, of course. Her prosing at me constantly will quite ruin the adventure."

"Do you know," Caroline said in a soft voice, "this quandary is not unlike the one we found ourselves in when we received your mother's invitation to come to London. Only then our problem was to find an abigail."

"What did you do?" Chloe said.

"Irene disguised herself as our abigail; Miss Proutie, she called herself. Oh, Irene always has her wits about her, you know. Martha hangs back a little, being somewhat bashful, but Irene never hangs back. I believe she is quite fearless!"

"Indeed!" Chloe exclaimed, deeply impressed. "I had not thought of her in such a light."

Caroline then confided the tale of Miss Proutie's encounter with Mr. Molyneux at the Bluebird, portraying her sister as a veritable heroine in defending a young maiden's honor.

This astonishing story quite raised Irene in Chloe's esteem. She exclaimed for some time upon Miss Sparks's boldness and concluded, "If she is so fond of dressing up in costume and disguising her identity, I think she will fall in with our scheme at once."

But Irene did not fall in with the scheme at once; moreover, she vowed to do her best to prevent the two girls from executing it at all. Too incensed at Caroline's heedlessness to weigh her words, she upbraided her with her ingratitude toward Lady Selby. "If her ladyship's feelings do not give you pause," she said, "Mr. Colton's improper suggestion should. How dare he require you to defy every stricture you have ever learned! What a villain he must be to demand you risk your reputation and safety to meet him."

Strengthened by disapprobation, Caroline pulled herself up to her full height and replied with offended dignity, "You have hated him all along. I did not see it before, for you have dissembled well. But you harbor an unreasoning prejudice against him, and because of it you are doing everything to ensure I spend the rest of my life in misery."

"Do not say so," Martha urged. "Oh, how it tears my heart out to hear you say these things to Irene."

"Don't pay her any mind," Muffin said scornfully. "That is not Caroline speaking. It is some mooning creature out of a novel."

"I find it most useful to quote from my reading," Beatrice interjected. "One should always endeavor, I think, to apply literature to life whenever possible."

At this point, all the ladies, with the exception of Chloe, burst into clamorous argument. Muffin and Martha loyally supported Irene, though the latter did her best to speak gently and sympathetically to Caroline, while the former informed her that she was completely odious. Beatrice took advantage of every pause to offer an epigram for the edification of the contenders; however, her pearls of wisdom were lost utterly on Caroline, who grew more obstinate with every word spoken. If a few hours before she had felt a little doubtful, she now felt wholly certain of the rightness of her actions.

When the ladies ran out of breath, Chloe stepped in with an entirely different view of things. "I believe Miss Irene Sparks has some very natural reservations," she said smoothly, "but once she hears what I have to say, I am confident she will volunteer to chaperon us."

The other ladies looked at her in amazement.

"My mind is made up," Irene said.

"I must tell you," Chloe went on blithely, "we, too, have our minds made up, and we will not be brooked. I must also tell you, Miss Irene, that it is your duty to protect us, however much you may dislike the scheme. I think it behooves you to do this for me in recognition of the enormous good I did you when I put it about that you were to receive a dowry of two thousand pounds."

"It was you!" Muffin cried.

"Yes, it was," Chloe stated with a proud sniff, "and what an inspiration it was, too!"

"I wish you had not done so," Irene said.

"I believe you meant it for the best, but it was ill advised and possibly harmful."

"Poof!" Chloe sneered. "Why, you saw yourself how quickly you were accepted by the ton. Do you think you could have accomplished that without my little fib? You should be thanking me for my help."

"Is it help to make us prey to fortune hunters?" Irene retorted.

"Mr. Colton is not a fortune hunter!" Caroline shouted. "How dare you imply he is."

Irene turned to Caroline with a rueful smile. "I never implied anything of the kind. That is your own conscience speaking. But it is of no importance, for I will not add to Chloe's falsehood by deceiving Lady Selby. There will be no Vauxhall outing and no deception."

"Those are very high-sounding phrases, Miss Sparks," Chloe said silkily, "coming as they do from one who is so accomplished in the art of deception. Indeed, I feel the injustice so keenly I shall probably be compelled to reveal to my uncle and mother the identity of that heroic abigail, Miss Proutie!"

"Who told you about that?" Muffin demanded. Receiving only a demure look in reply, she continued, "Oh, Caroline, how could you tell her? If you were married to

Mr. Colton this minute, it would not be punishment enough for what you have done this day."

"You must not say a word about Miss Proutie," Martha implored in an anguished voice. "Chloe, promise you will not say a word."

Chloe shrugged. "I do not think I shall be able to recall the smallest particle of information regarding Miss Proutie, as soon as Irene consents to be our chaperon."

"You must do as she says," Martha urged Irene.

"Humgudgeon!" Muffin said angrily. "So what if Chloe does blab? What is the worst that can happen?"

"There is no telling," Chloe replied slyly. "But, knowing Mama, I expect she will no longer be able to welcome the ladies of Hopewell in her house. It would be regrettable — I'm sure she would feel the loss profoundly — but to harbor scandal under her roof is more than my poor mother's health can sustain. She suffers from palpitations, you know."

Silenced by this threat, the ladies all looked at Irene to see what she would say. Irene herself wondered how to respond, for, with her back to the wall, she found it sorely tempting to make a clean breast of the whole affair. Of course, once Hammond heard of her masquerade, he would despise her. But that could hardly matter; he despised her already, as witnessed by his cold sarcasm at the ball.

Had she no one but herself to consider, Irene would have preferred to leave the protection of Lady Selby's house and live her life independently. There was no guarantee, however, that Lady Selby's wrath would confine itself to Irene — the actual perpetrator of the deception. No, she would be sure to hold all the Sparks sisters equally responsible and cast them all into the street. The result would be disastrous. For one thing, Muffin's education would end before it had begun. Although the dowager was not the sort of woman to renege on a promise, she could hardly be expected to sponsor the girl's schooling against the principles and morals of her only daughter. And there was Martha to think about, too. Despite her stubborn secretiveness, she seemed dreadfully vulnerable of late. She shied away from company, and had been so tender-hearted in the face of Chloe's warning as to beg Irene in the most urgent way to go along with the Vauxhall scheme. Finally, there was Caroline, who, driven by desperation and an image of love as self-immolation, seemed on the point of precipitating herself into a marriage with Mr. Colton. Much as Irene criticized the girl's heedlessness, much as she regretted her betrayal of family secrets, she loved her sister too much to see her bound for life to a man like Mr. Colton.

Compared to all these portents, an evening at Vauxhall seemed the lesser of two evils. Irene began to consider how she might even turn it to her advantage, using the opportunity it afforded to reveal to Caroline Mr. Colton's true nature. Indeed, the Vauxhall scheme might be the very means she had been seeking to prove the man a scoundrel. Perhaps it might be made a blessing in disguise. Whatever plans Colton had for Caroline at the Gardens, Mr. Molyneux was sure to be implicated. If Irene could discover the two of them together, she could disclose them to her sister as conspirators. Once Caroline's eyes were opened to the facts about her suitor, they might all rest easy again.

"Very well," Irene said in a calm voice, "I will do it."

Martha exhaled a breath of relief, while Muffin exclaimed wrathfully to Caroline, "I hope you are pleased with yourself now. You have the satisfaction of breaking Irene's heart, and I wish you joy of it."

From her expression, Caroline appeared not the least bit pleased with herself; however, she allowed an ecstatic Chloe to pull her by the hand to the attic to rummage through musty old trunks in search of costumes. As soon as they had gone, Martha dashed to her room, and Beatrice predicted that the upshot of it all would be a debacle of apocalyptic dimensions. "Nevertheless," she added, "I shall endeavor to see the scheme succeed, lest my sister bring shame upon the family, which might reflect adversely upon myself." So saying, she left to find solace among her books.

"Go to the attic," Irene instructed her youngest sister, "and find me a disguise with tiny sleeves or fitted ones, for I shall need freedom of movement. And be sure there is a pocket."

"What are you thinking?" Muffin asked. "Do you actually mean to submit to this scheme?"

Straightening her shoulders, Irene replied, "I mean to prevent this farce from ending in tragedy. The curtain may fall on a stage littered with corpses, but the bodies of the Sparks sisters shall not be among them."

Muffin considered her sister thoughtfully. "Do you have a plan, then?"

"It is not perfectly clear in my mind as yet," Irene confessed, "but yes, I mean to expose Mr. Colton and his accomplice."

"His accomplice?"

"Hurry, do as I bade you, my love. There is no time to lose."

Muffin moved to the door, then stopped as she recollected a horrifying thought. "I shall be in Brighton Thursday!" she exclaimed. "How will I know the outcome?"

The reminder gave Irene a pang, but she shunted it aside. "Thank God you will be safe," was all that she said. "You will hear the news — whatever it be — soon enough."

"I will go find your disguise," Muffin declared, "and anything else that may help you. But I doubt it will do much good, for Caroline means to ruin herself, and, in my view, she deserves to have her way!"

When Muffin had shut the door behind her, Irene tiptoed down the stairs to the library. She walked to a cabinet mounted on the wall and, turning a small key in the lock, opened the glass door. Inside were five pistols of varying shapes and sizes. She reached for the smallest one and found it attached securely to its mountings. The next largest, however, came loose with just a little coaxing. This she put in the pocket of her skirt and swirled around to test the feel of it. It was a trifle bulky, but, she decided, it would serve her purpose.

In an agony of impatience, Martha endured the carriage ride to Fleet Street. A placid young woman by temperament, she now found herself in a perturbation of spirits usually seen only in Caroline. When she threw open the door of Mr. Mowbray's business establishment, she looked so distraught that he came to her immediately and asked if she was ill.

"Please let me fetch you a glass of water, Miss Proutie," he said, "or a sip of brandy, perhaps."

He led her into a small chamber and, entreating her to sit, took a flask from a bookshelf, moving papers about in search of a cup. As he generally availed himself of refreshment directly from the flask, he was unable to produce anything suitable for use as a glass.

"It doesn't matter," Martha said, distracted. "There is only one thing I require. You must return my poems to me at once, and I must give over any intention of having them published."

Dismayed, Mr. Mowbray responded, "Oh, but that is out of the question, my dear lady."

As a dreadful apprehension filled her bosom, Martha inhaled deeply. "I must have them," she insisted quietly.

"But they have already been bound."

"Then they must be unbound."

Mr. Mowbray regretted that he had ever advised her not to be such a mouse. "I cannot do that," he protested. "Bound is bound."

Taking his check from her purse, Martha held it out to him. When he did not take it, she persisted, "You must accept the return of your sixty pounds and give me back my poems. I have no other choice, Mr. Mowbray, and I beg your pardon if this causes you any inconvenience."

Mr. Mowbray slunk down in his chair with a sigh. He had worried from the start that his dealings with the young poet had gone too smoothly to be trusted. Now, it seemed, he must pay for his unwonted good fortune. Licking his dry lips, he wished he dared to reach for the brandy flask.

"Inconvenience," he repeated forlornly. "I don't suppose it is much of an inconvenience to go round to every bookshelf and library in London demanding to have your poems returned."

"Do you mean the book is already out?"

she cried. "But you said it would not appear for some time yet."

"That was weeks ago," he protested. "Besides, Mr. Fiske insisted we print it right away. He said it would not do to put it off, and Mr. Fiske is never wrong about these things."

Martha looked so despairing at this news that he began to relent a little. "See here, Miss Proutie," he said. "It cannot be so bad as all that."

"It is as bad as it can be," she mourned. "You see, Miss Proutie is not my real name."

As Mr. Mowbray had never thought that it was, this piece of information did not shock him as much as Martha had anticipated. Instead he shrugged in puzzlement and said, "That ought to enable you to rest easy, then, for your identity will never be known."

"You don't understand," Martha cried helplessly. "It is too complicated to explain. All I know is that the appearance of a book of poems ascribed to Miss Proutie might ruin those I love most in the world."

The gentleman frowned, deeply sorry that her view of the matter was so tragic, yet not quite ready to allow that the situation was wholly devoid of hope. "It is a very small

folio, you know," he said in his most reas-
suring tone. "Hardly anyone will notice it. I
should be very much surprised if it is read at
all."

That observation appeared to comfort
Martha considerably. "I do pray you are
right," she said, "and that no one will ever
see it."

"Furthermore," Mr. Mowbray went on,
handing her back her check, "there is a great
deal that a little of the ready can do to offset
a tangle."

Martha looked at him with curiosity.
Then she looked at the bank draft, fingering
it gingerly.

Perceiving that she had caught his meaning, Mr. Mowbray said, "One can do much
with sixty pounds."

"Did you not advise me once to make a
killing on the Exchange?" Martha asked
slowly.

Brightening, Mr. Mowbray recalled the
incident.

"How does one go about making such a
killing?" she asked. "I should like to do so at
once, if at all possible."

"You must find a broker — a man of business. Do you know anyone like that — a
lawyer, or a banker perhaps?"

Martha racked her brain and answered,

"There is Mr. Uffingham. He administered my father's estate."

"He's your man!" Mr. Mowbray pronounced, feeling strongly inclined to celebrate with a swallow from the flask.

"Can you find me his direction?" Martha asked.

Seizing the flask, Mr. Mowbray dashed into the anteroom to set his scribes to finding the lawyer's direction. Then he found a corner where he might collect his emotions undisturbed. There he took several hearty swallows of brandy and toasted deliverance from unhappy authors.

Chapter XIII

Outside Selby House, the Earl of Hammond's coach waited, a trunk and two valises tied securely on the top. The steps had been lowered, and a footman stood at attention by the open door. Inside, the household gathered to bid farewell to Miss Mary Sparks. They were required to cool their heels for some time before she made her appearance, however, for she was engaged in the stables, saying a tearful goodbye to the hands and the frisky gelding. When at last she arrived in the drawing room, dressed in a pretty traveling suit cut in the military style, she greeted the solemn faces before her with a low-spirited sigh.

"I daresay you will be glad to be rid of me," she said to Lord Selby, who disputed this suggestion.

"That I shall not," he grumbled. "I could not have wished for a better companion at cards, for you never tired of playing, and you never drank a drop of port."

Muffin squeezed his arm and promised,

"I shall teach all the young ladies at Miss Oglethorpe's how to play commerce and loo, and if I don't like them, I shall fleece them of their pin money."

"Gracious," Lady Selby cried in alarm. "Do not say so! I'm sure his lordship will feel it very deeply if you do; it will reflect on him, you know, and everyone will say that he corrupted you." She then leveled a stern look at her husband, who squirmed mightily.

Beatrice and Chloe stepped forward opportunely to make their adieux to Miss Mary and to wish her good fortune at school. As Chloe moved to kiss her cheek, Muffin whispered vehemently, "I shall never forgive you. Do not dare to kiss me, unless you mean to give up this idea of going to Vauxhall."

In reply, Chloe laughed raucously, as though Muffin had made a great joke, saying loudly, "I shall miss you, too!"

Solemnly Beatrice presented Muffin with a slim volume of sermons and a pretty box. "They will both provide sustenance, I pray," she said, "for the essays contain much philosophy, and the box contains sweet tarts."

Thanking Beatrice for her goodness, Muffin turned to her sisters. Stiffly and angrily she approached Caroline, saying in her ear as she hugged her, "Give up your scheme. I don't care what happens to you. You can run off with Mr. Colton and never be heard from again, for all I care, but it is odious to drag Irene into your vile plot."

Caroline's eyes filled with tears. "Do not cast me off," she sobbed, hugging Muffin so affectionately that the girl could not help feeling sorry for her.

As the two embraced again, Muffin exhorted one last time, "Can you not see what is happening to you? You are a perfect sight. You are pale, where you used to be rosy and blooming. You have dark circles under your eyes. You hardly smile anymore. And all on his account."

Caroline pushed her sister from her roughly and ran to the window, where she wept into a commodious handkerchief for several moments.

"Partings are often painful to those who dwell on them overmuch," Beatrice observed. "One must endeavor to bear up bravely, so as not to distress the one who is leaving."

Taking no heed of this abundant wisdom, Caroline continued to sob as if her heart were cracking in two. The others shifted about, embarrassed, while Muffin took Martha into a private corner.

"You must talk Irene out of going to

Vauxhall," she urged in a low voice. "It is not too late to change her mind."

"I cannot do that," Martha said sorrowfully. "Chloe must not be allowed to carry out her threats."

"It is only that I am afraid for Irene," Muffin said. "She has a plan to expose Mr. Colton. What if it should go awry? Suppose he overpowers her? I am terrified at what might happen."

Martha bit her lip. "How I wish I were brave!" she said, hugging her sister. "But I can only do what it is in me to do. Believe me when I tell you I will do everything I can to prevent our family's ruination."

Looking into her sister's kindly face, Muffin allowed herself to be a little comforted. She would have turned to Irene for a kiss then, but was forestalled by a loud knock on the door. The footman announced that Lord Hammond had arrived on horseback and was ready to set out for Brighton.

Irene walked to her youngest sister and clasped her tightly in her arms. Though her eyes were wet and her throat was dry, her expression was bright and jovial. "You will do well at school," she said, with rather more hope than conviction, "and I shall think of you every minute."

"Write me," Muffin implored. "Tell me at

once what happens. I shall not shut my eyes till I know how it comes out."

With a nod, Irene promised, then followed the others out-of-doors to the waiting carriage.

Although he anticipated having Muffin join him on his bay for much of the journey, Hammond had ordered his coach equipped with pillows, throws, a basket of refreshments, a deck of cards, and a box of chessmen. He greeted his charge heartily, bestowing a cordial bow on the others and a somewhat wary one on Irene.

"You will take good care of her?" Irene whispered to him in a shaky voice.

"There will be no scrapes 'twixt here and Brighton, I can promise you," he answered.

A moment later Muffin was installed in the coach, hanging out the window to wave farewell. As the carriage pulled away at a brisk pace, the others gradually filtered inside again, leaving Irene alone on the street until she could see the travelers turn out of the square. Muffin no sooner was gone than Martha came out of the house. She hurried toward Irene, stopping breathlessly in front of her.

"What on earth is the matter?" Irene cried.

Blushing and stammering, Martha said,

"You must take this at once to Mr. Uffingham." So saying, she thrust a paper into Irene's hand.

Unfolding it, Irene said, "Why, it is a check made out to the bearer in the amount of sixty pounds. How did you come by it?"

"It is mine," Martha declared, "and I beg you, sister, to take it to Mr. Uffingham without delay."

"I do not understand. What is this check, and what has father's solicitor to do with it?"

"You must believe me, Irene. The money is entirely mine. I have not stolen it, I promise you."

"Of course I believe you," Irene said with a smile, "and I know you are not capable of stealing anything. But where did you get it?"

Martha bit her lip. Averting Irene's eyes, she answered in a quivering voice, "I sold the ring Mama gave me."

"You loved that ring," Irene said, considerably shocked. "It was the only memento she left. But what possessed you to sell it?"

At first, Martha looked about her helplessly, as though her reply might spring aloft from the cobblestones in the street. Finally, however, she managed to say, "It is this Vauxhall scheme. We must have something, you know, in case it goes awry."

Irene looked grim. "I see that this dreadful affair causes you as much anxiety as it does Muffin. Indeed, I am very sorry for it."

"But if you will take this to Mr. Uffingham," Martha pleaded, "he will turn it into a sum we all can live on. Then it will not matter about Vauxhall."

"If you are so set on this course, why did you not go to Mr. Uffingham yourself?"

"Because you have a fine head for business — everyone says so — while I hang back and look afraid of my shadow. Besides, you spoke with him about the estate after father died. He knows you and regards you as our family's representative."

Irene studied her sister's pale, tense face. "How drawn you have become since we left Hopewell," she said. "You were so plump and rosy before we arrived in London. Oh, I am sure we should never have agreed to come."

Martha blushed and looked distressed.

"What if Mr. Uffingham cannot perform a miracle with your sixty pounds?" Irene asked as kindly as she knew how. "Have you thought of that? Perhaps you would do better to take your money and redeem the ring."

"I can't do that!" Martha blurted. "I wish to place it with Mr. Uffingham and nowhere else. If you will not, then I must."

Startled by this outburst, Irene gazed thoughtfully into Martha's distraught face. "I will do it for you," she consented at last, "on one condition. You must not miss breakfast every morning, as you have been wont to do. And you must not stay indoors all day writing letters."

That brought tears to Martha's eyes. New ones streamed down her cheeks whenever she brushed the old ones away. Impetuously she threw her arms about Irene and hugged her, murmuring, "I do not deserve to be blessed with such a sister."

Smiling at this exaggerated praise, Irene patted Martha's back and stood away to look at her. "Now tell me what I am to say to Mr. Uffingham for you."

Drying her tears, Martha replied, "You must tell him to use this sum to make a killing on the Exchange."

Irene's eyes shone with amusement. "A most natural request. I wonder I did not think of it myself, with my fine head for business. And you are quite sure that Mr. Uffingham will agree to do this?"

"Of course," said Martha. "I have it on excellent authority that a solicitor is the very man to make our fortune."

"Our fortune!" Irene could not forbear smiling again. Looking at the check, she remarked, "I daresay I shall find the visit a vast deal more entertaining than poor Mr. Uffingham," and put the paper in her pocket.

"I shall go and ask for Lord Selby's barouche," said Martha.

"What? Am I to go this very instant?"

"Why, yes. If you intend to be at Vauxhall Thursday next, there is no time to lose."

"You expect, then, that we shall be homeless by Friday?"

Martha bowed her head and said nothing.

"Very well," Irene replied to this silent affirmation. "Send for the barouche. I only hope that Mr. Uffingham is as fond of making killings as you seem to think he is, and that he is accustomed to making them at a moment's notice."

Irene rode to Mr. Uffingham's law chambers in pensive mental conversation, berating herself one moment for agreeing to Martha's absurd request, and wishing the next that the solicitor might indeed fabricate for them a sum of money that would render the Vauxhall scheme harmless.

"Miss Sparks!" the lawyer greeted her. "I had no idea you were in London."

Irene related to him the events that had led to her family's installation in Berkeley Square.

"Lord Hammond has acted in the noblest manner," declared Mr. Uffingham. "I am greatly shocked to hear it."

"No less than I," replied Irene. "From what you told me, I expected conduct of a very different sort."

"Perhaps the earl has reformed his ways," the solicitor suggested. "His family will be greatly relieved to know it if he has. But his actions are not entirely without precedent. A colleague of my acquaintance knew of a squire in Northumbria, who had a brother near Cornwall, who heard of a similar action. The gentleman was later discovered to have corrupted his wards in the most dissolute manner. It was said that he turned the young lads into servants and the young girls into actresses!"

As he unfolded the details of the case, marveling all the while that its outcome was achieved without litigation, he escorted Irene to a small, well-appointed chamber and invited her to sit.

"I can assure you, sir, Lord Hammond has never taken advantage of our dependency," Irene said. "His treatment of us has proved unexceptional. His generosity appears to be as disinterested as it is surprising. I begin to think, Mr. Uffingham, that there has been some misreading of his character — that he may be, in reality, a moderate and sensible man."

"You are very outspoken for a young lady," he replied. "Certainly the earl is all that you say he is, if it is ever moderate and sensible to speak to the House of Lords on currency reform before testing the political waters!"

Irene regarded the solicitor for a moment. "Do you mean," she asked incredulously, "that the reputation you ascribe to Lord Hammond is not derived from any want of character on his part, but from his plan to make a speech?"

"Lord Selby informs me that such a reckless course can only end in Hammond's ruination, as well as his family's."

Irene smiled. Her eyes shone, and it seemed as though she would laugh out loud. "I am delighted he means to speak," she said. "You could have given me no happier news this day."

The lawyer raised his brows. "Do you anticipate with pleasure the ruination of your benefactor?"

But Irene did not hear him. She sat for a considerable time in rapt, smiling silence, until Mr. Uffingham interrupted her reverie to suggest, "Perhaps you ought to tell me why you have come today, Miss Sparks. How may I be of service to you?"

Recollecting herself, Irene said with a brilliant smile, "I have been asked to say that I wish to make a killing on the Exchange."

Mr. Uffingham's eyebrows elevated. "No doubt you do," he said. "So, in fact, does half the known world. But I am afraid a certain amount of capital is required before a venture may be undertaken."

Digging into her purse, Irene produced Martha's treasure and gave it to the lawyer.

Appraising the value at a glance, he said, "The amount is decidedly small. I am in the habit of advising investors to place their principal where it may be safe, and to risk only the interest on speculative schemes. This sum you have shown me is so insignificant as to yield hardly anything at all from the five percents."

"My sister expressly wishes to have a great deal of money as soon as possible," Irene said.

Again Mr. Uffingham's eyebrows climbed. "You surprise me, Miss Sparks," he said. "What has a young lady like you to do with killings and such affairs? You ought to be thinking of how to marry and bring up your babies and put up your strawberries and manage your servants."

"I have not had any offers of marriage," Irene replied. "Nor am I likely to."

The lawyer favored her with a disapproving glance and advised, "Well, you must continue with Lady Selby until you do."

"That may not be very long," Irene sighed. "Indeed, it is my strong apprehension that we will soon find ourselves without a home once again. When that happens, I must be prepared."

Mr. Uffingham appeared grim at this dire prophecy. It did not surprise him that Lady Selby had wearied of hosting the four lovely sisters; she had two daughters of her own to provide with husbands and did not need beautiful rivals to surround them beyond what London society already afforded. Irene did not lose any measure of his esteem by anticipating the need for an independence and endeavoring to provide for it. But sixty pounds could hardly be counted on to mushroom into a competence for four young ladies, and so he informed Irene in a deeply grave voice.

"Then you must speculate with the entire amount," she stated.

"You may as well bet it on a horse at Ascot," he exclaimed, "for you have as much chance of making your fortune at the track as you do on speculation."

Irene smiled philosophically. "There is no alternative," she said flatly. "My sister —

whose money this is — specifically wishes you to invest it. Besides, I have no means of traveling to Ascot, nor do I know how to go about laying a bet, interesting though it sounds. I am therefore wholly dependent on you, Mr. Uffingham, and I know you will do your best for Lord Sparks's daughters. That is all I ask. If the entire sixty pounds is lost, I shall absolve you of any blame, I assure you."

"Miss Sparks!" the lawyer argued. "You cannot simply deliver money into my hands and depend upon me to multiply it for you. How do you know I shall not embezzle it?"

Irene rose and gave him an arch smile. "I should feel very sorry for you if you did," she said, "for, as you have said, it is such a paltry amount."

Captivated by that smile, Mr. Uffingham relented, saying, "I hope I shall not one day find myself in the dock over this."

As he led her back to her coach, he warned, "I hope your sister does not depend too heavily on my making her fortune."

"I am afraid she does," Irene replied. "But I pray you will not let it daunt you, sir. You have given me news this day which cheers me beyond anything I could have hoped. It is not impossible, I think, that one day soon you may do the same for Martha."

Raising his eyebrows to his scalp, Mr. Uffingham bowed and handed her into the coach.

Hammond rode for two hours without hearing so much as a peep from Muffin. His favorite prattler evinced no interest whatsoever in his chestnuts, his tiger, his bay, or himself. When he offered to hand her aloft to join him on horseback, she declined, and when he ordered the coach to stop at a cathedral for a brief tour, she seemed hardly to notice the interruption.

"Are not those arches picturesque?" he asked her, to which she replied with a shrug of supreme indifference.

Their pause at an inn for a nuncheon did nothing to induce her out of her brown study. She ate her buttered bread slowly and touched only one bite of a roasted partridge.

"Have you been nibbling at the basket?" he questioned her.

Shaking her head and sighing, she explained that she was not hungry.

This was so unusual as to make his lordship suspect that Miss Mary was homesick. That being the case, he would do well, he thought, to let her alone to wrestle with her sorrow in peace. But by the time they had completed more than half the journey, he had seen no sign that solitude had restored Muffin's wonted vivacity. He therefore instructed the coachman to pull up by a stile, and he ordered the tiger to hitch his bay to the carriage. Then he climbed inside the coach and sat opposite his charge with folded arms and narrow gaze. "Do you want me to turn the coach around and go back?" he asked. "Are you that unhappy to leave your sisters?"

Muffin shook her head. "No, I am perfectly content," she said.

"Your happiness is every way apparent," he remarked. "I hear it in your pathetic sighs. I see it in your steady preoccupation and your uncommon loss of appetite. I feel it in your refusal to admire my horses as they deserve. Indeed, I congratulate myself on being able to inspire such contentment in a young lady."

This irony roused Muffin to explain, "Oh, you have done nothing, sir. It is my sister, who is a hateful, despicable toad."

"Your sister has made you so unhappy?" he said. "I find that difficult to believe. She cares for you very deeply."

"She cares for no one but herself," Muffin cried bitterly. "She is every way horrible. I believe she will not be happy until she has ruined us, and all over her precious Mr. Colton!"

"Colton!" Hammond said. "What has he to do with all this?"

"He has persuaded her to meet him at Vauxhall Thursday night. God knows what vile scheme he intends to carry out there, but I doubt not he means harm."

The earl's square jaw hardened. "I am surprised that Lady Selby has agreed to take her to Vauxhall," he said. "It is a place of which she claims to disapprove entirely."

Muffin gestured wildly in distress. "No, no," she exclaimed. "The scheme goes forward without Lady Selby. She refused at once."

"Your sister means to go anyway?" he said darkly. "Without Lady Selby's knowledge or approval? Deception, it would seem, pleases her excessively."

"I do not think it does," she replied thoughtfully. "It is only that where Mr. Colton is concerned, she is completely lost to reason."

Hammond's expression grew frigid. "Perhaps Lady Selby will not discover the scheme, and your sister's deception will not end in calamity. She is adept at carrying out masquerades, and I doubt not she will bring this one off to perfection."

"She may do as she pleases!" Muffin stated roundly. "She may go to the devil; in fact, I wish her there now. But to drag Irene into it — that is the outside of enough!"

"Irene!" he thundered. "I thought we were speaking of Irene."

Muffin looked at him in confusion. "We are speaking of Caroline," she said. "Who else would love such a stick as Mr. Colton?"

"Who else indeed?" he replied with a smile. "And how has she brought Irene into it?"

Here Muffin was obliged to tell only part of the truth, for to mention Miss Proutie's role in the scheme might represent Irene in a less than creditable light. "It is all Chloe's doing," she said acidly. "She has threatened to expose the plan to Lady Selby and to lay the blame for it at Irene's door."

"For one so young, my niece appears to be wonderfully proficient at extortion."

"That is not the worst of it, though," said Muffin. "Irene means to go to Vauxhall in the hope of exposing Mr. Colton."

"She dislikes him, then?"

"She says he is a fortune hunter who is after your blunt."

"Ah, yes," he remarked, "the rumored dowry."

"Which, by the way, got about thanks to Chloe, and not Irene, as you thought."

"But she hardly set your dowry at such a figure as to lure a fortune hunter."

"So Irene says, too, but she suspects he may be desperate, for he is in debt to someone — whom Irene calls 'his accomplice' — and may be forced to commit heaven knows what enormity because of it."

"Molyneux," said his lordship, more to himself than his companion. "But how does Irene mean to expose Mr. Colton?"

"I don't know." She sighed. "I don't think Irene knows, either. I only know that when I brought her cloak and mask into her chamber, I found a pistol half-hidden on her table. Oh, it is all such a muddle!"

"For the first time," he contradicted, "it is all very clear."

"Well, I am glad you find it so clear," she huffed. "As for me, I think it would be very wrong of them to hang Irene for murdering such a one as Colton. And yet, hanging might be preferable to a life in Newgate. God knows how long she will survive among the rats and fleas and vermin."

"We shall not let it come to that," Hammond said.

"How may we prevent it?" she cried.

"I shall do so," he assured her. "Thursday

night will find me at Vauxhall — even if I have to ride all night to get there."

Muffin grinned broadly at him. "You!" she exclaimed. "Of course, you will make it all right."

"Now you must tell me everything," he said. "I must be able to recognize the chief actors in the play."

She described to him as much of the plan as she had managed to learn, concluding with a description of the costumes to be worn by Mr. Colton and Caroline. "Irene is to be the Queen of Night," she concluded. Her voice had acquired a conspiratorial tone now, as she felt all the security of devising a stratagem with the Earl of Hammond.

"The Queen of Night," he mused. "I suppose half the ladies there will be similarly disguised."

Muffin's face fell.

"You must tell me every detail of her costume," he said.

Screwing up her face into a ponderous frown, she recalled that Irene's half-mask would be silver.

"If she does not cover her head," he said, "then her hair is sure to give her away. Perhaps the night will be warm and ladies will be forced to dispense with hooded dominoes."

"Oh, I hope so!" Muffin declared earnestly. "If what you say is true, and all the ladies there will look alike, I don't know how you will recognize her."

"I will know her," he said. "I knew her as Miss Proutie, and I shall know her as the Queen of Night."

"You knew her as Miss Proutie?" Muffin squealed, bursting into peals of laughter. "What a lark!"

"I daresay she thinks she's fooled me completely."

"I wish I could see her face when she finds out!"

"I fear she would be deeply mortified."

"Humgudgeon!" Muffin cried. "She'd be vastly relieved."

Chapter XIV

The warmth of the summer evening was mitigated by the breezes that blew over the Thames. As the waterman piloted the scull toward the shore, Irene could see the glow of light cast up from the Gardens.

"Will there be fireworks tonight?" Chloe asked Mr. Quince.

"I expect there will," he replied. "Dash it, this mask is pinching my nose."

"Here, let me adjust it for you," she offered. When she had retied it, she observed the effect as best she could in the moonlight and pronounced him all the kick.

Absently smoothing the folds of lace that cascaded from his collar, he replied in an undertone, "I do not mind telling you, Miss Selby, I don't like this. Why did your mother not come tonight?"

"As I told you before," said Chloe, subduing her irritation, "Mama felt dreadfully unwell tonight. She sent Miss Sparks in her place."

Irene glanced at Chloe briefly, then

turned her eyes back to the black waters of the river.

"Is that not so, Caroline?" Chloe called to her friend, who strained to catch a glimpse of the approaching shore. Caroline murmured her assent and opened her fan to cool her neck. Her serious expression was hidden beneath a spangled mask.

Like Caroline's, Irene's thoughts bent on the subject of Mr. Colton, and as she tried to project what the night held in store for them all, she felt about in her cloak pocket for the pistol. It would have been far better to carry it in her skirt, for the evening was hot and she might need to remove her domino. But the gown she wore was too filmy and thin to permit her to carry anything bulky in its pocket. She would have to make do somehow, she told herself, touching the cold metal of the weapon. This was playacting in earnest now; if she did not bring off her part to perfection, the consequences would be dire in the extreme.

At the shore, Mr. Quince handed the three ladies carefully out of the boat, cautioning them not to muddy their slippers or trail their hems in the wet grass. With Chloe on his arm and the other two following close behind, he led the way to the gate. After paying the price of admission, he bowed the ladies inside, where they admired the brightly colored globe lights lining the walks and heard the lilting sounds of music playing in the distance.

"I'm hungry," Chloe declared. "Let us find a booth."

"I can not leave the gate," Caroline reminded her friend. "I am to meet Mr. Colton just here."

"Very well," Chloe pouted, "but I don't know if I can sustain myself for very long on that boiled fish I had at home."

They waited in impatient silence as a number of dominoes passed by them. Many struck Irene as disreputable-looking figures — females who teased in loud and vulgar accents; gentlemen who walked unsteadily and ogled them rudely; pedestrians of both sexes who wore no costumes and studied the crowd as though looking to pick their pockets or rob them on the way home. Irene gave an imperceptible shudder. Then her eyes fell on a Punchinello who materialized from behind a hedge.

"At last!" Caroline cried with breathless pleasure. She took the arm he silently proffered and introduced him to Mr. Quince. This fastidious young gentleman bowed smartly in response to Punchinello's elaborate flourish. The amenities completed, the five strolled along the Long Walk, following the strains of the fiddlers. In a little while they came to some boxes arranged in wide semicircles; there they were invited by Mr. Quince to dine. Finding a booth with a view of the crowd, they seated themselves comfortably and called for a green goose and burgundy.

"Let us eat quickly," Chloe exhorted her companions, "for I am longing to dance." Throughout the repast she chattered in lively fashion, hooting with laughter as she became lightheaded from the wine, and returning the leers of the passing bucks with impudent winks.

While Mr. Quince endeavored vainly to contain the wild spirits of his companion, Irene surveyed Punchinello from under her silver mask. He said little or nothing, which Caroline apparently took as a sign that she must needs bestir herself to put him at ease.

"Well, I have done it, Mr. Colton," she said in a cheerful tone. "I am here."

"We are both here," Irene added.

This piece of obviousness provoked Punchinello into raising his goblet, holding it toward each of the Sparks sisters in a wordless toast, and draining the wine to the lees.

Having made short work of the supper, principally through Chloe's healthy appetite, the party left the booth to find the dancing. As they strolled, Irene noted that the Long Walk was frequently intersected by small lanes leading away from the crowds and the brightness of the lanterns. She observed, too, that pairs of lovers sought out these lanes, disappearing fondly into the seclusion of the trees and hedges.

Just off the Walk they came upon a large rotunda where the dancing was going forward. Without pausing to see to the others, Chloe pulled Mr. Quince toward the orchestra. Instantly the couple was swallowed up in the crush. Punchinello found a chair for Irene, then extended his arm to Caroline to lead her onto the floor.

"I thought you did not dance, Mr. Colton," Irene said.

He laughed softly and shrugged.

Uneasily Irene watched him put his hand on her sister's waist and swirl her gracefully between the other pairs with practiced skill.

For an appreciable time she sat in her chair, ignoring the dominoes who called out to her begging the favor of a dance. She kept her eyes on the dancers until at length Chloe and Mr. Quince returned. Chloe sank into a chair, noisily exclaiming, "Oh, I am hot to fainting! But it is wonderful, Miss Sparks.

You may dance with Mr. Quince if you like. I'm sure he will not mind, will you, Mr. Quince?"

Noting the young gentleman's exhausted air, Irene replied that he was very obliging, but she preferred to sit. "Where are Caroline and Mr. Colton?" she asked. "Have you seen them?"

"We saw them at the first," Mr. Quince told her, "but I do not recall seeing them again after that." He fingered the lace at his wrists, uncrumpling it so that it lay flat over his hand.

Chloe giggled a little unsteadily. "I think they have gone off," she declared mischievously. "I suspect they have found a quiet lane and lost themselves in it."

Irene sprang to her feet in alarm. "Did you see which way they went?" she exclaimed. "I must find them."

"Well, how is Mr. Colton to make the poor girl an offer if you intrude on them?" Chloe demanded.

"I appeal to you, Mr. Quince," Irene pleaded quietly. "Help me find them. I fear my sister may be in some danger."

"Good God!" Mr. Quince exclaimed. "Danger! I say, I did not bargain for any of that, I assure you."

"If you will look around the rotunda,"

Irene instructed him quickly, "I will make toward the gate."

"But what if they did not turn back?" Mr. Quince said nervously. "Suppose they have gone down to the Greek Temple?"

"I should have seen them if they had gone that way," Irene declared, though she was not quite as sure of herself as she sounded.

Mr. Quince shifted about on his feet, hardly knowing whether to obey.

"Do not waste another moment," Irene said earnestly. "I beg you to do as I ask."

"Come, Mr. Quince," Chloe invited. "You do not mind exploring a path with me, I hope?"

"I wish Miss Sparks might consent to come with us," he said. "I do not like her going off by herself."

"Do not concern yourself about me," Irene urged him. Descending the steps, she hurried in the direction they had come, and, conscious all the while of the bulky metal bumping against her thigh as she moved, she turned into the first path that greeted her along the way.

Caroline smelled the scent of flowering shrubs as she descended the lane, leaning her delicate hand securely on her companion's arm. The farther they walked, the sparser grew the crowd, until at last they came to an isolated corner ringed by a hedge, where there was no sign whatsoever of human presence. The air was quiet; indistinct now was the music of the fiddlers and the laughter of the revelers. In the distance the globe lights shone against the dark sky.

"I may not stay long," Caroline whispered. "I do not want to worry Irene."

Her companion sat down on a marble bench and, with a gesture, invited her to join him. Demurely she sat beside him and asked, "Did you think I would not come? Do you see that I do not fear to brave the disapproval of scandalmongers for your sake?"

"I see that you are the most delicious little chit that ever kept an assignation," said a cynical voice.

Startled, Caroline peered into the eyes behind the black mask beside her. That satyr's look was unmistakable, and she jumped up, backing away from him in fury. "How came you here?" she cried. "Where is Mr. Colton? What have you done with him?"

He laughed laconically at this. "Devil take Colton. Come, you cannot want such a bloodless fellow as that. You want a man of mettle."

As she made for the path, he seized her arm.

"I beg you to stay, Miss Caroline. I mean to have that kiss your abigail cheated me of."

"Why do you persecute me?" Caroline demanded. "You cannot love me. You cannot know what it is to love."

"You are pleased to be romantical, my dear," he observed. "There are sensations far sweeter than love. Revenge is the chief of these, I vow."

Defiantly, she spat at him. Wiping his face with his free hand, he remarked that he did not think the less of her for that gesture of contempt. "Indeed, your fire kindles one in me," he said, grasping her tightly. "I cannot permit you to throw it all away on Colton; why, the fellow is as indifferent to your charms as the frost is to the beauty of the rosebuds."

"How dare you speak of him!" Caroline hissed. "You are not fit to breathe his name."

Something in this taunt struck Mr. Molyneux as vastly amusing. He laughed sardonically, loosening his hold on her in the process, so that she was able to tear herself free of him. He managed to clutch hold of her cloak, the tie of which came undone instantly. Leaving him holding her patchwork, she ran into the lane and collided with another Punchinello.

"Mr. Colton! Thank God!" she said sobbing.

Molyneux, who had followed her with the domino in his hand, stopped at once when he saw the Punchinello protecting Caroline in his arms.

"Damme, what in thunder are you doing here?" Molyneux shot out. "You had your instructions. You will be sorry for this, I promise you."

In reply, Punchinello stepped out of Caroline's embrace and drew a rapier from beneath his domino. He sauntered toward his adversary, flashing the weapon once or twice so that it hissed in the air.

Holding open his cloak and grinning, Molyneux said, "As you see, my dear sir, I am unarmed."

The Punchinello placed the tip of his rapier at Molyneux's throat. Then, with a sudden movement he stabbed the blade into the patchwork cloak and lifted it up. Holding it toward Caroline so that she was able to remove it, he stared unflinchingly at Molyneux. Then suddenly he put up his weapon, wrapped Caroline gently in her domino, and led her down the lane toward the Long Walk.

Glancing quickly behind her to see if they were being followed, she begged him, "Please help me find Irene."

"I will," he murmured.

"And you must promise to say nothing to her of this."

Punchinello favored her with a solemn promise.

Irene saw nothing in the path she had taken, save an affectionate pair under a tree and a group of noisy revelers. She could not have missed Caroline, she told herself. Despite the seclusion of the many nooks, she must have seen her sister's spangled mask and patchwork cloak had she and her companion wandered in this direction. Shrugging off uncertainty, she rushed back along the lane, coming again to the main thoroughfare. With a brief glance about her, during which she saw no sign of any member of her party, she turned into another path, a much darker one this time, and one that she felt might well attract Mr. Colton by the privacy it offered.

Coupled with the heat, her frantic hurry had made her feel suffocated. She reached into the pocket of her domino and withdrew the pistol. Untying her cloak then, she draped it over her arm, thus hiding the weapon beneath in its black folds. A buck paused to ogle her bare white shoulders, tempting her sorely to aim the weapon at him and give him a well-deserved fright, but he moved on again with only an oath of regret, and she continued her search unmolested.

Apart from that one gentleman, she passed no other human creature. Observing the emptiness around her, she began to feel she ought to turn back. Nevertheless, she walked straight ahead until she came to the end of the lane. As she prepared to return along the same route, she thought she discerned a rustle of a branch. She stood motionless, waiting to see if a human figure would show himself. When none did, she began to walk quickly up the path. An echo of her footsteps caused her to halt and listen. Turning around, she saw nothing in the blackness. She began to run toward the Long Walk then, attaining its well-lit precincts in a few minutes. While she paused to catch her breath, a noise made her start, but it was only a rabbit, which scurried into one of the nearby paths.

Thinking that the rabbit might perhaps have been a fortunate omen, she followed it. A few lanterns dotted this lane, enabling her to discern a company of ladies and gentlemen approaching from the opposite direction.

"The fireworks!" one of them cried out.

"Let us find the water," another called. "There we will have the best view."

Looking after them as they rounded a bend, she thought she saw a silhouetted figure in a sombrero. When lengthy watch revealed no further evidence of the domino, however, she continued her walk. She rounded another turn and came face to face with Punchinello.

"Where is my sister?" she demanded. "What have you done with her?"

A satanic laugh answered this. "She has gone off with her lover, I expect. Ah, me, young love will have its way."

"You will tell me at once where she is," Irene said softly.

The imperiousness of her voice caused him to feign terror.

Uncovering the pistol, she said calmly, "I had a notion I should meet you here, and I have come prepared."

Molyneux's lip curled. "You are a clever girl," he remarked, "but you have been too clever this time. Your sister is not with me. Another Punchinello has claimed her, and I am, alas, completely alone."

Irene looked about in some confusion.

She could threaten to blow off Molyneux's head, she knew, but that was evidently not going to produce her sister. Caroline might in truth have gone off on another path. Or Molyneux might have left her somewhere by herself; he was quite capable of such a deed. But unless he had drugged her or knocked her unconscious, Caroline would in all probability have made her appearance by now. It occurred to her then that Chloe and Mr. Quince might have discovered Caroline and taken her under their dubious protection. As she examined these various possibilities in her mind, she involuntarily lowered the pistol. Seeing her hesitancy, Molyneux moved toward her, gripping her arm and wrestling with her until he had possessed himself of the weapon.

He slid it into his waistcoat and took her by the shoulders, laughing. "I do hope it wasn't loaded," he said, "else we might have attracted a good deal of notice, which I would not like at all. I would have been very sorry to miss an opportunity to resume our recent tête-a-tête, which was so unceremoniously intruded upon." Slowly he drew closer to her and would have performed a most unwelcome salute had not an affable voice behind him stated, "I believe you have something which rightfully belongs to the lady."

Whirling around, Molyneux swore. "You again," he said viciously to a tall gentleman in a black sombrero, a figure who, except for his half-mask, exactly resembled a highwayman.

"Nemesis, at your service," the highwayman said cordially.

Molyneux stood a moment in uncertainty. Then, pushing Irene from him so that she fell to the ground, he threw the pistol into a thicket and leaped over a hedge out of sight. Instantly the highwayman was at Irene's side, allowing Molyneux to make his escape. With the help of his strong arm supporting her back, Irene sat up and looked into the eyes of her rescuer.

"You are not hurt?" the familiar voice inquired.

Afraid he might recognize her voice, she whispered that no harm had come to her.

Handing her to her feet, he brushed off some leaves that clung to her arms and hair. "Do not be alarmed," he said. "I am not a highwayman — only the Earl of Hammond. May I be allowed to escort you back to your party? You have apparently lost your way."

Caroline led her companion to the rotunda, where the throng of dancers had dwindled to a few determined couples. Only a trio of fiddlers sawed at their instruments now, the others having joined the mob that had gathered to view the fireworks. After making a thorough search of the grounds, Caroline admitted helplessly, "She is no longer here. I suppose she has gone to look for me."

"Is she alone?" Punchinello asked.

"She is with Mr. Quince and Chloe."

"Then she is safe," he declared. "In that case, I shall take you home."

Caroline gave him a look of wonderment. "But I thought you wished to meet me here expressly that we might have a moment or two alone. I thought for certain you had something of a particular nature you wished to say to me."

"We can be alone in a hackney coach as well as here," he stated, and, offering his arm, he propelled her outside the gate, where a line of hacks for hire waited at the ready. Handing her into the neatest-looking one, he climbed in beside her, calling out to the driver to hasten to Berkeley Square.

"We crossed by water," she said unhappily.

"We shall take the bridge this time," he replied. His accent sounded so unlike what she had expected that she felt impelled to exclaim, "Please do not be angry with me,

Mr. Colton. I did not know Mr. Molyneux would appear. Indeed, if you are thinking that a rendezvous was arranged between us, you are very much mistaken."

"It is you who are mistaken," he returned, "for I am not Mr. Colton."

Untying his mask, he drew it off and revealed the stern visage of Mr. Charles Dale.

"You must stop the coach at once," Caroline commanded. "I am to meet Mr. Colton."

"I doubt that you would find him now, Miss Sparks," he said. "In any case, you will be safer at Selby House."

"But he must know I came," she wailed. "What will he think if he does not see me?" She leaned out the window to call to the driver to turn back.

"He will think you are too sensible to loiter very long at Vauxhall," he replied, reaching out his hand to draw the curtain over the window. After urging her to calm herself, he observed, "Mr. Colton seems to have a great aversion to keeping his appointments. I suggest, therefore, that you make do with the Punchinello available to you at the moment."

In high dudgeon, Caroline folded her arms over her bosom and tilted her chin obstinately.

"It is not really as bad as all that," he told her. "At least you are not constrained to ride with a Punchinello who makes love to you."

Caroline did not reply.

"How do you suppose that blackguard came to be dressed as Punchinello?" Charles wondered aloud.

"For that matter," she snapped, "how came you to be so dressed?"

"Why, you told me yourself how Mr. Colton meant to disguise himself. Did you inform that other gentleman as well?"

Tearing off her spangled mask, Caroline treated him to a look of withering scorn. "I hate you," she hissed venomously. "I hate you with all my heart."

Chloe, weary with searching in lanes, complained to Mr. Quince that her feet were tired, her head was hot, and she was about to be vilely sick to her stomach. "I detest burgundy," she said moaning. "I don't know why I drank so much of it. I declare, it was more vinegar than wine."

"I am very sorry," Mr. Quince apologized assiduously, not knowing what else to do for her. "You do not mean to be sick to your stomach here, do you, Miss Selby?" He brushed his coat of superfine cloth, as though she might soil it by her proximity.

"Oh, this is not at all what I planned to do at Vauxhall!" she lamented. "Indeed, we have danced only two dances and spent the whole evening marching up and down the place, looking for a pair of lovers who have no wish to be found. They have very probably gone home, without so much as a fare-thee-well to us."

"Gone home?" Mr. Quince repeated, much struck by this suggestion. "But surely they would stay to see the fireworks. They would not put themselves to all the trouble of coming here without staying to see the fireworks."

"I do not feel at all well." Chloe groaned in a nauseated tone. "I know I shall be ill, and I detest being ill."

"Perhaps you have caught your mama's sickness," the gentleman exclaimed. He stepped away a few paces to avoid any contagion that might spring from her person.

"Mr. Quince," she said with uncharacteristic sincerity, "I believe I cannot stay to see the fireworks either, for if you do not take me home this very minute, I will not answer for the consequences."

"But how can we leave without the others?" he asked in consternation.

"Irene is probably with Caroline and Colton by this time," she said. Then she let out a piercing moan, holding her stomach and retching in agony.

"Gracious, Chloe! Damme! Do not be sick, I beg you." He led her quickly to the gate, found a hack that did not smell so foul as to exacerbate her nausea, and installed her inside. Instructing the driver to fly across the bridge, he seated himself inside, as far from Chloe as he could. The coach drove off in a flash, jostling the passengers fearfully. Each time the wheels bumped on a pothole, Chloe grasped her abdomen and moaned, causing Mr. Quince to gulp and to wish that she would not look that odd yellow color. After watching her writhe for some time, he hit upon the idea of offering her his hat.

"There, Miss Selby," he said politely. "If you are inclined to be sick now, you may use that, for it is only a very old hat and a very plain one and not really much in the fashion anymore."

"I only want to die!" Chloe lamented piteously.

A little abashed, Mr. Quince looked at his hat and then at his companion. "I'm afraid I cannot help you there," the young man replied. "However, you are welcome to my hat."

"They may have gone to view the fireworks," Lord Hammond suggested to the

280

Queen of Night. "Do you wish to look for them by the water?"

Irene nodded.

"Then I suggest we find your pistol at once and make haste."

Silently the two of them approached the thicket and felt about among the twigs and brambles for the weapon. Irene, who had not worn gloves, scratched her hands on the undergrowth as she groped in the dark. Her skirt snagged on a clump of thistles, tearing a little as she struggled to free her hem.

Stephen found the pistol, holding it aloft for her to see. "I will keep it for you," he offered. "I promise to return it before you leave. But you must promise not to go about armed, unless you know precisely what you are about and are in no danger of having the weapon turned on yourself."

She bowed her head in acquiescence, and they strolled together along the walkway, Irene leaning wearily upon her companion's arm.

"How far is it?" she asked in a whisper.

"Quite far," he replied. "But perhaps we need not go all that distance. We might find them after the display is over, just by sitting in a box and observing all who pass by."

She nodded, grimacing as the thistles that clung to her hem pricked her ankles.

"Would you like to rest awhile?" he asked. "You are very tired."

Leading her into a nook, in the center of which stood a bench by a fish pond, he insisted that she sit down before proceeding any further. He took her mantle from her and laid it on the bench. She looked pensively at a water lily in the pond as she rubbed the scratches on her legs. Meanwhile, the earl regarded the same lily pad as it floated under the moon. He noticed a frog hop onto it and croak vehemently for his lady. The small creature called for some time, but to no avail. Finally he gave it up and dived back into the water, making a tiny splash and disappearing under the ripples.

"I wish you would tell me who you are," Hammond said softly, "and what has happened to cause you such distress."

In a throaty voice, Irene replied, "I wish I could tell you the answer to both those questions, but, indeed, I cannot."

Turning his eyes from the pond to her tense figure, he asked, "Can you not trust me?"

She raised her hand to her mask to make sure it had not worked its way loose. "I do trust you," she murmured almost indistinctly, adding quickly, "though you are a stranger."

"I will not add to your distress by pressing

you further," he said. "I will content myself with assuring you that I am at your service, and I ask that you not hesitate to call on me if you need anything."

Quietly, she thanked him.

"Your hem," he said in surprise. "It is covered with thorns. How have you managed to walk this far without scratching yourself?"

"I have not managed it at all," she said. "I'm afraid I have torn my ankles to shreds, besides ripping my gown."

In a trice, he knelt before her and began to pick the thistles out of her skirt. He paused once to remove his sombrero, whose brim cast a shadow on her dress. Then he set to work again, patiently locating the burrs and tossing them into a clump of dogwoods.

Irene looked from his dark hair to his methodical hands. She might tell him everything now, she thought, but she could not bear to break the spell. Nor could she bear to see his present tenderness transformed into scorn. Having become so accustomed to disguising her true self in his company, she could not now be certain how she would behave as Miss Irene Sparks, or whether his sudden discovery of her true identity would call forth his contempt. He was evidently much taken with the Queen of Night; but he might not find very much to inspire gallantry in the lady of Hopewell.

"That's the last of them," he pronounced, smiling up at her. Slowly he placed a hand on each of her cheeks and drew her face down to his. After kissing her a long time on the mouth, he let his lips wander to her ear, her hair, and her neck. He released her gently and stood up; extending his hand, he raised her up and folded her into his arms. He pressed his lips to hers, and, responding to the passion he had released in her, he tightened his grip on her.

Tossing in her bed, Caroline pounded her pillow and raged at Charles Dale. His high-handedness infuriated her so intensely that she could not close her eyes, let alone fall asleep, though she was tired to aching. The consciousness that she had probably lost his regard did nothing to mollify her, and the fact that she had precipitated her sister into a dreadful scandal by her foolish escapade only gave her further reason to attack the pillow with her fists.

What had become of Mr. Colton she could not imagine. The answers that suggested themselves were too dreadful to be seriously entertained. Yet, Mr. Molyneux had waited for her in the very spot Mr.

Colton had described, wearing the very same costume Mr. Colton had told her to look for. A logical explanation for such a coincidence did not come readily to mind. Instead, a fearful suspicion crept over her, and she wept tears of mortification to think that she might have been completely wrong about Mr. Colton and done her sister unspeakable harm on his account.

Suddenly another idea swept all doubts from her bosom. It occurred to her that Mr. Molyneux had poor Mr. Colton in his thrall, that he had somehow coerced her suitor into revealing the details of the rendevous, that Mr. Colton would never have permitted a word to pass his lips unless he had been subjected to the most horrible torments, and that even now he might well be languishing in a dungeon or attic whose equal had not been seen since Richard threw his two little nephews into the Tower.

The sound of a pitiful moan penetrated these anxious thoughts. Caroline threw off the sheet and tiptoed to the door, opening it the barest inch. In the corridor stood Chloe, looking a most astonishing shade of green and creeping unsteadily toward her chamber. Caroline took hold of her friend's waist, uttered a word of encouragement in her ear, and guided her to her bedchamber.

There she untied Chloe's cloak, relieved her of her mask, and hid the telltale apparel beneath the bed ruffs. Pulling down the counterpane, she helped Chloe into the bed and begged her to tell her what to do.

"Let me die!" Chloe wailed. "I detest being so miserable. I want to die."

Caroline rubbed her friend's hand, as if the friction might cause her ailment to vanish.

"Shall I fetch your mama?" Caroline asked.

"Oh, yes," Chloe cried miserably. "But first you must fetch me a basin."

Hammond and Irene gazed upward at the shooting sparks of colored light. The noise came from a great distance, permitting them to enjoy the fireworks in relative quiet. They waited to see whether the last spectacular shower signaled an end to the display. Seeing that it did, they left the nook with only one regretful glance, and headed in the direction of the Walk. There they found a booth, from which they scanned the crowd of returning revelers. Nowhere did Irene see a patchwork cloak or a spangled mask. Neither did she glimpse a humpbacked Punchinello or a figure trimmed out with lace at the neck and wrists. Soon the crush became a scattering of stragglers. In another quarter-hour, Irene realized that she and Hammond were among the last of the remaining visitors to Vauxhall.

"Your friends appear to have gone home without you," he said grimly. "The inference is troubling, but I do not know what other can be drawn from their failure to appear."

"I pray you are right," Irene said. "I would like to know that they are safe in their warm beds."

"And giving no thought whatsoever to your welfare."

"But I am perfectly fine, thanks to you."

He smiled at her, saying, "I will find a hack. A sedan might be preferable for privacy's sake, but a carriage is quicker."

"You know I must go alone," she said.

"Yes," he said, coming close to her. Draping the cloak over her shoulders and closing it snugly around her neck, he took her hand and led her away.

After he had paid the hackman, Hammond said to her, "Once you cross the bridge, you may give him the direction. There is no more for me to do but to give you back your pistol and wish you Godspeed." As she took the weapon from him, he stayed her hand with his. "I hope we may meet again," he said in a low voice. Then he closed the door firmly. At once she parted the curtain to look at him, and she did not close it again until the horses had sprung forward and his tall black figure had quite faded into shadow.

Roused by Caroline, Lady Selby scurried from her chamber to minister to her youngest daughter. At the bedside, she ascertained that Chloe was not at death's door, as the distraught Caroline had claimed, but only very nauseated and sick to her stomach. She sent for the lady's maid to assist in her ministrations and urged Caroline to return to her bed. "There is no need for you to stay awake any longer," clucked her ladyship. "Chloe will recover shortly."

Although she knew she would not shut her eyes the rest of the night, Caroline obeyed.

For an hour Lady Selby snapped brisk orders to the maid and applied the basin and a cool cloth as needed.

"I daresay that fish we had at dinner had turned a little," Lady Selby mused. "She will be bright as new in the morning."

She sent the maid back to her bed and remained at her daughter's side until the child settled into an easy slumber.

Removing the cloth from Chloe's forehead, she put it by and tiptoed out of the room, closing the door softly behind her. Turning toward her bedchamber she was astonished to see Irene stealing along the corridor, wearing a torn dress, a black domino, and a silver mask.

As the significance of that outlandish costume dawned upon her, Louisa set her hands upon her hips and furrowed her brow. "What is the meaning of this?" she demanded.

"As you see, I have been to Vauxhall."

"My God! This is not to be believed — that I have harbored a hussy under my roof. And did you go alone?"

Reluctant to speak either a lie or the truth, Irene lowered her lashes and held her tongue.

"I feel my palpitations beginning," Louisa cried. "Merciful heaven, and I thought you were the sensible one!"

"I am very sorry to have distressed you, ma'am," Irene said. "Shall I fetch you something? Your vinaigrette, perhaps?"

"You will do no such thing!" Louisa hissed, passing a fluttering hand over her eyes. "You will go to your room at once, and I wish you may have a pleasant sleep in your bed, for it is the last one you will have there, I can promise you."

Chapter XV

In answer to Louisa's urgent note, the earl presented himself at Berkeley Square the next day. The hastily scrawled summons, just barely legible, said only that she must see him at once upon his return; but it was enough to convey to her brother the height and depth of her outrage. Even if the missive had not forewarned him, he must have guessed, by the look on Holt's face as he admitted Hammond to the house, that her ladyship was in a state.

Stepping into the parlor, he saw his sister looming over a stiff-backed chair, where Irene sat as straight and unmoving as ice. Hammond's entrance interrupted Louisa in mid-sentence. When she glanced at him, he perceived that her blood was up. It would take all the cunning he could muster to damp the fires of her wrath.

Irene, taking no further note of Hammond's presence than a brief nod, stared impassively at nothing in particular. Her hands, showing two or three red scratches, were folded primly in her lap.

"How charming you look, Louisa," Hammond greeted her pleasantly. "You are in rare beauty today. That is a fetching cap. Is it new?"

"I did not send for you to talk of caps," she snapped.

"Naturally," he replied, "but that does not diminish the delightful effect of the one you have on. Where is Chloe?"

"Chloe is in her bed," Lady Selby answered. "She is most vilely ill and has been sick to her stomach since last night. I thought she would have recovered by now, but she is still in agonies."

With a great smile, the earl said, "What a pity! I wonder what can have brought on such an attack? Perhaps she went out and caught a chill. That is a risk, you know, particularly on a hot night. Have you had the doctor, Louisa? Mayhap a strong dose of physic will restore poor Chloe."

"Physic!" Louisa exclaimed. "Good God, Stephen, there is much more at stake here than physic. You are talking a farrago of nonsense, and I insist you stop it."

"I don't consider physic to be nonsense," he returned affably. "Nay, I have known it to cure an ailing hunter and bring him right up to snuff. You may recall that stallion I kept at Crown Leigh? He went punk, and it seemed for a time he would not ride to hounds, or a haywagon either. But a judicious application of physic brought him round in a day."

"Chloe is not a horse!" his sister reminded him indignantly.

"Ah, more's the pity."

"I assure you, I have done everything necessary for her."

"I do not doubt it, my dear." Out of the corner of his eye, he stole a glance at Irene. Seeing her lips quiver in a suppressed laugh, he continued in the same vein. "Did you know," he asked, "that Lord Volteface adds a pinch of physic to his receipt for snuff? I vow, I was appalled on hearing it at first. However, as soon as I sampled it, I was forced to admit it is a highly original notion."

"You are the most provoking creature, brother," Louisa cried. "I have brought you here expressly to discuss important matters, namely, Vauxhall."

"To be sure," he replied tranquilly. "That is a subject on which I flatter myself I am reasonably conversant. I was there only last night."

Irene's smile faded entirely away.

Lady Selby considered her brother with a

good deal of surprise. "I thought you were at Brighton," she said.

"I was, but I did not stay. It was Miss Mary, you recall, who was to stay." Walking to Irene, he addressed her directly for the first time. "Miss Sparks, you will be glad to know that your sister is pleased with school. She has named her pony Lark, an appellation more suitable to a member of the feathered species, I warrant, but one with which she is wholly enraptured."

Unable to look up, Irene thanked him succinctly and fixed her gaze on her hands.

"Miss Sparks was at Vauxhall last night as well," said her ladyship darkly.

"Did you stay to see the fireworks?" he inquired politely. "I did not see very much of them myself, being engaged at some distance from the water."

Before Irene could manage an answer, Louisa interjected in an overwrought tone, "Miss Sparks went to Vauxhall without my knowing it. And, as if that were not enough, she will not say who it was accompanied her. I should not be the least bit shocked to learn that she went alone."

Hammond studied Irene seriously. "Alone?" he said. "Well, it is lucky you returned unharmed."

"That is not the point!" Louisa exclaimed impatiently. "Why will you never see the point of an issue? Caps, physic — you are always wandering off someplace far afield. I declare, I could box your ears."

Stephen chuckled good-naturedly. "I shall sit down just here," he said, "and you shall tell me what the point is." Seating himself, he assumed an air of intense alertness.

"The point is that Miss Sparks has deceived me, and that she may have precipitated a scandal which will tarnish Beatrice and Chloe's reputation, should it be noised abroad that they had any part in such doings."

Hammond nodded solemnly, assuring her at the same time that Beatrice's reputation was beyond reproach. "No one who knows her could imagine her consenting to such a scheme, at least not without a punitive barrage of sermons on the subject. As for Chloe, her reputation is such that a rumor of her being at Vauxhall would not sully it. London knows very well what the youngest Miss Selby is capable of. I do not concern myself with them, therefore. My concern is for what will be said of you, Louisa."

Lady Selby gasped. "What could be said of me, other than that I was tricked by a scheming girl to whom I had opened my doors and my heart in the most disinterested spirit?"

"It will be said," Hammond replied pleasantly, "that you have been negligent, that in your preoccupation with the late ball, you gave your charges too free a hand implying they might roam at large, so long as they did not distract you from your purpose."

Louisa sank into a chair, overcome by this suggestion. Irene turned to Hammond and stated quietly, "That would be unjust, sir. Lady Selby could not know that we — that I — meant to steal out of the house in the dead of night when we — when I — ought to have been in bed. The blame is entirely mine."

"There, you see!" her ladyship cried. "The deception was all her doing; she admits as much herself."

"I am sure Miss Sparks's conduct has been everything that is reprehensible," his lordship remarked genially. "Nevertheless, when have we known rumors to be just? They will spill over and enmesh innocent parties, as you, my dear sister, pointed out so aptly only a moment ago. Are you aware, for example, that it is said I will provide these Hopewell ladies a dowry of two thousand pounds apiece?"

"I had not heard such a rumor," Louisa said, considerably disgusted. "Only a vicious mind could have conceived such an arrant falsehood as that. But it merely serves to confirm me in my conviction, Stephen, that you must remove Miss Sparks and her sisters from my house."

"I shall do so at once," said Hammond, rising.

Having anticipated a strong protest from her brother, Lady Selby breathed a sigh of relief. She had planned at the outset to withdraw her hospitality from the Hopewell ladies just as soon as the ball was over. But she had not allowed herself to hope that Stephen would support the move with such complacence. Smiling at him contentedly, she said, "I am very glad you see the necessity for their removal, and I forgive you for your digressions on caps and physic."

"What do you suggest I do with the ladies now?" Hammond asked amiably. "If you won't have them, I'm sure I don't know who will."

"I suppose you can find them rooms to let." Louisa shrugged indifferently.

"Who is to chaperon them?" he asked. "No, I have been over this same ground before, and a rocky, rut-filled road it is, too. Mother said if I brought them to London, they would find rich husbands, and although they have been here some time, still I see no such happy answer in the offing. You will not have them, Mother is too unwell to entertain, and so there is only one thing to be done. I must take them to Crown Leigh."

Irate, Louisa protested. "I meant to remove there myself this summer," she said. "You cannot expect me to go now, if they will be there as well."

"Dear me, did I invite you to Crown Leigh, Louisa?"

Looking a trifle conscious, Lady Selby hedged. "You did not invite me precisely — not in so many words. I merely assumed you would. Gracious, Stephen, since when do I need a formal invitation from my own brother?"

"Thank you for clearing that up," he said. "I was afraid I had made an invitation which slipped my mind. Believe me, dear sister, I never had any intention of extending an invitation to you. And, of course, now we must put aside all thought of your visiting me in the country. You may go to Lady Volteface instead. How fortunate you are to have an alternative."

"Lady Volteface," Louisa said with distaste. "I love Maria to death and think the world of her, but she is forever inviting rackety fellows and silly misses. One never knows whom one may encounter under her roof."

"In that case you must go to Selby's estate. You have not been there in years, I venture to say, and the change will do you good."

"You are detestable, Stephen!" her ladyship cried. "I have not deceived anyone. I have not behaved like a hoyden intent on raising a scandal. I have not been guilty of the least impropriety. And yet I am to be punished, while Miss Sparks is to remove with you to Crown Leigh!"

"It is lamentably unjust," Stephen allowed. "However, I trust Beatrice will scare up a bit of philosophy to console you." He then asked her to have the ladies ready to leave London as soon as possible, after which he quit Selby House and made his way to Grosvenor Square. As he walked, he decided that the role of noble heroine befitted Irene as forcefully as her Miss Proutie and as prettily as her Juliet, but not nearly as magnificently as her Queen of Night.

The journey into the west country took the travelers past the same countryside they had admired en route to London. They rode at a more leisurely pace this time, making stops at a number of sites where King Arthur and his associates were reputed to have dwelt. The conversation centered on Camelot, Excalibur, and the Holy Grail, so that Martha and Irene, who had set out from town wearing expressions of worry, were soon lulled into enjoying a respite from care.

Caroline was not so readily won from her discomfiture. Although legends and knights might be thought to appeal to her more than either of the others, she regarded the ruins and relics with little curiosity and less joy. Hammond guessed that pangs of conscience prevented her from lending herself to the charm of the sights. He knew she must be feeling the shame of having let Irene take all the blame for the Vauxhall scheme, and he was glad to see that she was not so lost to all sense of what was right as to be perfectly happy. Still, the image of her lovely face clouded over with wretchedness, and the sight of her violet eyes ringed with black circles compelled him to speak in a more kindly tone than he felt she really deserved.

"I believe you are familiar with the writings of Mr. Scott," he said.

She assented glumly. "I have read them all," she sighed, "and more than once."

"Then you must find the claims of this castle most romantic, for the legend that King Arthur held court here at Cadbury is said to be grounded in fact."

Observing the castle and its environs, Caroline sighed again. "Yes," she replied indifferently, "it is very romantic."

As long as they found themselves hard by Somerset, said his lordship to the ladies, they may as well make a stop at Hopewell. They might like to pay a call on some of their acquaintances at Botherby, or come with him to view the restorations he had initiated at Hopewell.

This last suggestion was greeted with cries of pleasure. Even Caroline evinced a certain enthusiasm for the journey. To Botherby they went, therefore, peeking out the windows of the carriage to catch the first glimpse of its wattled roofs. When at last the coach trundled down the main road, they waved to the villagers, who gaped at the earl's equipage and its occupants with conflicting emotions. There were those who considered the Sparks sisters enviably fortunate in having lost a worthless father and gained a nabob for a guardian in the space of a few short months. This contingent was heard to remark that some good fairy must be looking out for the ladies of Hopewell otherwise they would surely be found in the most desperate condition. Another, less benevolent view held that no proper moral could be drawn from Lord Sparks's depravity if his daughters did not suffer as a result of it, and while the purveyors of this upright opinion bowed and smiled to the passing coach with the same assiduity as the other party, they whispered among themselves that the sight of the ladies trimmed out in the French style was an affront to England and to decency.

As the carriage rolled toward Hopewell, Irene noticed a difference in the farmlands surrounding the approach. Fallow for so long, they now appeared rich and fertile. Rows of crops striped the hills and flats. Farmers stood in the fields, pausing in their labors to wave at his lordship's coach as though it were a familiar and welcome sight. The earl stopped his horse to exchange a few words with several of the tenants. He stayed so long to chat that when the coach stopped in front of the house, Irene saw they had left him far behind.

Followed by Martha and Caroline, she descended the steps of the carriage to see Hopewell's facade crisscrossed with scaffolding. Masons on platforms busily applied bricks and mortar to the crumbling walls. Workmen dotted the roof, laying a new covering in the exact style and color of the old one. Gardeners hoed the rose beds, which teemed with yellow and purple blooms.

The coachman banged the new brass door knocker and spoke to the benevolent-looking woman who answered his summons. Coming forward to greet the ladies, she introduced herself as Mrs. Cherrie, the housekeeper, and said that his lordship had sent a message ahead to expect them. With a kindly gesture, she invited them to come inside to drink a cup of tea and inspect the improvements.

The three sisters, impatient with curiosity to see the house, could not sit passively and await the tea tray. They examined every inch of the parlor Mrs. Cherrie had led them to, exclaiming over the fineness of the new brocade curtain and the elegance of the furnishings.

"If you like, I can wait the tea until his lordship arrives," said the housekeeper. "Meanwhile you may see what he has done to the house. I know you will prefer to find your own way about, and so I will leave you to yourselves."

Although they started out together, the

sisters' individual preferences soon took them in different directions. Caroline made her way up the newly carpeted staircase and sought out her old bedchamber. Martha caught up with Mrs. Cherrie and accompanied her below stairs to view the modern new roasting range in the kitchen. Irene dawdled in the corridor, peeping into rooms along the way. Everywhere she looked she found something to admire — rosewood cow-hocked chairs, a papier-mâché-cased cabinet, a japanned screen, new brass inlays in the sofa back, clawfoot tables, shining gilt on the picture frames, small touches that demonstrated taste and care, large flourishes that demonstrated daring and an interest in comfort rather than show. The cleaning and repairs had been thorough. Yet, the house had in actuality undergone few changes. It was the same Hopewell Irene knew intimately; only now it was sparkling, sturdy, and commodious. Hammond had even retained the portraits of her father, her mother, and their forebears, a mark of respect that moved her profoundly.

Opening the door to the library, she found the room almost exactly as she had left it. Apart from the high polish on the wainscoting and the dust-free condition of the furniture and shelves, the only difference lay in the window glass, which, having been washed to a shine, now let in a bright sunbeam. The books she had sent to the vicarage had all been brought back and now stood in their former place. The ladder leaned against the shelves as though no one had moved it in her absence. She approached it to test its steadiness and found that it had been repaired. As she thought back to a time when she had nearly fallen from its highest step, she heard the door open.

"Will you come have tea now?" Hammond invited. Following the direction of her eyes, he glanced briefly at the ladder. After a pause, he said quietly, "The vicar has called. I believe Miss Martha has persuaded him to join us."

"Will you stay a moment?" Irene said. "I have something I would like to say to you."

He came inside, closing the door behind him.

"I want you to know," she said, "that I did not go to Vauxhall alone. There were two other ladies and a gentleman with me."

"I see."

"I did not tell this to Lady Selby because it would only have led to questions I could not answer. Unfortunately, I am not at liberty to tell you, either, who my companions were. But I wish you to know that if I had only myself to consider, I would not hesitate to tell you everything."

"You honor me by your confidence," he said gently.

"Please do not think I have taken advantage of your family's kindness to my family, or that I have repaid you for it by disgracing myself. I want you to understand that I did not wish to go to Vauxhall but was constrained to do so against my will."

He smiled and seemed as if he would draw closer to her. "Is there anything else you wish to tell me?" he asked

"Yes, there is," she said. "But I cannot."

"Then I thank you for the trust you have exhibited thus far. Tell me what you think of Hopewell. Are you pleased with it?"

"Indeed I am," she replied with a warm smile. "What you have done is more than tasteful; it is accurate."

"Perhaps you have some suggestions for additional improvements?"

"I have several, I think."

"Good. I am glad you do not mind coming today," he added. "I was afraid that bringing you might stir painful memories and remind you of your loss."

"On the contrary," she replied. "This visit is exactly calculated to revive me after my ignominious banishment from Berkeley Square."

They exchanged a smile and then stared at the floor.

"How odd it is to be chatting so complaisantly together," she said with a lightness she was far from feeling. "And to think, it has all come about from my confiding to you that I could not confide in you."

"Your saying as much as you did was a great deal, believe me," he said. "And it is far preferable to having you thank me yet again."

"I have been preoccupied of late," she explained. "Otherwise you should not have escaped so easily. Tell me, sir, do you mean to settle at Hopewell?"

"I am advised to sell it at a great profit."

"I suppose you might," she agreed, "though I hardly think you would bother to reclaim the farmlands and marshal the tenants around you if you did not intend to stay."

"It may be that I am not the sort of fellow to see good farmland lie fallow. Perhaps my pride does not allow me to sell off a piece of property which is in less than first-rate condition."

"Or perhaps you wish to prove that you are not an undeserving interloper at Hopewell."

He laughed and asked affably, "Now why on earth should I wish to do such a thing as that?"

"I can't imagine," she said, smiling, "but if that was your intention, you have succeeded admirably."

Mr. Eccles, the vicar, was drawing up a chair to the tea table when the earl and Irene returned to the parlor. Hammond greeted him with a joyful heartiness that astounded the old gentleman. Inviting Martha to pour and Caroline to hand round the sandwiches and cakes, his lordship smiled expansively at the little gathering as though he was perfectly content with the world. Then he whispered to Mrs. Cherrie to bring them a plate of cold meat and some fruit, saying, "I believe we shall not dine at the inn or spend the night there after all, unless, of course, it will be too much trouble to you to have us here."

Mrs. Cherrie, scorning the idea of his lordship's sleeping anywhere but in his own house, insisted that he not mention the inn again. "I am sure the young ladies will like to be in their old beds again," she added, and bustled off to find some substantial victuals for the travelers.

As they ate, the vicar and his lordship became engrossed in the subject of fly fishing, while the ladies, deriving a feeling of comfort from their familiar surroundings, listened quietly. The vicar never mentioned a particular way of tying a fly or an anecdote from his angling experience that did not fill the earl with great delight, and although Hammond's smiles rested on Irene as often as they fell upon his interlocutor, still the vicar began to preen himself considerably on his powers of entertaining a fellow fisherman. The conversation culminated in an invitation to the vicar and his wife to visit Crown Leigh, where the fishing was unrivaled. Mr. Eccles agreed to come in three weeks' time, and then, congratulating himself on having amused Lord Hammond so cleverly, he took his leave of the ladies.

Very soon afterward, the Sparks sisters adjourned to their quarters, for although it was early yet, they sought the luxury of a good night's rest in their childhood beds before embarking once again for a destination that was not home. Stephen, meanwhile, sat up reading in the library, which he found the most congenial room in the house. Soon he dozed off over his book and slept peacefully until the morrow.

Chapter XVI

Crown Leigh, situated half a day's ride from Devon's red cliffs, was a plain structure of mellow brick. The oldest part of the house dated from the tenth century and sported a neat line of dormers over the eaves and three equally neat rows of windows underneath. In contrast, the "new" part of the house — added during the reign of Charles I — boasted two arrogant turrets, a tower, and a carefree, haphazard arrangement of windows.

The approach was lined with sculpted hedges and flower beds. Before the entrance of the house, at a few yards' distance, lay the remains of a moat, now a duck pond. A rising parkland behind the house was thickly covered with trees, and the greenery there had been allowed to grow as nature directed. On the other side of the rise ran a young stream, invisible from the house, yet audible in the quiet of night.

Inside, the mansion contrasted sharply with Hopewell. The latter was dark with wood and heavy wainscoting, while the former was light and sunny. Though the windows were far from large, they faced south and looked out on well-groomed gardens. The walls were painted in a soft cream color, matching the marble of the fireplaces. An intricate network of beams supported the high ceilings, from which hung gaily decorated banners of a chivalrous time. The furnishings were spare, simple, and elegant. His lordship's taste in pictures ran heavily to vignettes of the sporting life. Duck hunters, fox-hunting parties, and fishermen plied their vocations on prominently displayed canvases, while the likenesses of a long line of Hammonds were exiled to the stairwells.

In this comfortable setting, the Sparks sisters fell easily into the quiet routine of country life. Here there was time to indulge many of the simple pleasures for which London days had left little room — reading, drawing, playing the pianoforte, singing, walking, sewing, and daydreaming. With Lord Hammond, they rode on horseback to Dartmoor for a stroll through the enchanted forestland. On another occasion they rode by coach to a harbor village on the ocean. Twice they journeyed to Hopewell to inspect the restoration. In the evenings the earl and his guests entertained themselves and one another by reading aloud. Except for Caroline, who could not resist putting in a word for *The Castle of Otranto* and other writings in the gothic mode, the small company invariably elected to read plays — especially comedies — with which the earl's library abounded. Irene and Hammond vied with each other for the roles of the villain, the fool, and the drunkard, while Martha and Caroline enacted the hero and heroine.

Although these activities provided many pleasant hours, they did not afford another opportunity for a private interview between Irene and Hammond. Nevertheless, the two of them appeared content with their new understanding, and they seemed pleased, if not surprised, that it lasted more than a day and extended beyond the confines of Hopewell.

Upon her arrival at Crown Leigh, Irene had written to Muffin, apprising her in detail of the consequences of her expedition to Vauxhall. Not long afterward she received a reply, which contained much to cheer and something to astound.

My Dear Irene,
I think I have not slept a whole night through since I left London, worrying every minute about you. But I rest easy now, knowing you have not killed any-

body and that you are safe with his lordship. I get on tolerably well with my studies, excepting history, which is a great soporific. Miss Oglethorpe says I am highly proficient in mathematics and if I apply myself, I may study the calculus with a tutor. She tells me I am very spoilt and show all the signs of being the youngest child of a family which has petted and babied me excessively. Lark is a good-natured animal, a sleek and handsome pony, though a trifle tame. You will not tell the earl about this last, I trust, for I would not like him to think me ungrateful. I have learnt a good deal about riding, having always thought before that I had nothing more to learn about it, and I have acquitted myself creditably at a show. I have been too occupied to miss you as much as you miss me, though you are constantly in my thoughts. I have taught myself to forgive Caroline, and I hope she is only a little miserable after what she has done. I sometimes wish I might hear one of Martha's tales again, or snuggle close to you, especially when it is raining and I am confined indoors. You may give my love to my sisters and to the earl as well, for he is a right one, and I hope you are learning to like him better.

Your affectionate sister,
Mary Sparks (Muffin)

P.S. I forgot to mention that Lord Hammond knows you and Miss Proutie are one and the same. What a lark!

Irene set this letter down and laughed. She sought out his lordship to tell him of its contents — all excepting the postscript — and learned that he had received a similar communication. "Your sister is the most entertaining correspondent I have ever had," he said.

"Have you received other letters from her as well?" she asked.

He evaded this question smoothly, saying only that as she must want to share Muffin's letter with her sisters as soon as possible, he would not keep her. It was strange, she thought as she went to find Caroline, that he had never said anything to her regarding Miss Proutie — strange, and lucky, and immensely considerate. If he meant to save her uneasiness by avoiding any mention of the abigail's name, she was deeply grateful.

She discovered Caroline sitting by the pond, holding an unopened book in her lap.

Listening half-attentively to Irene's summary of the letter, she gazed into the still water with an expression of wistfulness. After reading aloud the postscript, the significance of which Caroline did not grasp, Irene mused, "How do you suppose he saw through my disguise?"

Caroline sighed. "What does it matter?"

"I am glad he knows," Irene said. "I only wonder what else he may have guessed."

Perceiving Caroline's preoccupation, she inquired gently if she was well. "You must not dwell on Vauxhall," she urged. "It is done with and no real harm has come of it."

"You can say so," Caroline replied, "for you have not deceived anyone. Your conscience on that score may be clear, while mine stabs me every minute."

Irene flushed a little at this reflection. "I wish I were as candid as you make me out to be," she said. "Still, I cannot, in this lovely summer garden, brood over the past — not when I look about me and see a baby swan waddling among the daisies."

"Even if my conscience did not weigh on me so heavily," Caroline said, "I should be oppressed by my thoughts of Mr. Colton. I cannot make him out, no matter how I try."

Kneeling beside her, Irene said, "Believe me when I say I understand how you must be feeling now. It is exasperating to try to sort out a man's character when his words and actions appear contradictory. A gentleman may seem generous and noble one moment and threatening the next, gentle and charming in the evening and then sinister in the morning's light. Only time can reveal his true nature."

"I must give Mr. Colton time, then," Caroline stated resolutely.

Irene was disappointed that her sister still cherished hopes in that quarter, but thinking her perfectly safe from his addresses, she said only, "You must give *yourself* time. As for Mr. Colton, I think his character is clear."

A trace of the old defiance animated Caroline's face. "I am not ready to convict him," she said stoutly. "I hold firm to the belief that he loves me and that he will find a way to explain his actions."

Since it was futile to remonstrate with her, Irene simply patted her sister's shoulder and went off in search of Martha, whom she found seated on a bench by a topiary tree plying her drawing pencil and rapt in woolgathering. After informing her that Muffin had written, she dropped the letter into Martha's lap and sat down beside her.

"What have you heard from Mr. Uffingham?" Martha asked anxiously.

"Why, nothing at all," Irene confessed. "Indeed, I had forgotten all about him."

As her sister frowned pensively, Irene peered at her sketch pad which Martha had taken care to close upon her arrival. "May I see your picture?" Irene asked.

Silently, Martha showed her the paper, which contained not a sketch at all, but a poem. Irene was not a great reader of poetry, being so very partial to the theater; nor did she in general esteem poets very highly, considering them a mooning, brooding lot, by and large. But she thought her sister's lines were exceptionally fine.

"I did not know you were so accomplished," Irene said. "I hope you will write more of these, for you have captured my feelings perfectly."

Martha's cheeks dimpled in a bashful smile. "I am happy you like it," she said. "In truth, I have a trunk-full of poems. I am forever scribbling them at the oddest moments."

"Do you mean to tell me that while I have suspected you of secretly corresponding with a beau, you have actually been conducting a courtship with the Muse?"

"I am afraid so," Martha said, "and I hope

you are not disappointed in me, for I know how much depends upon one of us finding a beau and marrying him. And I did try. I honestly did. But then I began to think of publishing my poems." She scanned Irene's face to see how she would receive this news.

"A capital notion!" Irene exclaimed. "You must publish them at once. I hope you will not delay a moment longer. It would be a great pity if this lovely poem were to turn to dust in a trunk and never be read."

Martha felt her heart grow full. She essayed a few words by way of introduction to a full confession, but suddenly she stopped in mid-phrase. Her eyes fell on the letter open in her lap. The words Muffin had appended leaped off the page at her. Rising abruptly, she murmured that she must go and write a letter at once. Assuming that the inspiration for a lyric had seized Martha, Irene bade her a pleasant goodbye and picked up the missive, which had fallen to the earth.

Martha was prevented from writing to Mr. Mowbray, as she had intended, by the arrival of Mr. Eccles and his wife. The vicar's lady cornered her by the staircase as the footmen hauled valises inside, and subjected her to a thorough interrogation for fully half an hour. No detail of London life, of Lady Selby's household management, of Muffin's school, or Beatrice and Chloe's finery was too petty to be belabored. Mrs. Eccles insisted upon hearing every scrap she could glean regarding the Earl of Hammond. In particular she cross-questioned Martha about her beaux. Had the town gentlemen taken to her? Had anyone offered for her as yet? She hoped it would be an older gentleman, a widower perhaps, with a gaggle of young children for her to mother. Martha ought to waste no more time in finding such a husband, if she had not already done so, for she was made to bear children, and it would not do to begin too late. Children were a great joy, she asserted, though she herself was childless, and they would bring Martha to the fulfillment of what everyone knew was her destiny. Only when the earl entered to greet his newly arrived guests was Martha able to make her escape.

On the next day, the Sparks sisters were forced to submit to a vigorous interrogation by Mrs. Eccles. The gentlemen, having gathered their tackle at dawn, had gone down to the stream, leaving the ladies to themselves. As they sat together in a sunny parlor, Mrs. Eccles took advantage of the opportunity to examine Caroline on the subject of her marital prospects. In the space of a few minutes, she wore down the girl's resistance and emerged from the inquisition with the name of Mr. Colton, a complete description of his manners and person, and a certainty that Caroline would soon be wearing his wedding ring. With these facts in her possession, Mrs. Eccles next bore down upon Irene, who, taking a page from the Earl of Hammond's book, responded to every home question with a digression on lace caps and physic.

"If you persist in dwelling on such trivialities," the vicar's wife declared at last to Irene, "you will never get yourself a husband."

"I have no thought of marrying," Irene replied primly.

"It is exactly as I have always said," the good woman pronounced. "You will end by living out your life as an aunt to your sisters' children."

"Nothing would please me more," Irene returned. "If I could see my sisters happily established, I should count myself very fortunate."

Mrs. Eccles gave a noise of disdain and turned to Martha, who trembled lest her secret come tumbling out before this skilled inquisitor. Sensing her sister's uneasiness, Irene said loudly, "Martha, do you not have a letter to write to Muffin? I suggest you go finish it at once. Mrs. Eccles has promised to show me a pattern for a bonnet. I mean to enlist Caroline's assistance with it, too, for I hope to send it to Muffin when it is finished. Be sure and forewarn her of it."

Gratefully, Martha availed herself of the chance to escape, while the three others embarked on their cutting and stitching. As they worked, Mrs. Eccles made numerous hints to the effect that Muffin's bonnet would end up in the dirt of the stables within a day of her receiving it. She interspersed these allusions with sly remarks about Caroline's forthcoming nuptials, Martha's maternal air, and Irene's blatant spinsterhood.

After a steady diet of this routine over a week's time, Irene resolved that the gentlemen should claim their fair share of Mrs. Eccles's scrutiny. To this end, she gathered her sisters, her sketch pad, her sun hat, and a picnic, and set out for the stream where the two fishermen recreated themselves. Mrs. Eccles scurried after her, hoping, in as many words as possible, that his lordship would not be angry at this unconventional interruption.

His lordship, as it turned out, was very glad indeed to see them all, especially as the catch had been exceedingly poor that afternoon. He had waded in the stream for many hours to no avail, and the diversion of company was particularly welcome. He added that he admired Irene's foresight in bringing some bread and cheese in a napkin and some cool wine in a crock. Clearing a spot for the ladies under a shady alder, he rejoined the vicar in the water and resumed the hunt for fish.

"We shall not talk," Mrs. Eccles assured him loudly. "We do not wish to frighten your quarry away."

"Silence is not necessary," Hammond said. "I have no opinion of a fish who is scared off by the conversation of ladies, and I would not for the world hook such a contemptible fellow."

Irene wandered to the edge of the stream to watch Hammond ply his rod and reel. Seating herself on a rock at the water's edge, she observed his every move, as if memorizing his technique. Finally she asked if she might try her hand at a cast.

Mrs. Eccles gasped at this bold request, but seeing that his lordship was pleased by it, she held her tongue. Hammond waded ashore to stand next to Irene. Patiently he demonstrated the manner of holding the rod and using a wrist motion to throw out the line. While she practiced the cast, listening carefully to the earl's advice and encouragement, Mrs. Eccles grew bored enough to inquire into the subject of Caroline's book. "Dear me!" she said when she saw the title. "It is one of those novels about secret passageways in haunted castles." Not finding this any more to her taste than her own book, she peered over Martha's shoulder to ascertain the progress of her sketch. "How very odd," she remarked. "That is not a picture at all. In fact, it looks just like a poem."

Reeling in her line, Irene called out, "Martha has a considerable talent, I think. She ought to have her poems published."

"Miss Sparks," Hammond said, "fishing requires your complete attention. In that respect, it is very like dancing. You see the result of your distraction now. You have caught your line."

While Irene concentrated on unsnagging the fly from a twig, Mrs. Eccles declared that she hoped Miss Martha would certainly not publish her poems. "A book of sonnets was sent me some weeks ago by a friend who lives in London," she said with a sniff. "She says the volume has set the town on its ear. Its title is most scandalous, and I have no doubt the contents will prove equally improper."

"If it promises to be offensive," the vicar said, "you ought not to read it, my dear."

"Of course I shall read it," she said. "How else am I to know what is unfit for the young people to read?"

"Perhaps its contents are not at all offensive," Martha ventured.

"With such a title, they must be," Mrs. Eccles stated. "Besides, the author has put her name to the book, instead of remaining anonymous. Let me think now. What did she call herself?"

"I have hooked something!" Irene exclaimed in delight.

"Reel in slowly, then pull," Stephen counseled her. "If you have only snagged another twig, you will not want to break the line. I shall lose one of my best flies if you do." He moved close to her in case she should need his help.

In another minute, they saw it flapping and splashing in the water.

"It's a fish!" Irene cried. "Now I must land him."

Following his lordship's patient directions, she reeled in her catch, and when she had him in the net, she and Hammond burst into uncontrollable laughter, causing the others to draw near with looks of curiosity.

"You are amazing, Miss Sparks," Stephen

said, holding up the line so that all might view the prize. "You have caught him by the tail. In all my years of fishing, I have never witnessed such a feat."

Still laughing, Irene said, "I suppose I hooked him just as he was out for his afternoon exercise. Poor fellow! You must put him back in the water, sir. He is just a baby."

"You may put him back yourself," his lordship replied, "with instructions for him to grow up and learn the proper manner of impaling himself on the Earl of Hammond's best fly."

As the others looked on, Irene removed the hook from the creature's tail and placed him gently in the rushing stream.

"That is what comes of teaching a lady to fish," Mrs. Eccles said.

"It does give one pause," Hammond replied, gathering the tackle and preparing to return to the house. "She not only outfished two experienced, empty-handed anglers, but she outfoxed the fish himself."

Chapter XVII

The Sparks sisters waved farewell to the vicar and his wife with little regret, and within days of their departure three new visitors took their place. Charles Dale escorted the dowager to Crown Leigh in compliance with Hammond's request that his mother be brought to the country as soon as she felt well enough to travel. Miss Simpson attended her ladyship, anticipating her needs and ordering her to rest in her bed as soon as they arrived at the earl's estate.

Stephen had ordered a room to be prepared for her on the main floor, and as he carried her to it she bussed his cheek, saying prettily that she hoped he appreciated what she had added to his entertainment by coming in such state to his house. "Country life may grow tedious unless one has something to fuss over," she said. "I have alleviated the tedium by giving you the very thing — myself." After Hammond had seen his mother comfortably installed in her chamber, Miss Simpson chased him out again, scolding that madam had better nap a while so as not to exert herself overmuch.

Hammond walked out to the sitting room to find Charles unusually animated. The secretary confided to the earl that he had brought much news. Mr. Dabney had been to Grosvenor Square, charging him with a message for his lordship. The speech was to be delivered in the House within a week, and so he must return to London at once. Hammond heard this news with surprise. Was it possible that the minister had scheduled his speech for the opening session? And why now, of all times, when he was finding the country so uncommonly salubrious and the company so amazingly complaisant? "The timing seems a little odd, don't you think?" he observed.

"Mr. Dabney has his reasons," Charles said. "He will tell you them when he sees you."

"I shall leave at once," Hammond said with a sigh, and would have ordered his valet to commence packing on the spot, had not Charles detained him with another piece of news.

"I saw this in the *Times*," he said gravely, handing his employer a scrap of paper.

As Hammond perused it, a look of grimness crossed his face. "I know you will tell her gently," he said. "I will tell Miss Irene Sparks."

"Caroline hates me bitterly," Charles protested. "She told me so in no uncertain terms. I doubt very much I am the one to tell her."

"Who could hate such a charming pudding-head?" his lordship answered pleasantly, and went in search of Irene.

Charles discovered Caroline sitting in a shady glade hard by the park. On hearing approaching footsteps, she glanced up from her page. Then seeing who was the source of the sound, she fixed her eyes on the book and set her lips tight.

"I had hoped you would have forgiven me by now," Charles said, standing near her and looking down at her luxuriant dark hair.

"I have nothing to say to you, Mr. Dale."

"I have something to say to you, Miss Caroline."

"Then I beg you will say it and leave me in peace."

He sat down next to her and drew the *Times* report from his pocket. "What I have to tell you will give you pain," he began. "Please believe that I take no satisfaction in bringing you this news, though I am sure you will think my intention is to gloat."

Caroline neither answered nor looked at the paper.

"Mr. Colton is married," he said softly. "This announcement appeared just days ago."

She took the scrap from him then and read it uncomprehendingly.

"Mrs. Colton is the daughter of a tradesman in Newcastle," he said.

"This cannot be true!" Caroline cried. "It is a gross mistake. I don't know how the *Times* could have printed such a lie."

Taking a breath, Charles continued softly, "I'm afraid it is true. After meeting with you at Vauxhall, I inquired a little into Mr. Colton's circumstances and found that he has been deeply in debt for some time. This marriage is his way of extricating himself."

"Then you think he was a mere fortune hunter. Irene thinks so as well."

"This would seem to prove it," he said as gently as he could.

"You wish me to think he never loved me at all," Caroline cried, "but I do not believe you. He may have been forced to make a prudent marriage, but he can still love a penniless girl."

"He did not think you were penniless at first. Hearing of your rumored dowry, he thought to come by some of Lord Hammond's fortune through marrying you."

She colored an angry shade of red. "Then why did he not do so? Why did he not even so much as offer for me or form an engagement? Why did he fail to appear at Vauxhall? Why did he marry another?"

"Because the man to whom he was indebted got in the way of it all. I am sure you recall Mr. Molyneux. I have learned that he applied pressure on Mr. Colton to woo you. But Molyneux changed his mind at the last, thinking to have you for himself."

"Mr. Molyneux is not the sort of man to take so much trouble over a female," she retorted. "He may have any number of willing paramours without bothering himself over a lady who despises him."

"Your contempt intrigued him, I collect. But you are right. Love was not his principal motive. He had a more forceful one — namely, revenge."

"He wished to punish me for spurning him? It seems a lot of trouble for very little satisfaction."

"He wished to punish Hammond for humiliating him on more than one occasion. He meant to seduce his lordship's protégée, embroil her in a scandal, and demand he pay dearly to keep it under wraps."

Caroline stood up. "This is mere conjecture," she said. "You cannot know for certain that Mr. Colton was in league with Mr. Molyneux. You have no right to accuse a gentleman of such corruption without any evidence."

"I have all the evidence I need," said Charles, standing up and facing her. "I have Mr. Colton's own testimony as witness."

"He confessed this to you?" she asked incredulously.

"He did, and in a manner wholly devoid of remorse."

Caroline inhaled and closed her eyes.

"Are you all right?" he asked.

"I am perfectly fine," she stated.

"You are very white. May I take you inside to your sister? Perhaps I should fetch you a glass of water?"

Caroline shook her head. "No, I do not require anything."

"Let me do something," he pleaded. "I cannot stand to see you looking so."

"I am neither a child nor an hysterical female," she said firmly. "I have no need for your solicitude or your presence." So saying, she produced a racking sob and ran blindly toward the house.

When Irene accepted Hammond's invitation to walk out with him, she did not think he had anything of a particular nature to disclose. Their acquaintance had developed to where they were on terms of easy friendship with each other, and so the invitation was not at all remarkable. Irene never spent a moment in his company without recollecting a certain meeting with a highwayman, but she had taught herself to maintain a facade of equanimity, an attitude his lordship facilitated by speaking only on the most comfortable topics and never alluding to Miss Proutie or Vauxhall.

As they paused on an outcrop overlooking a vista of rolling hills, they discussed improvements at Hopewell. Irene had several suggestions to put forward, all of which he received with close attention. "But it is so charming here at Crown Leigh," she said. "I don't know when you will visit Hopewell."

"When Louisa comes here," he said, "I shall go there."

She laughed and allowed that sisters were sometimes a trial.

He turned to her with a grave look and said, "Charles Dale has brought me some information which affects your sister Caroline."

"What is it?"

"A report appeared in the *Times* announcing Mr. Colton's marriage."

After absorbing his news, Irene confessed,

"I cannot say I'm sorry to hear it, but Caroline will be greatly distressed. I must go and tell her at once."

"Mr. Dale has taken it upon himself to do that," he said. "I imagine he is telling her even as we speak."

Irene frowned. "I wish he had not assumed that office without speaking to me first."

"I urged him to tell her."

"You? I wish you had not presumed so, my lord. It ought to be done by someone close to Caroline, someone who understands her heart."

"That is what I thought, too. That is why I encouraged Charles. He is that very person you describe; he is in love with her."

"Does she know?"

"He has told her, but she does not return his affection."

"No, I don't suppose she can," Irene said. "She is still infatuated with Mr. Colton. But now she will be forced to put all thoughts of him aside. His marriage is the only good he has ever done her. I hope it teaches her to see Mr. Dale in a proper light."

"Charles is an excellent young fellow," he said, "steady, prudent, and kind-hearted. In two years he comes into an estate which will permit him to settle comfortably with a wife."

"Two years is a long time," Irene replied. "I only hope it is enough for Caroline to forget her disappointment. She has strong opinions of how one ought to behave when crossed in love. More than that, she is passionately loyal. Once she has given away her heart, she will not easily reclaim it."

"I am convinced Charles will do his utmost to help. He is a patient sort and will not be deterred by her pining for another. At any rate, it has not deterred him so far. I am glad you approve of him."

"I do," she said with a smile, "but I am not quite so sure I approve of you. You ought to have consulted me, you know, before sending Mr. Dale to my sister. But now I must go back and see what may be done for her."

"Please do not go yet. There is something else I wish to tell you."

"Gracious!" she said archly. "What marriage will you announce next?"

He looked thoughtful. Then he answered briskly, "None at the moment. What I have to tell you is that I must leave for London at once."

Bowing her head, Irene answered, "I am very sorry to hear it."

"Are you, indeed?" The question, as he asked it, did not sound at all rhetorical.

In some confusion, Irene responded,

"Why, yes. I would not say so if I did not mean it."

"Will you come with me, then?"

Irene caught her breath. "I ought to decline, sir," she said. "My sister will need me, and I am sure that you can find someone else to accompany you."

"I can tell you, I will need you far more than Caroline does," he said warmly. "She will be comforted by my mother, who is the soul of gentleness in such cases, and by Charles, who means to embark on a lifetime of looking after her. I, on the other hand, am obliged to rely solely on you."

Irene stared at him as he made this astonishing speech.

"You are joking, my lord," she said, though she did not appear the least bit amused. "I cannot possibly be of any use to you. Moreover, I am obliged to tell you that I do not take kindly to this officiousness. It is one thing for you to abrogate to yourself the authority to guide Mr. Dale as regards my sister; it is quite another thing for you to try to cajole me into coming to London."

"Then I ask you to recall my promising I would one day demand repayment for all my generosity to your family."

" 'Repayment *in full*' was how you phrased it, I believe."

"Ah, yes," he replied affably. "Well then, this appears to be the day I spoke of."

An expression of fury blazed across Irene's face. She could not produce a rejoinder, being too stunned by his perfidy. She excoriated the gullibility that had induced her to trust him these past weeks. "Am I permitted to know what form this repayment will take?" she managed to get out finally. "Or do you expect the recipients of your beneficence to bow meekly and do your bidding without question?"

"I know you too well, Miss Sparks, to expect anything like meekness and blind obedience. Indeed, I infinitely prefer the opposite. But I am afraid that in your present state of mind you would feel it a point of honor to refuse me. I expect that once you are in London, you will prove a good deal more receptive."

Outraged, Irene flashed, "How can you speak this way? Apart from the fact that I am needed here, there are other very solid objections to my going. For one thing, to travel alone with you would give rise to gossip. For another, I have no place to stay when I reach the city."

"You will have two days after I am gone to comfort your sister," he said. "And Martha will ride with you in the coach to prevent gossip. As to your lodgings, I flatter myself that I shall be able to convince Lady Selby to welcome you once again to her home and hearth."

Irene gave out with a bitter laugh. "I doubt her ladyship would willingly set eyes on me again, let alone welcome me."

"Trust me, Miss Sparks. I shall bring her round."

"I believe you, my lord, for you have the means to constrain any number of people to do just as you please. But trust you? That, I can promise you, is beyond your power to demand." Following this taunt, she left him and made her way swiftly back to the house.

On the very next day, Hammond set out on horseback for London, leaving behind instructions for the two ladies to follow in forty-eight hours. When he reached the city, he stopped at Grosvenor Square just long enough to change his travel-worn buckskins and topboots for a suit of the finest camel-colored cloth. He then paid a visit to Mr. Dabney, whom he found seated with his stalwarts, perusing a page of numbers. The moment the earl was announced, Mr. Dabney stood to greet him. The two party members rose as well and echoed their leader's salutations.

"Charles gave me your message," Stephen

said. "Now tell me, what has happened to make my speech suddenly a matter of such importance?"

"The Prince wants to hear it, don't you know," explained the chancellor. He gave an expansive chuckle as his followers repeated this startling tidbit.

"When did His Grace conceive a fondness for currency reform?" inquired Hammond.

"Some weeks ago, His Majesty was gracious enough to invite us to his villa in Brighton."

"Brighton," the supporters said.

"I happened to mention your speech to him, and he was much taken with the idea that he asked to hear it at the opening session."

To the earl's look of skepticism, Dabney replied, "You see, he very much wishes to hear a speech in the House which has nothing whatsoever to do with Boney, or Ireland, or the exasperating colonies in America — the former colonies, that is."

"America," chimed the faithful.

"In short," Stephen observed with pleasant irony, "he wishes to hear something of little pertinence and less moment."

"Exactly!" cried the chancellor, vastly pleased with the earl's quickness. He raised his hands to quiet his factotums. "Do not be discouraged on that account," he went on. "Regardless of what the Regent or anyone else may think, the subject is not without significance. Long after our treaties have withered with age, and the generals who signed them have turned to dust under their monuments, guineas and pounds sterling will still be very much with us, and we must see to it that their value does not wither and dry up as well. We cannot do it all in one speech, don't you know, but we may make a beginning." With a raised forefinger he signaled to his associates that they were now at liberty to repeat his utterances, which they did with energy.

"That is how I see it," Hammond stated, "and why I have brought this." He drew some papers from his breast pocket and spread them on the desk before his mentor. "There it is," he said. "Now, let us make it worthy entertainment for a Prince."

For upward of an hour, the gentlemen hacked away at the speech, honing it to a precise few pages. Then, leaving it with the chancellor's associates to be copied, Hammond made his departure and went straight to Berkeley Square.

"You look exhausted, Stephen," Lady Selby declared when she saw him. "I daresay there has not been much rest for you at Crown Leigh. It is too bad you did not come to Selby's lodge with us. You would have had nothing but rest, day in and day out, until you had gone quite distracted with it."

"I have come to prepare you, Louisa," he said. "In a few days, Miss Sparks and her sister Martha will be taking up residence with you again. You will want to alert the household, I expect."

His sister glared at him. "Do you imagine I will have them here after what has passed? You have taken leave of your senses, brother."

"Yes, I do think you will have them," he said, "when I tell you that Miss Irene Sparks did not go to Vauxhall alone. She went with her sister Caroline and your daughter Chloe. Indeed, it was Chloe who insisted that Miss Sparks act as chaperon, and she threatened her with expulsion from your house in order to force her to do what went sorely against the grain."

"Now I know you have taken leave of your senses," she retorted angrily. "How dare you implicate Chloe, an innocent girl who is hardly out of the schoolroom and your very own niece. If this were true, why would you wait until now to tell me?"

"It was Miss Sparks's wish to protect

Chloe and save you further distress. I merely obliged her by keeping mum. But I find I cannot do so any longer; and if you want proof, then send for your daughters, ma'am. We will see what they have to say for themselves."

Beatrice and Chloe appeared before their mother in answer to the butler's message, and seeing the look of sternness on her face, they shifted about on their feet and studied the pattern of the carpet. Louisa related to them the charge their uncle had leveled, and for a time the only reply vouchsafed her was the ticking of the clock on the mantel.

Suddenly Chloe blurted, "Oh, I am sorry I ever thought of such a scheme! I was sick to dying for days afterward, and I am sure it was all due to that horrible burgundy, which was nothing but vinegar, you know, else I should never have been so ill from it. And the upshot of it all is that Mr. Quince has thrown me over for an heiress with red hair. Indeed, Mama, I shall never go to Vauxhall again, not even if I am positively begged on bended knee."

Aghast, Lady Selby swayed on her feet and put her hand to her palpitating breast. Beatrice helped her to the sofa, while Chloe ran out of the room and returned with the salts. When Beatrice saw that their ministrations restored her mother a little, she confessed, too. "I did not consider it my place to disclose this deception to you, Mama," she said. "I thought it the duty of the guilty parties themselves. I hope, therefore, that any punishment you mete out will not fall on my head, for as you can see, I am wholly blameless."

"It must have occurred to you," said Hammond, "that Miss Sparks was also blameless. Yet you allowed her to shoulder all the blame herself."

Looking profoundly remorseful, Chloe burst into tears. Beatrice remained calm, remarking that it was indeed lamentable that Miss Irene had been so foolish as to protect Caroline and Chloe. "While her actions may appear somewhat noble in a certain light," she intoned, "I believe that Truth is a higher good than any other. As a mere bystander, however, it behooved me to let others unfold the Truth."

"Get out of my sight!" Louisa moaned. "I shall deal with you later."

Making their curtsies, the girls disappeared as quickly as their legs could carry them, while Hammond waited patiently for his sister to revive.

"I knew the day they arrived, and their sister knocked over my china vase, that no good could come of it," she wailed. Pulling herself up to a sitting position, she asked, "Could you not keep them at Crown Leigh, Stephen? Why must they come here again? You are not insisting on it just to plague me, I hope?"

"Much as I dearly love to tease you, Louisa," he said, "I have a serious reason for wanting them here. I am to make my speech in the House at long last, and I particularly want Miss Sparks to be there to hear it."

Lady Selby moaned and sank down onto the cushion again. "Your speech!" she exclaimed in despair. "As though our family did not have sufficient folly to occupy it already!"

"I am very sorry you feel that way about it, my dear," he replied. "Happily, the Prince Regent feels otherwise. He is most eager to hear it."

Her ladyship jumped up from the sofa. "You don't mean the Prince will be there — and that he approves?"

"He will, and he does."

Louisa brightened, patting her ruffled person and adjusting the folds of her skirt. "Then it is all right," she pronounced. "You may make your speech. But why Miss Sparks must hear it I am sure I don't know."

After a brief pause, the earl replied, "She is a sensible, well-informed young woman, and I value her opinion."

His sister held her arms akimbo across her bosom and treated him to a quizzical look. "Fiddle!" she said at last. "You must be in love with her. To be sure, why else would you champion her so and foist her on your only sister?"

Stephen did not answer.

"Well, why don't you simply marry her and be done with it? At least then you would know where to put her when she came to London and not have the bother of scaring up lodgings and sponsors."

"As things stand now," he said, "she would not accept me."

"Not accept you!" she scoffed. "My dear, you are an extraordinary catch. A girl would have to be as mad as you are to refuse such an offer."

"In any case, I cannot marry her until she is willing to trust me with the whole truth."

"Trust!" Louisa laughed. "What has that to do with marriage? You are hoaxing me, brother. You do not love her at all. You hate her and mean to punish her by making her listen to a speech. Well, it will not do, Stephen, for the instant she is seen in the gallery, her name will be linked with yours in the most insinuating manner, and then you will be forced to make her an offer."

At this suggestion, Stephen looked troubled. "I hardly think her presence will be remarked," he said.

"Ordinarily it would not," Louisa replied, "but if the Prince is to be there, then so will the cream of the ton. In that case, the lady who enjoys the Earl of Hammond's generous sponsorship will not be overlooked."

Stephen paled somewhat and said, "Damn, Louisa. For once in your life, you are right!"

Chapter XVIII

Before departing Crown Leigh, Irene begged Lady Hammond to look after Caroline.

"Of course I shall do so," the dowager replied, as they prepared some rose petals for drying. "Who could do less than be kind to her? She is so red-eyed and sighs to break one's heart."

"I wish I could be here," Irene said, "but his lordship insists upon our going to London."

"To tell the truth, I am surprised. What can Stephen mean by it, I wonder? He will be wholly occupied with his speechifying."

"He said nothing to me about the speech."

"Perhaps it has unnerved him. It is very important to him, you know, though he endeavors to make light of it."

Irene took this in without comment, feeling once more her old sense that the Earl of Hammond was a mass of contradictions.

"At any rate," her ladyship continued, "if he has asked you to go to town, he has good reasons."

"That may be," Irene replied, "but he has not condescended to make me privy to them."

"He will in good time," the dowager stated confidently. "In the meanwhile, Mr. Dale and I will do what we can for Caroline. His regard must eventually win her away from grief. And I am not entirely inexperienced in the art of consoling disappointed lovers. I have a daughter who broke her heart many times before she married. It is from her I garnered my store of expertise in that line."

Smiling, Irene asked what her secrets were, to which the dowager replied, "It will be much easier once you and Martha are out of the way. Your continued presence here encourages Caroline to cosset herself and avoid the company of others outside her family. As soon as you are gone, she will have to depend upon those of us who are left. Then the first thing I shall do is permit her to cry her eyes out. It is ridiculous to try to suppress such tears, you know. They will out eventually. We may as well make it sooner than later. Afterward, I shall distract her with my complaints. Miss Simpson will be seized with a cough and have to take to her bed. Caroline will have to look after me then, and, I assure you, I can be a vast bother when necessary!"

346

"There is nothing so well suited to a girl of Caroline's temperament as ministering to the sick. The self-sacrifice it requires is precisely to her taste. I thank you for hatching such a plot. It will answer famously."

"Now you may go to London with an easy heart," said the dowager, "for if you worry any more about your sister, I shall be mortally offended."

Unlike Irene, Martha said goodbye to Crown Leigh without reservation. As the carriage rolled past the pond and descended the approach, Irene taxed her sister with insensibility. Martha flushed rosy red and replied that Caroline would get on much better without two sisters to coddle her. "Besides," she added, "we have business in town. You must see Mr. Uffingham, and I intend to look into the publication of my poems."

This suggestion cheered Irene considerably. "If you can manage that," she said, "then I shall consider our stay in London as not such a great punishment after all."

To her irritation, no word came from Hammond for several days after their arrival in Berkeley Square. Although Lady Selby's demeanor proved surprisingly gracious, and the Misses Selby expressed the fervent conviction that they would not be so bored now their dear friends had returned, still Irene could not but bristle at his lordship's inattention. However, she took advantage of the time at her disposal to pay a call on Mr. Uffingham.

When Irene presented herself in his chambers, the lawyer said he was relieved to see her. He had been endeavoring for the better part of a fortnight to locate her, as he had something of a delicate nature to communicate, but since her quitting Selby House, he had not known where to reach her. She followed him into his private room and took the chair he held out for her.

"I have been at Crown Leigh," she said.

"Good God!" the solicitor exclaimed, raising his brows.

Alarmed, Irene looked at him.

"Then you will be all the happier for the news I have to give you," he said. "You will want to leave Lord Hammond's protection as soon as possible."

"I should like that excessively," Irene agreed.

"You have heard, then. He means to speak this very day."

"The speech has been alluded to," she said, "but not by his lordship."

"Let me assure you, it is true, and therefore I am pleased to be able to tell you that your account with me has grown prodigiously. In fact, you are now richer by seven hundred fifty pounds."

"Is that all?" Irene responded.

"Egad!" Mr. Uffingham ejaculated. "When you consider the amount of your original investment and the short time which has elapsed since you placed your capital in my hands, I should say I have done exactly as you asked. This sum represents a killing in the truest sense, Miss Sparks, which is precisely in line with your instructions."

"I thank you with all my heart," she said. "It is only that my sister counted on its being more."

Regarding her closely, the lawyer shook his head, declaring that he had not thought her so greedy. "The return on your investment, when calculated to the percent, is more than respectable."

"Well, I suppose we must take what we can get," she replied. "Martha may yet decide to continue to place a portion of it with you. If so, I will return here another time."

"Do you not know any other man of business who might invest your money for you? Perhaps there is someone who can do better for you than I have. I hope so, at any rate."

Irene favored him with an innocent smile.

"I would not have anyone but you make my killings for me," she assured him. "Although this sum will not support four females over a lifetime, with frugal habits and diligent husbandry we may do very well. The great thing is that we may be independent now. It is very hard, you know, to have to impose on others in order to survive in the world."

"I daresay you are overly scrupulous," he remarked. "The world exists by imposing on others for survival. It is called 'credit.' I do not know if our nation could last a day without it. But I must not bore you with philosophy. Here is your money, Miss Sparks, and I wish you and your family good health."

Taking the proffered check, she inquired, "May I know what is the source of this sum? I am only curious, and will not presume to cavil at your choice."

Here Mr. Uffingham cleared his throat in embarrassment. "French champagne," he answered succinctly.

Irene scanned his face in some perplexity. Then her eyes sparkled and she laughed. "Smuggling!" she said, clapping her hands.

"I prefer to designate it as *imports*," he corrected. "After all, I did not actually row the cargo across the Channel. I merely availed myself of the opportunity to purchase it once it reached English soil."

"Do not apologize," Irene said. "I have no objection to smuggling. It is ever so much livelier than the five percents and a vast deal more dashing than laying a bet on a horse."

Mr. Uffingham sighed, resigned to the fact that the eldest Miss Sparks might always be relied upon to voice remarkably unconventional opinions. When she rose to take her leave, she made him promise he would let her know the second he heard of another shipment of champagne, saying, "Since husbands appear to be pretty scarce, we may have to content ourselves with *imports*."

Irene returned to Selby House to find the Earl of Hammond closeted with his sister in the parlor. His state of mind was such that he seemed hardly to notice her entrance.

"You are on your way to the House?" Irene heard Louisa ask.

"I must spend an hour with Mr. Dabney first," he replied.

"My lord," Irene interrupted with barely controlled anger, "have you forgotten that you insisted upon my coming to London?"

Approaching her, he said, "No, I have not forgotten."

"You demanded we make all haste about it, and now you appear to have lost sight of the reason for it."

"I have changed my mind," he answered. "You will be glad to hear that you may return to Crown Leigh at your earliest convenience."

Shocked, Irene was on the point of upbraiding him for his capriciousness, when he looked at her intently and asked, "Will you wish me good fortune on my speech, Miss Sparks?"

A shade of hauteur froze her face. Deigning not to reply, she turned her back on him.

"Well, I shall wish you good fortune," Louisa interjected gaily, "if you promise to overlook my former objections to your orating. Indeed, Selby is ashamed he ever raked you over the coals for it. You must go now and present your speech and make us all very proud."

With a brief glance at Irene's rigid back, he left the house.

The moment she heard the door shut, Irene turned to Louisa in fury. "I do believe your brother does not know his own mind," she cried. "He is thoughtless, officious, and completely devoted to his selfish whims."

Louisa sighed. "He is incorrigible," she agreed. "However, I must say that there is some extenuation for his oddities today. Doubtless the excitement of addressing the Lords has taken its toll on his faculties."

"To bring me here against my will, and then to dismiss me without so much as an explanation — that bespeaks a good deal more than 'excitement,' ma'am."

"Oh, that," Louisa said deprecatingly. "That is nothing. He merely wished to ask you to hear his speech. In fact, if I did not abhor politics and such, I should go and hear it myself."

"He never asked me any such thing," Irene responded.

"Thanks to me," Louisa said. "He was primed to ask you. Happily I dissuaded him in time."

"How did you contrive to dissuade him? I should like to know, for I have always found him to be a most obstinate gentleman."

Louisa mourned the sad truth of this. "Obstinate he certainly is, and he will never stick to the point of a thing. I live in fear, I can tell you, that his speech will wander all over the place and hit on physic or some subject which will insult the Prince. But Stephen is no fool. I represented to him all the notice which must follow your attendance in the gallery. He saw at once that gossip, scandal, and speculation would result, and, not liking to subject you to such tittle-tattle, he gave up the scheme. You need not trouble to thank me, my dear. Not for the world would I allow your reputation to be tarnished. I know how much depends upon your finding a husband for one of your sisters."

Irene's mind raced with a thousand ideas, one of which gave her deep dissatisfaction. "And I turned my back on him," she said ruefully. Then, excusing herself hastily, she dashed from the room.

Louisa saw her again in the vestibule some ten minutes later and gaped at Miss Sparks's outlandish appearance. In truth, she hardly recognized her in a wide-brimmed black hat with a heavy veil pulled under her chin and a dense shawl bundled around her neck. Her daunting aspect silenced Lady Selby for an instant, until she found the voice to cry out, "I demand to know what this means."

"It means," Irene declared with a lively air, "that while Miss Sparks cannot hear his lordship's speech, Miss Proutie can."

"Miss Proutie?" Louisa repeated, her eyes bulging out of her head.

Dropping a curtsy, Irene answered demurely, "At your service, ma'am. I am an abigail, and a mighty bold one, too." With that, she poked the astounded butler in the ribs with her parasol, exhorting him to go outside and find her a hack without delay. With a lighthearted farewell to Lady Selby, she quit the house.

Considerably dazed, Louisa returned to her sitting room and racked her brain for the cause of so much lunacy under her roof. She wondered who next might suddenly exhibit a readiness to take up residence at Bedlam. Bethinking herself of something else then, she walked to the end of the room and picked up a slim volume that lay on a table. After digesting the contents of the title page, she threw her hands up in the air and gave herself up for lost.

Escorted by Mr. Dabney and his henchmen, the Earl of Hammond made his way through the crowd. It had gathered early at Westminster to catch a glimpse of the Prince and now blocked ready access to the Palace. The chancellor's vigilant associates proved their indispensability here by elbowing a path through the human sea, so that Hammond and his mentor might attain the House before having their cuffs entirely torn from them or their cravats sullied by the crush. Breaking free of the throng, Hammond came face to face with Molyneux, who greeted him insolently. "I look forward to hearing your speech," he said with a slit-eyed grin. "You must look for me in the gallery."

Brushing past him without a word, Hammond recalled that he had hoped to have a very different supporter in the gallery. Shrugging off regret, however, he entered the House. Very few of the lords had as yet taken their seats. One of them lay stretched out on a bench, snoring blissfully. Another, who sat on the opposition side, peeled an orange and hummed a lively air. The gentleman next to him cracked nuts and stowed the shells under the bench. A fourth gentleman stood at the table in the center of the hall, arranging papers.

Soon a parade of guards entered to flank the throne at the end of the hall. Glancing up into the galleries on either side of the chamber, his lordship took note of a scattering of visitors. Molyneux was not among them, he saw. He sat down in one of the front rows and waited for the hall to fill.

During the following quarter-hour, the sleeping lord was awakened by a kick from a well-aimed spur and bid to make room for the arriving lords. The gentlemen of the opposition were prevailed upon to put away their fruit and nuts before the Prince should enter. At the center table, the Prince's closest allies took their seats, while in the gallery, the benches grew full to brimming.

Lord Selby entered the unfamiliar precincts of the House to wish his brother-in-law well and enjoin him not to make a cake of himself. Then he took a seat and strove to look as if he knew precisely what he was about.

The entrance of the heralds silenced the House, stopping several of the lords in the act of coming or going. After a stirring announcement of his many names and titles, the Prince Regent strode inside the hall and, with a look of amusement at all the pomp and ceremony, eased his elegant person onto the throne. He gave a debonair gesture of welcome and declared the session of Parliament open. His words were neither many nor weighty; yet, his graceful bearing cast an air of reverence upon the onlookers. The lords on the benches and the visitors in the gallery whispered that Prinny was in devilishly fine fettle that day, and even the gentleman of the oranges looked attentive.

The archbishop then rose to welcome His Royal Highness with remarks calculated to inspire considerable applause and foot-stomping from the floor. Receiving these marks of respect with his accustomed graciousness, the Prince nodded and only five or six times drummed his fingers on the arms of the throne. A number of members stood to eulogize His Majesty, the Prince's father, and all Their Majesties past and future of the House of Hanover. Every speaker vowed death to Bonaparte and any other upstart who should have the audacity to challenge the supremacy of the British navy or call himself by his first name. At length, one of the lords, following Mr. Dabney's instructions, introduced the Earl or Hammond, who removed his notes from his pocket and rose to speak.

He began well enough. Allowing himself a period of time in which to warm to his subject, he trained his thoughts on his theme rather than on the expression of interest on the Prince's face. He was nearly a third of the way through when a movement in the gallery caught his eye. Without pausing in his text, he saw Miss Proutie elbow a spectator, forcing him to make room for her on the first bench. The sight of the abigail so startled his lordship that he was forced to cough into his hand for a bit. When he put down his hand again, he was smiling broadly. With a merry twinkle in his eyes he resumed his thread of argument, interspersing his sentences with so many chuckles that Lord Selby felt impelled to poke him in the arm. "You had better get a grip on yourself, man," Selby whispered. "You were doing well; don't spoil it now."

Hammond endeavored to regain his composure and proceed with more dignity; however, another look at Miss Proutie set him off again, causing the lords on both sides of the House to wonder how the devil their esteemed colleague contrived to find so much humor in the subject of currency reform. They glanced at one another in puzzlement, hoping that the novice was not about to disgrace himself, when they heard a loud snigger emanate from the direction of the throne. The Prince, taking his cue from the speaker, roared with amiable laughter. Hearing that rumble, the members instantly followed suit, slapping their knees and exchanging knowing looks.

The earl paused to allow the noise to die down stealing another peek at the black-hatted female in the gallery. Just at that instant he saw Molyneux enter and take the seat behind Miss Proutie. Molyneux leaned forward slightly and said something in the abigail's ear that made her start violently and clench her hands. The smile faded from the earl's lips. His eyes grew stormy and his expression hardened. When he took up his speech again, his voice shook powerfully. At this change of tone, his listeners perked up their ears, conscious of a new force in his voice. It implied that although currency reform might indeed have its risible aspects, it was nevertheless an issue of the most supreme urgency.

The words flowed quickly now. Soon Hammond was racing through his speech at alarming speed, hurtling toward his conclusion as though he could not stand a minute longer to see England languish under the present monetary system. When he had uttered his final word — one that stunned his hearers with its passion — he did not stay to receive his applause. Pushing his way out of the hall, he found a stairwell and bounded up the steps two at a time.

Molyneux, perceiving Hammond's intent, seized Miss Proutie by the arm and hauled her to her feet. Dragging her from the gallery, he found a small chamber nearby and flung her inside. The violence of his thrust propelled Irene against the mantel of the fireplace, where she hit her head and sank to the floor. Ignoring her, Molyneux closed the door and positioned himself close to it with his rapier drawn.

Slowly the door creaked open as Hammond stepped cautiously inside. Molyneux banged the door shut behind him and greeted him with a ghastly smile. "I congratulate you on your oratory," he said. "You have a gift, I observe. What a pity your debut should also be your swan song."

Turning his back on Molyneux, Hammond went to Irene and gently raised her head from the floor. "Are you conscious?" he asked quietly.

When she nodded, he asked her whether she was hurt. "I am unharmed," she told him, "but I am heartily ashamed at being caught off guard."

After helping her to rise, he faced Molyneux, whom he found poised at some distance, flashing his weapon in a prefatory way. Easing Irene behind him and moving away from her so that she stood out of the line of danger, he approached Molyneux. "Do you mean to kill an unarmed man?" he inquired affably.

"I would not have resorted to such a cowardly means of retribution," Molyneux replied, "but I have exhausted my alternatives. Colton has found a way of buying back his notes without running off with Miss Caroline, and I have been prevented from doing it myself by the interference of a stranger. I am therefore obliged to take what avenue is left me."

Molyneux and Hammond circled each other. Irene, meanwhile, inched carefully in front of the fire irons. Reaching behind her, she grasped a poker and stepped forward, holding it close to her back. The gentlemen continued to stalk each other and as Hammond moved in her direction, she cried out, "Stephen take this!" He looked at her and, with a reflexive motion, caught the fire iron she heaved at him. Grasping it firmly, as though it were a sword, he assumed the en garde position, aiming the weapon full at Molyneux. "Good God, Irene," he said, "how am I supposed to defend myself with this?"

"It is just like a reel," she called back. "It is all in the action of the wrist."

Molyneux sneered at this exchange. "If Miss Proutie were not a female, and an eminent poet to boot, I believe I should challenge her as soon as I had dispatched your lordship."

"You are raving," Hammond replied, thrusting the poker so that it ripped Molyneux's sleeve.

"Have you not witnessed her proficiency with the fire iron, my lord? I have been so privileged on at least two occasions, but she probably told you about that. And no doubt you are equally admiring of her poet-ical prowess. I must congratulate you on your book, Miss Proutie. It is the talk of London."

Hammond pressed his advantage against his adversary.

"Be careful, Stephen!" Irene cried, as Molyneux lunged at him.

"Such a scandal as those sonnets have caused," Molyneux went on breathing hard. "One would hardly think them the work of a proper damsel." On that he made a thrust and parry that Hammond just managed to evade by leaping aside. Before Molyneux could recover his foil, the earl hurled the poker at him, hitting him soundly in the stomach.

The door opened and Mr. Dabney appeared in the entrance with his loyal associates. "Seize that villain!" the chancellor ordered, rolling the syllables off his tongue with great relish.

Instead of repeating his words, the two stalwarts hastened to obey. Firmly they took hold of Molyneux, who was doubled over and coughing, and carried him outside. "Take him off to Bow Street," Mr. Dabney called after his men. "We don't hold with violence of that sort here. If he objects to a member's speech, let him write a letter to the *Times* like a decent fellow."

"Bow Street," came the echo as they disappeared down the stairway.

Irene straightened her hat and pulled her veil under her chin. She hung back while the chancellor engaged Hammond in talk. "I say, Hammond, you have had a remarkably eventful day," Mr. Dabney observed.

The earl laughed and thanked him for his fortuitous arrival.

"Prinny sent me to find you," he said confidentially. "He wishes to congratulate you on a fine speech. He says you are a powerful orator as well as a humorous one, and he looks forward to more of the same from you."

"I shall go to him at once," Stephen said. He invited Miss Proutie to join him and the chancellor, which, after a moment's hesitation, she consented to do.

The Prince strolled leisurely outside the House with a large contingent of courtiers. Brushing them aside, Mr. Dabney came forward and presented Hammond.

"I never suspected, when Mr. Dabney spoke of you, that you had such stunning gifts," said the Prince. "I understood barely half of what you said, of course, but you said it all with such élan that I was sure it signified a great deal."

Gravely Hammond thanked him.

Pointing to a spot behind the earl, the Regent asked, "Who is that female standing there? I declare, she is the most formidable creature I have ever clapped eyes on."

Glancing at Irene, his lordship replied with a smile that her name was Miss Proutie.

"Miss Proutie — the poetess?" the Prince exclaimed. "I am excessively fond of her sonnets. If she did not look such a dragon, I should ask to meet her."

"Is it true, then? She is the author of a book of poems?"

"I should say she is," Prinny answered emphatically, "and if you have not read them, you must go and do so at once, for a man who has made a speech such as you have done just now is bound to make a good deal of sense out of her rhymes."

At that invitation, Hammond bowed, took his leave, and went to collect Miss Proutie.

Chapter XIX

Caroline kept to her chamber for several days after her sisters' departure. Then a note from the dowager begging her company at tea drew her from her isolation. Without referring to any oppression of spirits Caroline might be feeling, her ladyship wrote of her own need for the solace of companionship. This unexceptional invitation, hinting strongly as it did of the dowager's loneliness, brought Caroline to the tea table. She perceived immediately that the dowager was alarmingly pale. Her well-wrapped leg was raised on an ottoman, and she coughed a number of times. Concerned, Caroline inquired if there was anything she could do for her ladyship, to which Lady Hammond replied that, yes, as a matter of fact, she would appreciate the girl's assisting Miss Simpson in the preparation and application of a plaster for her chest.

Directly after tea, Caroline threw herself into the work of ministering to the dowager. The plaster was no sooner completed than it became evident that the earl's mother was fast succumbing to a very bad cold accompanied by sneezing, aching, and inflammation. As evening wore on, Miss Simpson grew alarmed at the intensity of the cold. She whispered to Miss Caroline that her ladyship had been kept awake several nights in a row with a racking cough, and now a cold had settled in her head, making everything a thousand times worse. Using a receipt of her mother's, Caroline mixed a cup of lemon, honey, and hot blackberry wine, a syrup that the dowager found so soothing to her throat that she beseeched a glass of it every hour.

"I meant to distract you with my complaints," the dowager confessed to Caroline, "but I never meant to be sick in earnest."

"You have distracted me, my lady," Caroline said. "Now I must thank you by helping you get well again."

"You can thank me by leaving me to a nap while you go find Mr. Dale. I declare, that young gentleman is in a sad case."

Caroline smiled a little. "Should I mix him a plaster, do you think?"

"Ah, you have made a joke!" the dowager exclaimed. "That is an excellent sign." She was then obliged to submit to a fit of coughing.

Caroline answered with a succession of sneezes.

"Good God, you have caught my cold!" the dowager exclaimed. "Soon you will be as puffy as I am, and then Mr. Dale will not be half so receptive."

"Mr. Dale is probably sick himself," Caroline remarked, "sick to death with dangling after an ungrateful girl." At that she sneezed again, adding between sniffles, "I should not be at all surprised if he decamped for London very soon."

"Then you must speak to him before he goes," Lady Hammond urged. "And you must leave me to my nap."

Caroline came upon him as he stood in a sunny grove, occupied with smoothing a mound of leaves with the toe of his boot. He leaned against the trunk of an elm, engrossed in his enterprise as though it were a matter of the greatest moment. He glanced up and, seeing who approached, applied a vigorous kick to the leaves, scattering them abroad.

Not knowing what to say to him, Caroline watched him as he concentrated on his task. A series of violent sneezes forced her to blow her nose into her handkerchief, following which she conveyed Lady Hammond's salutations in a nasal tone.

"How does her ladyship?" he inquired.

"I'm afraid she will feel worse before she feels better."

"You appear to have caught her cold."

"So it seems, but, like other afflictions, I feel sure it will pass."

"Some afflictions never pass," he said forlornly. "Or if they do, they often leave heavy scars."

"One must bestir oneself to heal the scars," she replied. "Otherwise much time will be wasted in lamenting what cannot be changed."

Something in this speech encouraged him to take a step toward her. "Do you foresee that your scars will heal?" he asked.

"I think I can safely say that I am on the mend," she said. At that she burst into a spasm of coughing, and when she had done, she smiled a little at him.

Drawing closer to her, he said he hoped she was not very ill.

"Not at all," she reassured him brightly, producing a ferocious sneeze. "I have never felt so well in my life!"

He offered to walk with her back to the house.

"Do not come so close, Mr. Dale," she warned softly. "You will surely catch my cold if you do."

"If I do catch it," he said, taking her hand in his, "it is only the first of many I propose to share with you."

Irene flung into Selby House with the earl hard on her heels. Bursting into the sitting room, she gave Louisa and her daughters a jolt of surprise. Angrily she tore off her black hat and shawl and threw them onto a chair. The Selby women watched in fascination as his lordship stalked in behind her and the two confronted each other with fiery looks.

"Kindly have the goodness to make yourself intelligible," Irene said. "I haven't the faintest notion what you are talking about."

"Why didn't you tell me about Miss Proutie?"

"Because you already knew. Muffin wrote me that you've always known. If you wanted to speak of it, why did you not say so?"

"I knew you were Miss Proutie," he said darkly, "but I did not know the truth about her."

"I could not tell you she meant to come to hear your speech," Irene said. "There was not time. She thought it would please you to see her there. Believe me, sir, had she any inkling that you would fly into a temper over it, she never would have gone to the trouble."

"Whatever pleasure I may have experienced at the sight of Miss Proutie has been completely overset by her deception," he shot back. "She ought to have told me about her poems. Why, I ask you, could she not have trusted me with that piece of information?"

Lady Selby and her daughters looked from one combatant to the other. At first they did their best to adjust their faces in an attitude of shock. With this last taunt, however, they gave up the effort and allowed themselves to be hugely entertained.

Hands on her hips, Irene thrust her face toward Hammond. "Do you mean to tell me you take the word of a blackguard like Molyneux? You speak of trust, and yet you do not trust my word that I have never heard of any poems, nor did I ever write one in my life."

He turned away to lean his hand against the mantel. Then, banging his fist on it, so that a Limoges figurine tottered precariously, he said in a low voice, "How in thunder am I to marry a woman who will not trust me, who disguises and deceives at every opportunity, and will not disclose even the most innocuous secrets?"

"I have often observed," Beatrice intoned, "that one may say things in the heat of anger which are regretted later, when one has recovered one's senses."

Her mother gasped. "He would not marry her," she prayed aloud, "not after what she has written! Oh, Chloe, I must have my vinaigrette."

"Later, Mama," said Chloe, completely engrossed in the drama before her.

Irene stared at Hammond in disbelief.

"Did you assume I would disapprove of your writing?" he demanded. "Did you presume to answer for me without giving me a chance to answer for myself?"

Louisa lay back against the sofa and fanned herself rapidly.

"Did you say marry?" Irene asked.

Hammond composed himself, curling his lip ironically. "It's ridiculous to think of making you an offer now. I would never know to whom it was made, would I? Miss Irene Sparks hardly exists apart from her many assumed identities."

"It is just as well," Irene replied caustically, "for you've made it perfectly plain that you hate all of us."

"I wish I did hate you," he flashed on his march to the door. Pausing with his hand on the knob, he said, "I bid you goodbye, Miss Sparks, and I wish you joy of your poems and your masquerades." Then he was gone.

Irene sat down hard in a chair and shook her fists in vexation.

"This is the outside of enough, Miss Sparks," Louisa said with a shriek. "This time you must go, and nothing will persuade me to take you back."

"Is it true?" Chloe asked, drawing near. "You did not write these poems?"

Taking the slim folio Chloe held out to her, Irene scanned the cover. Her expression tensed with suspicion as she leafed through the book, stopping every once in a while to read a portion of its contents whenever a familiar reference caught her eye. Returning the book to Chloe, she said, "Where is Martha?"

"I expect she is in her chamber," Beatrice answered, "and I hope she may comfort you, Miss Sparks, for, sisterly spats notwithstanding, one must always seek out one's closest relations in times of trial."

"Seek her out is precisely what I mean to do," Irene declared.

Bunkers interrupted Lord Hammond at his solitary dinner to announce that a caller awaited him.

"Send the fellow away!" the earl snapped. "If I have to endure one more pat on the back for my witty and powerful speech, I shall rue the day I made it. In fact, I rue it already, and it is not yet over."

"The caller is a lady," the butler replied with an upward roll of his eyeballs.

"If it is Louisa, tell her I have caught the plague and am not receiving."

"It is not her ladyship," Bunkers persisted with supreme patience. "She gave the name of Miss Martha Sparks."

"Oh, very well." Hammond sighed. "Show her into the library. And then do not disturb me again."

Martha blushed handsomely when his lordship entered the library, and she apologized for intruding on his dinner.

"How can I help you?" he inquired politely, annoyed at himself for not being able to cast off his charges as indifferently as he wished.

"I have not come to request your help," she replied. "In fact, I have come to tell you that your help in regard to my family, while all that is generous, is no longer required."

The earl regarded her with interest and asked her to sit down. When she had done so, he invited her to proceed. In a sweet and modest style, she began, "I am pleased to inform you, my lord, that we have acquired an income which will enable us to support ourselves." As if to prove her assertion, she showed him the check Mr. Uffingham had inscribed in her name.

"I congratulate you, Miss Martha," he said sincerely. "Independence is always preferable to reliance on the goodwill of others."

"I knew you would understand," she said, "and I'm glad I was right, for I would not like you to think us ungrateful for your kindness."

"I believe I have heard enough gratitude to last me a lifetime," he said. "Therefore, I beg you will say no more on that head." He expected her to depart then, but she remained seated. Opening a black satchel, she removed a book and propped it upright in her lap.

"We have come by this income in ways which must shock you," she said. "It started with this." So saying, she handed him the book. After he had looked it over and absorbed its significance, she said, "I hope you will accept this copy with my compliments."

He smiled. "Miss Proutie is a woman of parts," he remarked.

"Naturally my poems were not so remunerative as this check would suggest," Martha continued. "Irene placed the payment I received with Mr. Uffingham and asked him to make a killing with it."

"Good God!" he said, laughing. "And what did he say to that?"

"He very kindly obliged, as you can see by the bank draft there."

"You have been amazingly enterprising," Hammond observed. "It appears to be a family trait. I only wish I had known earlier of your book. In that case I would not have taxed your sister with its authorship."

"I regret that deeply," Martha said. "I have no excuse but my own cowardice. However, the news is out now; the scandal I feared has come to pass. The ton talk of nothing but my poor jingles. Lady Selby says that this is positively the last deception she will support from us. And yet it is not so very dreadful as I anticipated, at least not so dreadful as to prevent me from writing another book. But I wish I knew how to patch it up between you and Irene. I'm afraid that there I have done irreparable damage."

"Let us hope it is not irreparable," he said. "We shall give it time — perhaps fifteen or twenty years — and by then she may have learned to forgive us both."

With a bashful smile, she rose to take her leave, saying she trusted it would not be as long as that. After wishing her good fortune, he watched her close the door behind her, feeling as though it were an act of finality.

Stephen opened the volume of poems at random and read a sonnet. He liked it well enough to read the next and then the next. For some time he allowed himself to become rapt in the poetry, until his attention was recalled by a throaty voice saying, "I have come to tell you all my secrets."

He looked up to see a tall figure in a black domino and silver mask. Slowly she unclasped the hooded cloak and removed it, revealing honey-colored hair and a black dress cut low in the front and torn at the hem.

Approaching her, Stephen said, "I had hoped we would meet again." He reached his hands behind her head to untie the mask. Then he took the cloak from her arm and tossed it with the mask onto a chair.

"Burn them," Irene said. "I have no further use for disguises."

"I am too fond of this one to burn it," he replied. "I have often thought of the Queen of Night since meeting with her, and now that I have found her again, I mean to persuade her to stay."

"Tell me the truth. Did you know?"

"From the start."

"Then my coming here tonight was unnecessary."

"Oh, but it was very necessary," he contradicted. "I would be greatly remiss if I did not congratulate you on your late good fortune."

"I need no longer be on the lookout for a rich husband," Irene observed. "I may be perfectly independent now, it seems."

"You have never been anything else, I think."

"But I have not been ungrateful, I hope."

He sighed. "The Lord knows you have not been that."

"Good," she said, looking up into his eyes with a soft smile. "Then you will not be surprised to hear that I intend to repay you — in full." She touched her finger to his cheek.

Drawing her to him, he kissed her. Slowly his lips moved into her hair and he whispered, "Juliet, Miss Proutie, Your Grace, Irene — I love you, all of you."

"Of course you do." She sighed contentedly, nibbling his ear. "Why else would you kneel at my feet to pick the burrs out of my hem? To love and love alone may such devotion be ascribed. But I confess, Stephen, I have one more secret to unfold. I love you, too."

"That has not been much of a secret lately," he murmured into her neck. "Nevertheless, it will do very nicely."

Epilogue

To the great delight of the villagers at Botherby, the Earl of Hammond and his bride were wed at Hopewell. In addition to the profits accruing from the sumptuous nuptials, there was the pleasure of seeing the four Misses Sparks return to the place of their birth and permit its inhabitants to ponder the hand that Fate had dealt them in the months since they had been tragically orphaned.

As they reviewed the various predictions made in bygone days, Mrs. Eccles and her neighbors could not but congratulate themselves on their perspicacity. They had always known, it seemed, that Miss Mary would turn out a fine young miss one day. They nodded approvingly as she dismounted her bay with dignity and let no more than a few giggles escape her lips as she glided gracefully into the church.

The vicar's wife allowed that in former days Miss Caroline had been a great favorite with the gentlemen, giving rise to her reputation as a beauty who was always surrounded by beaux. Mrs. Eccles and her confidants had never been deceived by this silly prattle, though, and so they smiled upon the sight of the young lady, very pale and subdued, clinging to the arm of one young gentleman who clearly doted on her.

Bashful and rosy, Miss Martha gave them equal cause for complacency, having turned out just as they had foreseen she would — an author of scandalous rhymes and a spinster.

As for Miss Irene Sparks, she most of all bore witness to the townspeople's sagacity. She had made an advantageous match, and it did not in the least surprise Mrs. Eccles that such a vivacious and beautiful lady had landed herself a peer of the realm — moreover, no less a personage than the heir to her ancestral estate.

Indeed, the only thing that succeeded in astonishing the good folk of Botherby was the sight of the happy couple as they took their vows, for the earl smiled broadly as he pronounced them, and his bride threw her arms about his neck, permitting him to kiss her ardently on the mouth.